MIND PREY
The *New York Times* bestseller by
JOHN SANDFORD

"A thriller through and through . . . impossible to put
down."   —*Houston Chronicle*

"Sandford conjures up the high anxiety his earlier works
are known for . . . This lone psychopath is among
Sandford's most chilling."   —*San Francisco Examiner*

"His seventh, and best, outing in the acclaimed *Prey*
suspense series."   —*People*

"Crackling, page-turning tension . . . great, scary fun."
                                          —*New York Daily News*

"Nonstop action, an offbeat milieu, and a host of
three-dimensional characters—all make for one of the
best *Preys* yet."   —*Kirkus Reviews*

CONTINUED . . .

EYES OF PREY

Davenport risks his sanity to stalk the most brilliant and dangerous man he's ever known, a doctor named Michael Bekker . . .

"Savage . . . suspenseful . . . gripping from start to finish."
—*Kirkus Reviews*

"Engrossing . . . one of the most horrible villains this side of Hannibal the Cannibal." —*Richmond Times-Dispatch*

"Relentlessly swift. Genuine suspense . . . excellent."
—*Los Angeles Times*

SILENT PREY

Michael Bekker, the psychopath Davenport captured in Eyes of Prey, *escapes. And the nightmare begins again . . .*

"*Silent Prey* terrifies . . . just right for fans of *The Silence of the Lambs.*" —*Booklist*

"Readers will speed through the surprise twists . . . Sandford delivers." —*Publishers Weekly*

"Superb." —*St. Paul Pioneer Press*

CONTINUED . . .

WINTER PREY

The brutal murder of a family in rural Wisconsin brings Lucas Davenport face-to-face with the ultimate cold-hearted killer—the Iceman . . .

"Vastly entertaining . . . a furious climactic chase . . . one of the best *Preys* yet."
—*Kirkus Reviews*

"An intense thriller with an unlikely killer." —*Playboy*

"Fresh . . . original . . . extraordinary."
—*Detroit Free Press*

NIGHT PREY

Davenport stalks his most elusive opponent—a master thief who becomes obsessed with a beautiful woman . . . then carves her initials into his victims.

"Strong on atmosphere and suspense . . . potent and compelling."
—*Kirkus Reviews*

"Action aplenty . . . Sandford is in top form."
—*Minneapolis Star & Tribune*

"*Night Prey* sizzles . . . positively chilling."
—*St. Petersburg Times*

JOHN SANDFORD

THE FOOL'S RUN

(PREVIOUSLY PUBLISHED UNDER THE NAME JOHN CAMP)

BERKLEY BOOKS, NEW YORK

THE FOOL'S RUN
(previously published under the name John Camp)

A Berkley Book / published by arrangement with
Henry Holt & Company, Inc.

PRINTING HISTORY
Henry Holt & Company edition published 1989
Berkley edition / December 1996

The Putnam Berkley World Wide Web site address is
http://www.berkley.com/berkley

ISBN: 0-425-15572-2

BERKLEY®
Berkley Books are published by The Berkley Publishing Group,
200 Madison Avenue, New York, New York 10016.
BERKLEY and the "B" design
are trademarks belonging to Berkley Publishing Corporation.

PRINTED IN THE UNITED STATES OF AMERICA

10 9 8 7 6 5 4 3 2 1

For Roswell and Emily

"Whereas crime has traditionally occurred in environments of manual human activities, some crime is now perpetrated inside computers in the specialized environment of rooms with raised flooring, lowered ceilings, large grey boxes, flashing lights, moving tapes, and the hum of air-conditioning motors. . . . A new jargon has developed, identifying automated methods such as data diddling, Trojan horses, logic bombs, salami techniques, superzapping, piggybacking, scavenging, data leakage, and asynchronous attacks. . . . Utility programs such as Superzap are powerful and dangerous tools in the wrong hands. They should be kept secure from unauthorized use."

Computer Crime,
a Criminal Justice Resource Manual,
U.S. Department of Justice

Prologue

I T WAS HARD work, which he hadn't expected. The thief removed each leaf from the blueprint book, squatted and centered it between tape markers on the rug. When it was in place, he stood up, squinted through the camera's viewfinder, and tripped the shutter. Then he did it again, ninety-four times, a long half hour of deep knee bends.

As he worked, he talked to himself: "Ooo, that's got it, Danny . . . Awright, motherfucker . . . Let's move this sucker a _leetle_ bit this way. . . ."

When he finished, he was sweating. He turned off the photo-flood and lit a cigarette.

The thief was tall and sandy haired, with a long English face, beaked nose, and china-blue eyes. His ruffled-front shirt was buttoned and cuffed with onyx studs. He wore tuxedo trousers, a black cummerbund, and patent leather shoes. A tuxedo jacket was folded over the back of a visitor's chair.

The thief was working in his own office. The desk was real oak, the carpet real wool. The two regulation plants, a palm and something else, were plastic, but exceptionally authentic.

At the back of the office, an old-fashioned drafting table stood beneath a window. He didn't use it; it was a harmless affectation allowed an upper-middle manager. A swing-arm lamp was mounted on the drafting table, though, and that had been useful. The thief replaced the lamp's 100-watt incandescent bulb with a floodlight and maneuvered the lamp out over the carpet. The light on the blue prints was flat and even. The pictures would be perfect.

After a dozen drags on his cigarette, the thief snubbed it out and began rebinding the blueprints. As he clipped the pages in place, he paused occasionally to listen. Except for the odd *plonks* and *plunks*, the building was quiet. When he finished with the blueprints, he set them aside and turned to a second book.

This book was also loose-leaf, but smaller, the size of a telephone directory. Its 706 pages were covered with computer code. He could photograph four pages at a time. The pages would be out of order on the film, but that made no difference as long as he got them all. It took him two hours and fifteen minutes to make the copies.

"Jesus Christ," he muttered as he picked up the last two pages. His knees cracked when he stood,

and his lower back ached. He lit another cigarette, stretched, and looked idly around the office.

He had spent a thousand days in it, but never
breached its built-in anonymity. Memos, business
cards, and procedure statements were thumb-
tacked to a bulletin board beside the desk. A
photo of himself, riding backward on a bicycle at
a company picnic, was pinned in the lower corner.
A cartoon from *The New Yorker* was mounted
next to it. A gold-framed photo of Margo, with
Tammy and Ben on her lap, sat on his desk, next
to an onyx ashtray from Cancun. There was little
else that was personal.

When he finished a second cigarette, the thief
picked up the code book and the unwieldy blueprint binder and stepped into the darkened hallway. The executive suite was empty. The annual
directors' dinner began in an hour. All the hustlers
and hotshots would be there early.

"All the hustlers, Danny," he muttered through
his teeth. He would be late and would miss the
cocktails. But he wasn't so important that his tar-
diness would be noticed, he thought with a touch
of bitterness.

Down two floors was the security library. The
thief carried the books down the fire stairs and
through another dark hallway and opened the library door with a key from a steel ring. Inside, he
went to a separate room in the back, opened the
fire door with another key, and put the books

back on the shelves from which he'd gotten them three hours earlier.

As he shut and locked the library door, he was seized by a graveyard chill. Footsteps? No. There was no one there. He pulled the key out of the lock and hurried—*scurrying,* he thought, *like a rat*—back to his office, suddenly afraid of the dark. Afraid that somebody would step out of a doorway and say, "*We know what you're doing. . . .*"

Inside the office, his heart pounding, the thief put the original bulb back into the drafting lamp, dropped the floodlight into a brown paper sack, and crushed it under his heel. He would dump the sack in a trash basket on the way out.

The film cassettes he tucked under his cummerbund, like so many bullets in a cartridge belt. The camera, on a short strap, went over his shoulder, under and slightly behind his armpit. With the tuxedo jacket covering it, the camera would be invisible. Satisfied, he turned out the light, picked up his alligator briefcase, and rode the elevator down eight floors to the lobby.

The guard at the front desk was watching an Orioles–White Sox game on a grainy black-and-white television. He turned his head at the sound of the elevator.

"How are we doing?" the thief said as he crossed the marble floor.

"Down three to two, but we're coming up in

the eighth." The guard pushed the sign-out register across the desk. "You going to the big party?"

"Yes." The thief glanced at his watch. Right on time. The guard checked his briefcase, deferentially opening the half dozen file folders inside. They contained routine personnel papers. Nothing technical.

"S'okay, and have a good time," the guard said. "Don't do anything I wouldn't."

"I'll be careful," said the thief, with a quick, pleasant smile. His teeth were white against his dark face. Sharp dresser, the guard thought as the thief went down the steps and out the door, though his tux was a little too full in the shoulder.

The guard looked at his watch and sighed. Five hours to go. He opened the drawer that held his lunchbox where a package of Hostess cupcakes waited. He knew if he ate them now, he'd regret it at lunch time. He opened the box and took out the cellophane-covered cupcakes and stared at them. Chocolate frosting with pink squiggles. God, it was a lonely job.

Chapter 1

S HE WAS TALL and lanky and wore an expensive white summer suit with a complementary cream-colored shoulder bag and jet-black wraparound fuck-you sunglasses. Her ash-blond hair just touched her shoulders.

She would fit in nicely with the Concorde crowd. On the river, she was wildly out of place. Her business heels dug into the side of the levee as she came down. The summer suit, light as it was, clung to her thighs like wet paint. At the base of the levee she brushed through a screen of head-high willows, took a few steps out on the sand, kicked off her shoes, and scooped them up with one hand. She walked like an athlete, like a long-distance runner.

I was working on a sandbar below the St. Paul Municipal Airport, where the Mississippi curls away from the Twin Cities. It's a rough river off the bar, deep and muddy brown. It smells of dead carp, rotting wood, and diesel fuel. A half mile upstream, the St. Paul skyline soars over the river, the buildings more impressive for the hundred-foot bluffs beneath them.

A gravel road ran behind the levee, so it was possible to get in by car, as the blonde had. I'd come by water. The boat was tied off on a driftwood stump, and the easel sat out on the sand, facing the bluff across the river.

I work in watercolor and sometimes pastel. A newspaper critic once wrote that "Mr. Kidd paints in a colorful representational style borne of the Second Generation of New York School Abstract Expressionism." One of the basic rules of life is that artists don't question favorable newspaper reviews. But I brood about that *borne* when I've had too much beer or gotten stuck on a tough painting. Did he mean *born?* Or did he really mean *borne?*

I had to give up on the day's painting. This bluff was a monster. The rock was mostly a golden yellow, crossed halfway down by a band of pink. Weedy little saplings sprouted from crevices on the rock face, and the mix of green leaves and pink rock set up uncontrollable vibrations. Then too, I'd made a couple of bad moves. I said "shit" and stopped. The painting was gone.

"Mr. Kidd?"

The only other person who ever came to the bar was a snuff-chewing catfisherman with a plastic drywall bucket for a seat, a half-pound of spoiled chicken livers for bait, and a face like an English walnut. He'd sit and spit and never say a word.

"Yeah." She'd looked good coming down the levee. Up close, she looked even better.

"I'm Ann Smith." She took off her sunglasses with one hand and stuck out the other. I shook it. Her hand was cool and soft, a business hand with short squared nails, no polish, no rings. We have an abundance of good-looking blondes in Minnesota. Even so, she was a head-turner. Green eyes with gold flecks. Square chin. A few freckles on her too-tidy nose. Surgery? Maybe. The most delicate scent floated about her, a mix of iris and vanilla. "A woman at your apartment building said you were working down here. I hope you don't mind the interruption. It's important."

"I was finishing up." I took an X-acto knife from the tackle box and cut a triangle from the center of the painting.

She frowned, took another step forward, and cocked her head to look at the painting. "Why'd you do that? Ruin the picture?"

"It was already ruined. If you leave bad paintings laying around, they wind up on walls." I tossed the knife back in the tackle box. "What can I do for you?"

"A job," she answered promptly, her eyes still on the wrecked painting.

"Ah. A job."

She put the sunglasses back on, hiding her eyes.
"A computer job."

"A computer job. I'll tell you, Miss . . ."

"Smith."

"I charge outrageous prices. And I hate consulting work. I can recommend a reliable freelancer—"

"We're not looking for bugs," she said flatly.
She opened her purse and took out an envelope.
"I have a retainer here."

I tried again. "Look, I've had a good run of paintings—"

She interrupted again. "Last year you made seventeen thousand dollars on paintings," she said. Her dark glasses gave her a hostile power. "That will barely pay your mortgage. You might make twenty thousand this year. You spend a month fishing in the Northwest Territories. You spend another month on Biscayne Bay, out of Miami. You go to New Orleans to paint. You'd like to buy a permanent place down there. Your karate costs a thousand. You have to eat. So you'll have to take computer work. And we don't care about your outrageous fees. We can afford them."

My easel is a homemade contraption, designed to disassemble and fit in the boat. It's held together by a bunch of butterfly-sized wingnuts. As she was talking, I dropped to one knee and reached in to loosen one of the nuts and to hide my face while I thought about what she said.

She looked too rich to be a cop. And she was too direct to be political. Political people ooze butter even when the knives are out. That left two possibilities. She might be private. Or she might be federal, working for an agency I didn't want to know about.

Whichever it was, she'd seen my tax return. That's the only place she'd find the amount of seventeen thousand dollars, because it was phony. I made a lot less than that, on the painting anyway, but declared seventeen. It accounted for income that couldn't be hidden and that I couldn't afford to explain.

So she had some clout. The business about a place in New Orleans was harder to figure. It suggested surveillance, though I hadn't felt a thing.

"You want more?" she asked, showing off. "Your friends say you're odd. That's the word they use: *odd*. You have a bachelor's degree in electrical engineering. You have a master of fine arts in painting. You should have a Ph.D. in software design, but you skipped your orals to go fishing in Costa Rica."

"They were biting," I said lamely, trying to slow the recitation.

"That's bullshit," she said crisply.

"Yeah. But it's the simplest explanation that fits all the facts."

"Occam's razor."

"A good guy, Occam," I said.

"Your friends say you stay up all night and sleep until noon. You paint and do computer programs and know a lot of politicians who come to your apartment with sacks full of money. Sometimes shoeboxes."

"Only rarely. Shoeboxes, I mean."

She rolled on like a Vandal. "Your friends say you have a wonderful nerd act. You dress up like an engineer with a white shirt and string tie, and put a calculator on your belt and nine ballpoint pens in a white plastic pocket shield. That's how you went to the Beaux Arts ball last year with Bette what's-her-name. But you don't quite make it as a nerd. You worked with the Strategic Operations Group out of Saigon during the Vietnam War. And I have a fuzzy television monitor photo of a man who looks quite a bit like you—couldn't prove it, but it's close—going over the three-strand wire at Belkap MicroTech. He's not dressed like a nerd at all. He's dressed in an Army urban camouflage suit that's supposed to be sort of secret. He left a little blood behind on the wire, type A-positive, which happens to be your type. You want more?"

"No." The wingnut came loose in my hand. I looked at it and wondered who had designed such an elegant, useful thing. It might be something to draw. "It's all pretty much of a fantasy anyway."

She took another step closer, until she loomed over me. "I don't think so. We have excellent sources of information. You were recommended by Jack Clark at Clark Foods. He gave you high marks for solving his problem, whatever it was."

If she'd talked to Jack, there was one more thing she'd know, but hadn't asked about. It was coming.

"There's one more thing," she said.

"I thought there might be."

"A couple of people said you do the tarot. That makes us a little nervous."

"It shouldn't. You don't know how I use it."

"The job we have is critical. We don't want it done based on the stars, or whatever."

"I'm probably less superstitious than you are," I said. I stood up and it was too close for comfort; she backed off. "I use the tarot my own way. You wouldn't understand it, and I'm not inclined to explain. If you don't like it, you can hike back over the levee." I pulled the easel apart and laid the uprights in the boat.

"We just don't want it to get in the way," she said.

"Is that a royal We? Or do We have an employer?"

"You'll get a name when you agree to work with us. That's what this is for." She unfolded the envelope, and showed me the money. She was a big woman, her eyes level with my chin, and the sun and the light breeze turned her blond hair into a halo. Behind her, on the water, a tow pushed a string of rust-colored barges upstream. A bare-chested deckhand in grimy jeans sat on the lead barge and watched us. "We will give you five thousand dollars to ride in to Chicago with me this afternoon. I've got a plane waiting at the airport. We'll buy you a return ticket."

"Convincer money," I said.

She shrugged. "Free money, Mr. Kidd. All cash, no record, no taxes."

"I declare all my income, Miss . . ."

"Smith."

"Right." If her name was Smith, I'd eat my brushes. "How much for the main job?"

"You'll have to talk to my employer about that. If you take it, you won't have to worry about financing a place in New Orleans. You'll be able to buy it outright."

She was cool, superior, and slightly snotty. A male friend, if she had time for one, would have a hard body, a great tan, a gold chain, a two-seater Mercedes-Benz, and no sense of humor. A commoner had little chance of peeling off her shorts. Should it happen, she'd do it purely for the experience, like shopping at Kmart or sniffing glue.

She knew what I was thinking, of course. And she knew she was reaching me, with her information, money, and long athletic legs. All management tools, properly deployed, well under control. It was mildly irritating.

Letting it percolate for a moment, I looked down at the battered, grass-green fiberglass hull of my boat, the brilliant white D'Arches paper, the black handles of the watercolor brushes. It was all I really wanted to do; I didn't want to fool with some rich guy's computers. But a bigger boat would be nice, and money would buy more time to paint. And New Orleans is a pleasurable place.

"It sounds illegal," I said after a while.

"I don't know what you did for Jack Clark," she said, "but I got the impression that the police wouldn't be happy about it. When I talked to him, he was grinning like the cat that ate the canary."

"I could call Jack and ask who your boss is," I said.

"He wouldn't tell you," she said promptly.

"Five thousand?" I'd been rubbing my hands with an old T-shirt, now a paint cloth. She handed me the envelope, absolutely sure of herself.

"In twenties and fifties," she said. "See you at the airport in an hour?"

"Make it an hour and a half," I said, giving up. I tucked the money into my hip pocket. "I've got to pull the boat out of the water, and make arrangements for the cat . . . take a shower."

She looked at her watch and nodded. She

started to walk away, then changed her mind and turned back to the ruined painting.

"I went to an opening a few weeks ago," she said. "Oil paintings, though, not watercolors. They had holes cut in the middle of them. Like that one. My friend and I spoke to the artist. He said the holes represented his contempt for the conventional form that has trapped painting for so long. He said the American Indian, for instance, often painted on irregularly shaped war shields. . . ."

It was the kind of talk that gives me headaches.

"Miss, ah, Smith?" I said when she slowed for a breath.

"Yes?"

"If we have to fly to Chicago together, if I take this job, do me a favor?"

"Yes?"

"Don't talk to me about art, okay?"

Her face froze up. Offended, she looked down at her watch and said, "An hour and a half. Please be prompt."

She started stiffly across the sandbar toward the willows, but loosened up after a few feet, and even gave it a little extra effort, knowing I'd watch. Which I did. At the base of the levee she stopped to put on her shoes, glanced back, and nimbly climbed the bank.

I keep a pair of 8 x 50 binoculars in the boat, so I can get a closer look at landscape structures.

When she disappeared over the levee, I got the glasses and jogged after her. A car door slammed as I scrambled up the levee and put the glasses on her car's license plate. It was a Minnesota tag, probably a rental. Back at the boat, I wrote the number on the cash envelope with a nice vibrant black made of alizarin crimson and hooker's green.

Then I went off to call Robert Duchamps, pronounced Doosham, and usually called Bobby.

Chapter 2

THE CAT, A tiger-striped tom, had moved in a few months after I bought the apartment. He was waiting now on the back of the living room couch, gazing out the window toward the river. He was doing the same thing one day when a pigeon, one of the big blue and white numbers, smacked headlong into the glass. He came off the couch like a bullet and hid under the kitchen sink for the rest of the day. He hasn't trusted a pigeon since.

"I'm going out of town," I told him. "I'll leave the flap open. Emily will feed you." He looked at me, yawned, and turned back to the window.

Emily Anderson lives in the apartment below mine. She's seventy years old and a damn good painter. Most Wednesday nights we hire a model and drink beer and draw and argue. I walked down the stairs and knocked on her door. When she answered, I told her about the trip. She agreed to take care of the cat.

"Though you ought to pay me for taking care of the smelly thing."

"Jesus Christ, you drink enough of my beer to float a battleship," I said.

"Yeah, and make sure there's a six-pack in the fridge," she said as she shut her door. We get along famously.

I live in a sprawling apartment in the northeast corner of a converted red-brick warehouse, four floors up. The painting studio is on the north side, under a lot of glass. There's also a study, a small living room that looks east toward the rail-yards and river, a tiny kitchen with a dining bar, and one bedroom.

Most of my time is spent in the studio or the study, which is dominated by three walls of books and a bunch of personal computers. There's an IBM-AT that's been collecting dust lately, one of the IBM PS/2s, a Mac II, and my favorite, a full-bore Amiga 2000. A Lee Data dumb terminal is stuffed under a book table next to an early vintage Mac. A few old-timers from Commodore, Radio Shack, and Apple sit in boxes in a corner with power cords wrapped around their disk drives. I work on the big machines when I need money, but prefer the small ones. Power to the people.

I turned on the Amiga, loaded a communications program, and typed in Bobby Duchamps's phone number in East St. Louis.

Bobby lives in the phone wires. We met one night in the late seventies, by accident, deep inside the General Motors design computers. We had a nice chat, and he gave me a number in Chicago. The number didn't exist as an independent phone line, but it triggered an intercept. Bobby was a phone phreak before he started hacking.

Bobby specializes in databases. He's deep into Arpanet and Milnet and BNeT and a half dozen other international and intercontinental data networks. He knows the credit company computers like the back of his hand. If you need something from a phone-wired database, chances are he can get it.

Other than that, I didn't know much about him. I was down in New Orleans once and hadn't hooked up my portable, and he called me on a voice line. He sounded like one of those soft-spoken Delta blacks, in his teens or twenties. He had a speech impediment, and hinted that he had a physical problem. Cerebral palsy, something like that.

Since then I've called him at half a dozen different numbers in the biggest metro areas east of the Mississippi. I don't know whether he actually moved or somehow changed area codes. You can get him personally, twenty-four hours a day, if you know how.

The East St. Louis number rang without an answer. I counted the rings to eight, and pressed the "a" key before the ninth ring. It rang twice more, and then the carrier tone came up. If I hadn't pressed an "a" between eight and nine, it'd have rung forever.

After another moment, a *?* came up on my screen, and I typed in a pseudonym. After another moment, a WHAT? appeared.

I typed, *need info 45 minutes max on driver rental car (unknown agency but probably from St. Paul Muni) XDB-471 white Ford.*

It sat there on the screen for a moment before he came back with $50, his price for the information.

I typed *OK* and he came back with LEAVE ON RECEIVE. I typed *OK* again and a second later the modem signaled a disconnect. I switched the modem to auto-answer and hung up.

Bobby doesn't take cash. His patrons sign up with SciNet, a science-oriented data-processing service, and give Bobby their account numbers and passwords. He uses their time, up to an agreed amount. He never cheats. I have no idea what he's using SciNet's mainframes for. It might be a money-laundering shuck of some kind.

While Bobby looked for data on the blonde, I showered and brushed my teeth.

As I was brushing, I stared at myself in the mirror, something that I seem to do more and more often as the years go by. Searching for signs of immortality, finding signs of erosion; the lines on either side of my nose get deeper and my hair is shot through with gray, which I like to pretend is premature.

I thought about growing a mustache again, but the last time I tried, the experiment ended in embarrassment. A woman friend was teasing me about the new growth, saying I reminded her of someone. But who? I modestly mentioned a few movie stars, and she started laughing. Things were moving right along until halfway through the evening, when her forehead wrinkled and she pointed her index finger at the brush above my mouth. "I got it. Mark Twain!"

Mark Twain was a wonderful guy, but in the picture everybody remembers, he was thirty years older than I am. Twenty, anyway. I lost the mustache.

When I finished brushing, I changed into a clean pair of jeans, a blue oxford-cloth shirt, and a fading linen sport coat. Then I went out to the kitchen, opened a can of chicken feast for the cat, and unlocked the flap so he could come and go. I was stuffing underwear and a couple of clean shirts into an overnight bag when Bobby called back. The computer answered, and data began running down the screen.

Margaret Ellise Kahn, dob 2/18/52, 80023 Indian, Evanston, Ill., eyes green, height 5'9, weight 135, no corrective lenses, registered owner silver-gray Porsche 911. Speeding tickets September 120 in 55 zone paid $150 fine; charged 112 in 55 November dismissed; charged 114 in 55 April dismissed; employed Anshiser Holding Corp. Chicago-Los Angeles personal sec Rudolph S.

Anshiser; reported income $297,000 last year's fed return; credit ratings AAA all services; bank balances $15,000 checking, $268,000 CDs and passbook; accounts with Merrill Lynch amounts unknown; Cook county court shows divorce Margaret Ellise Kahn Harcourt from John Miller Harcourt prof. U. Chicago economics, 2-24-80, shows no Cook County marriage license; Margaret Ellise Kahn grad U. Chicago economics BA 1974 MA 75 Ph.D. 78. Personal sec. Anshiser 1980–present . . . can print full divorce proceeding, full credit reports?

I typed back, *No.*

Much more around, if need more; lots of files & leads.

No thanx, may call back. Going Chicago, will take portable. Plenty credit SciNet, talk to you later.

Later.

The screen flashed disconnect. I sent the data to the printer, ripped off the sheet that burped out, stuck it in my coat pocket, and shut the system down.

The first part of Bobby's information came from a driver's license record. He's into the car rental agencies' data banks, and he got the license and credit card numbers there. Once he had those, he was on his way. Credit records, government records, Social Security—they're all open books, if you have the right opener.

He'd given me something to think about. Anshiser was serious money: a billion or two. if *The Wall Street Journal* knows what it's talking about.

I subscribe to twenty-five or thirty magazines and newsletters that touch on my work, everything from *Artnews* and *Byte* to *PC World* and *Vector Reports*. Any issues of particular interest get tossed in a closet. If I wasn't mistaken, *Business Week*, sometime in the past year, had done a profile of Anshiser and his businesses. I opened the closet and started sorting through the accumulation of paper. I found it six months down.

Anshiser, according to *Business Week*, directly controlled Anshiser Holding Corporation, which in turn owned a dozen major companies. On the industrial side was Anshiser Aviation, where he got his start during World War II, building up a company bought by his father during the Depression. There was also an avionics company, a small aluminum specialties mill, and a string of scrap yards. The holdings on the service side, where Anshiser had been most active in the past twenty years, were even more impressive. They included a hotel chain, two franchise restaurant chains, one of the nation's biggest garbage-hauling firms, and Kelmark Vending, a building and distributor of candy- and cigarette-machines, coin-op pool tables, and similar equipment.

Anshiser was known for his willingness to take risks and to delegate authority. If he gave you a company to run, and you ran it well, he made you rich and kept his hands off. Executives who failed to measure up were ruthlessly weeded out.

He was also a force in Republican politics, particularly in the upper Midwest. And that, I thought, was where he got my name. Most of my political money is Republican. That has nothing to do with personal preferences. The Republicans simply have more cash. As far as I'm concerned, the two parties are about as different as Curly and Moe.

Before leaving the apartment, I stepped into the studio and sat down at the drawing table. I keep a tarot at hand, wrapped in silk in a wooden box from Poland. The deck is a common one, a popular variation of the Ryder design. I did five quick spreads, and the Fool showed up in critical positions in three of them. The Fool represents a major change that occurs as a natural and inexorable part of life, without your volition, because of the way you live. I wrapped the cards in the silk cloth, put them back in the box, and slipped the box into my overnight bag. Something to consider.

THE MUNICIPAL AIRPORT from my apartment is across the Robert Street Bridge, down onto the flats along the river. Kahn was waiting for me in the terminal, smiled perfunctorily when she saw me coming with the bag and the portable, and headed out the door.

"We're right out here," she said over her shoulder.

It was a red-and-white Anshiser-built business jet with a charter logo. I hate traveling on small jets. You feel like you're in a mailing tube. The pilot and copilot were already in the cockpit.

"I'm surprised it's a charter," I said. "I'd have thought you'd fly it yourself, Margaret. Like you fly the Porsche."

She turned her head and looked at me. Her eyes unfocused a bit, and before we got to the waiting plane, she said, "The rental car. You got the license number."

"Very good," I said. The data said she was smart. The data were right.

"You've got a friend at the rental booth. The redhead?" she asked as we stopped at the steps to the plane.

"No. Database. The redhead wouldn't know about the Porsche." I gave her my best smile.

Her forehead wrinkled. "So you know who my employer is?"

"Rudolph Anshiser."

"Hmph," she said, and led the way to the jet. At the top of the stairs she turned and said, "It's not Margaret. It's Maggie."

Chapter 3

I N WHAT SEEMS like another century, I was a first lieutenant in the U.S. Army. The unit was small, and eventually all but four of us were dead or in pieces. I lay in an Army hospital in San Francisco, tried to rationalize my part in the deaths, and failed. Since then, I've had an aversion to organization. For the most part, I simply want to be left alone. That's not as simple as it should be.

I paint during the days, and late at night I sit in front of a computer terminal and make statistical models. In the early evenings, there are workouts at the Shotokan dojo on East Seventh Street.

I like my cat, a couple of women in town, fifteen or twenty Twins ball games a year, fishing out of Miami in the winter and on a Canadian lake in the summer, and the music and food in New Orleans. I go to New York and Chicago for gallery openings and to hustle my paintings.

It all takes money. Only a small fraction of my

earnings comes from painting, but the fraction is getting larger. A bigger chunk comes from the computer models. The models predict political behavior, using social statistics, a cynic's view of history, and a variety of small computers. If you want to be a state legislator, governor, congressman, or U.S. senator from Wisconsin, Minnesota, or several other states of the upper Midwest, you can buy a Kidd election model and run it on your own IBM office machine. You crank in a political position, and out comes a result in terms of vote shifts. If you don't like the answer, you can crank in a different position. A model like that will cost five to twenty grand, depending on how rich you are.

Sometimes, especially in political off-years, I take less conventional computer-related jobs. They pay the best of all.

I TOLD MOST of this to Rudolph Anshiser himself three hours after Maggie and I flew out of St. Paul. We were met at the O'Hare general aviation terminal by a gray Mercedes limousine. The chauffeur wore a blue pinstriped shirt and rep tie. He looked like he might own a company or two himself.

We drove north and east out of O'Hare. Forty-five minutes after we left the airport, the chauffeur turned off the arterial highway into a four-lane street through an expensive neighborhood. It may

have been Evanston, but may also have been a bit
farther north. Eventually we left the four-lane
street for a two-lane through an even more expensive neighborhood, and finally turned onto a
blacktopped lane that twisted and turned past
gated entries and vine-covered walls. We stopped
at a brick gatehouse with wrought-iron gates. The
chauffeur pressed a button on the car's dash-
board, and the gates rolled open.

Behind them were two acres of crisply land-
scaped grounds dotted with oak, ash, and the distinct forms of gingko trees. Here and there were
the stumps of departed American elms. The
house, a pile of ivy-covered brick, covered another quarter acre. Lake Michigan broke against
a seawall in back.

The chauffeur stopped at the arched front
entry, and Maggie led me across a red quarry-tile
porch, through a dimly lit, walnut-paneled entry
hall and into an old-fashioned parlor. She pointed
at an overstuffed chair.

"I have to report. We'll have you up in five
minutes," she said.

She left, and I sat down and looked around the
room. It had the peculiar stillness that comes with
a lack of living-in. It was a waiting room, but few
people waited in it. There was a blocked-up fireplace, flanked on both sides by bookshelves
loaded with obsolete business texts. Another wall
featured a narrow window with heavy brocade

drapes drawn back to show a thin slice of green lawn. Little, sparkly dust motes glimmered in the shaft of sunlight that came through.

A German Romantic oil painting hung over the fireplace, and my eye kept skipping over it. From the corner, beside the bookshelves, a much smaller painting made noises at me. I finally heaved myself out of the chair and went over to look at it. Then I got down in front of it.

Damn. A Whistler. One of the pastels from Venice. A street scene with strollers and a garbage-eating dog. The buildings, outlined in black chalk on gray-toned paper, leaned out over the crowd, and were brought to life with a few simple touches of color. In the lower left-hand corner was his butterfly signature. I'd never seen it before, not the real thing. The painting was hung five feet off the floor and I was practically down on my knees peering at it. The light was terrible. I didn't hear Maggie come back.

"Like it?"

I jumped and turned.

"Jesus. This is a Whistler."

"Uhh-huh." She was not interested.

"Yeah. I like it." I went back to it. How did he make it so real, with so few lines and so little color? I looked at it until Maggie started fidgeting.

"Okay," I said, and followed her out of the parlor and up a curving walnut staircase to the second floor. A long, carpeted corridor crossed the stairs at the top, running both ways the full length of the house. We turned left, past bedrooms now converted to offices. There were people in some of the offices, working over computer screens or stacks of paper. They didn't look up as we passed. Halfway down the hall, Maggie knocked at a heavy oak door and went through.

This room was a complete contrast to the waiting area. Anshiser had opened up the rear wall with huge glass windows. The lake made a sharp, dark horizon line as far as you could see to the north; to the south you could sense the great cul-de-sac at South Bend.

Anshiser, in wheat jeans and a blue rough-silk sweatshirt, sat behind an ornate table, his back to the windows. Another man, dressed in a gray business suit, white shirt, wine tie, and wingtips, sat on a side chair, one leg crossed over the other. Maggie and I plodded across a pond-sized carpet, and Anshiser stood to shake my hand.

"Mr. Kidd." His face had once been craggy, but the crags were softening with age and erosion. His eyebrows were thick tangled mats hanging over the pale blue eyes of a born killer—a man who lived on energy, but his energy, betrayed by the flesh, was beginning to fail. He gestured to a leather chair. As I sat down, facing him across the table, I noticed that his hand shook.

"This is Mr. Dillon," he said, indicating the man in the side chair. Dillon nodded.

Two computer terminals squatted on Anshiser's table. One was a dedicated stock-trading link, its screen covered with lists of numbers in tiny amber print. The other was a general-purpose IBM showing a dense block of text, a report of some kind. As he introduced Dillon, Anshiser reached out and tapped a key sequence, and the screen went blank.

"Tell me how you identified us," he said. "I don't want any trade secrets, just in general."

I told him, without mentioning names or phone numbers.

"Hmm." He pulled at his chin when I finished. "Suppose somebody like your friend wanted to get into my company files. Is there any foolproof way to protect them?"

"From the outside? Sure. Don't hook them up to a telephone. Your little IBM there"—I nodded at his desktop terminal—"is absolutely secure from telephone interference as long as the modem is turned off. If you set it to auto-answer, because you have people calling in, then you could have a problem. And I assume you're hooked into a mainframe, which means that it has incoming lines, so that could be vulnerable."

"Everything important is protected by randomly generated passwords."

"There are lots of ways to get passwords."

"Tell me one."

I told him several, and, since he lived on a lake, mentioned work done in the Netherlands involving the processing of images projected onto computer monitors.

"Everything that shows up on a monitor is the result of a high-speed beam that scans back and forth across it—letters, words, pictures, everything. As the beam switches on and off it creates an electromagnetic pulse, sort of like a radio wave. It's weak, but with the right gear, it can be picked up, amplified, sorted, synchronized, and reproduced on another screen, up to a few hundred feet away. Or further, if there isn't much interference. A boat on the lake would do quite well. They wouldn't have independent access to your files, but they'd see everything you see."

When I finished, Anshiser glanced out at the lake, then over at Maggie, who was sitting at a side table with a leather-bound book.

"Check this," he said briefly.

She nodded. "I'll call that FBI fellow who helped on the container ship contamination problem. He should know somebody."

Anshiser turned back to me, contemplated my face for a minute, and then decided. "Have you had any contact with the aviation industry?"

I shrugged. "Not much. I did some work on Boeing's economic and political clout in Seattle, and plugged the data into a political model. It didn't come to much."

"Why not?" he asked curiously.

"It wasn't a vote discriminator. Nobody in Seattle fools with Boeing. The discriminators involved other issues."

"Hmph." Anshiser pivoted his leather chair and peered out the window toward the lake. It was getting dark, and the line of the horizon was splitting deep blue sky and black water.

"I have a problem," he said, after a moment. He sighed and shook his head and pivoted back to face me. "It's the biggest problem of my career. It could destroy or badly damage the heart of this company. More than forty years of work for me, and twenty-five more for my father."

"I can help?"

He grunted. "Maybe." He turned the chair again, to look out over the lake, gathering his thoughts.

"About ten years ago, it appeared that there would be an opportunity. An opportunity to design a cutting-edge, all-weather fighter aircraft. It would be a half-step after the F-15, F-16, F-18 generation, but earlier than a really operational F-30 hypersonic plane came on. There was a lot of skepticism back then, in and out of government, about new military fighters. We were paying huge amounts of money for tiny increments of advantage."

He laced his hands behind his head. "In any case, the big defense aviation companies were focusing on the hypersonic aerospace fighter. To a few of us, it seemed that a gap might open, and we could slip into it with a privately built plane. So we started working on one. Just concepts at first, springing some engineers here and there to do studies and try out new ideas.

"We weren't the only ones doing that. Whitemark Aerospace had its own project going, and the bugs were out of it. They tried building private fighters and got burned. They got burned even though they did a hell of a job. But they weren't working with the same kind of gap that we are now."

He paused and looked at his hands, as though he would find words in them.

"Anyway, it was us and Whitemark. These things get complicated, almost philosophical, but we took different routes to the new fighters. They went with a heavy bird, called it *Hellwolf*. Big weapons platform, lots of armor, lots of computer assist. It's a brute. We went with a light bird, the *Sunfire*. Not much armor, limited amounts of weaponry, although it could take a good variety—cannon, rockets, smart bombs, air-to-air and air-to-ground missiles, area-denial canisters, the full spectrum. It has an exceptional stealth configuration and selectively malleable wings that make it into a hell of a lifting body, with great idle time. It can go out and hang there, waiting. It's as fast as the Whitemark entry, Mach 3.4 at thirty-five thousand feet, 1.3 at treetops. But it has half again the combat radius, better than twenty-three hundred miles."

"Sounds unbeatable," I said, uncertainly. "Though I don't know much about fighter specs."

"It looked good," Anshiser said. There was a bitter note in his voice. "For a while, at least."

He turned and looked at me. "There are reasons to build light birds, and reasons to build them heavy. Pure speed is good, but it's not everything. Dogfighting speeds are a lot lower than full-burn running. If you're trying to maintain air superiority over a ground fight, you've got to stay over the killing ground. Whitemark figured that for practical purposes, in dogfights, *Hellwolf* would be as maneuverable as our *Sunfire,* with the advantage of the armor and the extra weaponry. They also knew that the American defense establishment has always gone for the heavy fighter when it had a choice. So Whitemark thought they had an advantage. But we had something they didn't."

"And that was?"

He hesitated. "I haven't told you anything secret yet. I'm aware of your old military security clearance, but you've got to know that some of this is classified."

"I don't talk."

He nodded. "What we had was a genius.

Walter Markess. He was a synthesizer. They're pretty rare among engineers. He took some stuff from Navy submarine design and some stuff from the Corps of Engineers, God help him. He did some research of his own, and he had access to all the work on air target acquisition. He came up with a thing that he called 'String,' for Selective Targeting.

"You see, the maneuverability of a fighter is not limited so much by its design as by what the pilot can endure. Above certain turn rates, you get pilot failure. They're crushed by the high-g turns, they black out, they red out, their reactions go to hell, they get confused and disoriented. String targeting was a system that used laser tags, radar imaging, and even acoustics to get a target and hold it. It didn't make any difference what altitude the enemy plane was in, or your plane, what speeds or directions they were going. Once the target was acquired, String would hold it, and relate it to your plane, until it was so far out that it was no longer a factor. Just like you had a string tied to it.

"Then Markess took the whole thing a step further. He designed a control system using limited artificial intelligence software that could gameplay the opposing fighters, given selections made by the pilot. In other words, the plane could fly by itself. It could make intelligent choices by considering a whole array of data: type of armaments and remaining supply, remaining fuel, number of opponents and their armament, actions of allied and enemy aircraft, prospects of success, the importance of success, and so on. And the thing is, you see, a pilot could opt to let the plane go beyond his own control. Even beyond his blackout point. He could say to the plane, 'Take it. Run it to x number of gees, and it's okay if I go out for a while, because you can handle it.' And the plane would stay short of lethal maneuvers.

"You see the advantage that gave us? No matter how fast their *Hellwolf* turned, we could turn inside it in critical situations. We could run with it, climb with it, and outwait it on target. We could do maneuvers *Hellwolf* couldn't even consider. Maneuvers never seen before. We could attack and keep attacking when the pilots themselves were completely out of it."

"What happened?"

Anshiser had become more and more animated as he recited the qualities of the *Sunfire*, but suddenly he was still, almost frozen. The hush lasted for five heartbeats before he moved again, to lean forward on his desk.

"Those sonsofbitches at Whitemark stole String from us." He slammed a big fist on the desk, his face tense and pale. "Stole it. Paid some sonofabitch to copy plans and carry them out of our corporate headquarters. They built their own String. The specs for their early system designs even had our mistakes, because they didn't know enough to identify them."

"You didn't have any legal protection?"

"It's not the sort of thing you get a patent on," Anshiser snorted. "If we went to court, we might prove something fifty years from now. But after they figured out the system, they started altering it. Every time they found an alternate way to do something, they took it. If you went out right now and looked at the plans for our system, and their system, you'd probably feel the *resemblance*. But you'd have a hard time proving that their system is a copy."

He suddenly switched direction.

"How old do you think I am?"

I figured seventy or seventy-five, but gave him five years out of courtesy. "I don't know. Sixty-five? Seventy?"

"Thank you." He grinned. "I'm eighty-three. I don't have much time left. I've been feeling . . . hollow. I can't explain it, but it's worse than being sick. Not that I've been sick that much. The doctors say it's stress, and Dillon and Maggie say it's this *Sunfire* thing.

"My wife is gone, my kids are okay but nothing special. They'll each inherit a couple of million or so when I die, and turn into the fossilized dipshits you see standing around country clubs. I can see it in my grandchildren. They're okay—

most of them—but I'm not very interested in them.

"So I'm eighty-three, and the company is all I'm leaving behind. Now I might not leave that. In this business, development costs are so high that if you don't win the contract, if you don't get to build the plane, the whole company can go down.

"Right now, we employ thirteen thousand workers in our aviation division. If *Sunfire* wins the competition, we'll hire ten thousand more. If we lose, and all we have left is the corporate jet division, we'll be down to five thousand by the end of the decade. The corporate jet field is saturated, competition is getting worse, and we have nowhere else to go. There are eight thousand people, more or less, who could lose their jobs because of a rotten little thief. I'm not going to stand for it. Not if I can do anything about it."

"Do you know who the thief is?"

He glanced at Dillon. Dillon stared back impassively, and when Anshiser turned to me again, I got the feeling he was about to tell a lie. "No. We have some ideas. But right now, we don't know."

"Okay. So where do I come in? What do you want me to do?"

"A couple of things. Everything we do, from design to production to cost estimating, we do on computers. It's all so complicated, there is no other way. If somebody smart got into our computer system, I don't know how, but did it, he could hurt us. Badly."

"And you think it's the same with Whitemark."

"I know it is. There simply isn't any other way to do the work. Whitemark has about three months to integrate the String system with their *Hellwolf* avionics. Then they have to demonstrate to the Navy and Air Force that it will work. As it is, they might not make the deadline. They've got a crash program going, but they started late. I want you to slow them down. I want you to get into their computer system and screw it up. Be subtle, be obvious, I don't care. But I want you to push them to the wall—I want you to jam them up so they can't move. If they can't demonstrate their system in three months, and we can, we're back in the ball game."

"What's the other thing you want?" I asked.

"Revenge," he said, his killer's eyes glittering in the dying light. "I want revenge on the bastards who stole my baby."

Chapter 4

I SPENT THE night in a Chicago hotel, watching a bad movie about teenagers and thinking over the job proposition. Anshiser was a maniac, of course. He knew what he was doing, but he was clinging to a thin edge of control, like a grunt with battle fatigue. Would a crisis crack the control, or harden it? It could go either way. Maggie was something else. She was precise, measured, cool. She knew what she was doing, and she was nowhere near the edge. She apparently agreed with Anshiser. Dillon was a cipher.

Their proposition was not entirely novel. There have been several hushed-up incidents in which businesses were damaged by computer attacks. Most of the time, the object of the attack was theft or embezzlement, and the damage was an unintentional byproduct.

A major railroad was burned when a group of techno-thieves, as they were called in the FBI report, began shuffling and relabeling boxcars. The intent was to send certain cars, loaded with high-value consumer items like televisions and stereos, to remote sidings, where the gang would crack the cars, load the loot onto trucks, and haul it away. The most serious damage came when they tried to cover their tracks. Three thousand boxcars were mislabeled and sent to the wrong destinations. The result was chaos. Perishable products rotted, time-critical shipments were late. It cost the railroad millions to straighten out.

In a few of the known raids, the damage was intentional. In every case, though, the attacks were from the inside—guerrilla hits by employees against their own company. Anshiser's proposition was altogether different. He was proposing a war, an act of naked aggression, an attack to the death by one corporation on another. As far as I knew, there had never been anything like it. A war that was business by other means, to paraphrase a famous Prussian.

MAGGIE CALLED AT eight o'clock.

"Jesus," I said with a yawn. "When you said morning, I thought you meant like eleven. Where are you?"

"Downstairs," she said briskly. "I have three warm bagels, a small cup of cream cheese, a plastic knife, two Styrofoam cups of coffee, and your room number. What do you think?"

She looked like she'd been up for hours. She

came in, sat in one of the chairs, and ate one of the bagels while she watched me finish the other two.

"You look like you've been dragged through hell by the ankles," she said. "Any thoughts yet?"

"It will take a while," I said, scratching my day-old beard. "I wonder about Anshiser."

"If he's crazy?"

"I might have picked a different word."

"But that's what you want to know," she said. "The answer is, no, he is not crazy. He is extremely anxious. This might be our last card. If we're going to play it, we have to do it soon. In six weeks, or two months, it will be too late."

"Hmph." I drank the last of my coffee. "Let me shave and take a shower, and we can get out of here."

She came and leaned on the bathroom doorjamb while I shaved, still nibbling on her first bagel. "I used to watch my father shave when I was a little girl," she said as I wiped the last of the shaving cream off my face.

"You watch your father take a shower, too?" I asked.

"Of course not." A tiny frown.

"Well, if you'll move your elbow, I'll shut the door and spare you the experience," I said, and she grinned and moved off across the room.

• • •

THE ANSHISER RESEARCH plant was somewhere out by O'Hare, a nondescript, modernoid
building. It looked, as somebody clever once said,
like the box the building should have come in.
The director didn't quite slaver over Maggie's
hand, but he personally took us down to the labo-
ratory level, where a String package was being as-
sembled.

The lab looked like the world's cleanest machine shop, with concrete floors and a lot of
noise. The String package was in a back room.
Entry was through three sets of glass doors, and
for the last two the director needed different-
colored key cards.

String was the size of a console television. It
was mounted on a testing gyro that allowed it to
swivel freely. There was nothing tidy about it.
Wires and electronics boards stuck out at all an-
gles. There were nozzlelike protrusions here and
there, and cylindrical openings where other nozzlelike protrusions would fit. A dolly full of testing equipment sat next to it, and nearby, two
engineers in blue smocks argued about readouts.
They stopped when we walked in.

Maggie introduced me as Mr. Lamb and told
them I was cleared for all access. "What do you
think?" she asked me.

I walked around the instrument package and
shook my head. "Beats the shit out of me," I said.

"We could give you the Bigshot show," one of

the engineers suggested. He had tape wrapped around the bridge of his glasses, which gave him a slightly crazed look. "It'd take about two minutes to rig up."

"Sure, why not?"

The testing equipment was quickly disconnected. The two engineers rolled in a dolly that carried what looked like a cartoon fishbowl, except that it bristled with short metallic rods. At the end of each rod was a glassy bubble. The engineers fitted the fishbowl around the String package like a Plexiglas jacket, and plugged in a half dozen multicolored flat cables.

"Okay," said one of the engineers. There was a keypad with a tiny digital LED panel on the side of the package. He punched a few buttons and peered at the readout, punched a few more, and nodded.

"Mr. Lamb, if you could stand right here." He pointed at a spot on the floor and I stood there. "Okay. Now look at this screen."

He turned on a monitor. It showed what looked like a head as painted by a two-year-old.

"That's your head as interpreted by high-frequency audio waves, infrared sensors, radar and laser rangers. Right now we're looking at the laser sensing. You can read it like a contour map. The brightest yellow part is your nose, then it moves through the red, green, and blue as it goes further back.

"Now here," he said, flipping on another monitor, "is a simulated three-dimensional readout of your head, and its direction, size, range, velocity, and probable identity shown down here in the corner of the screen."

Most of the numbers were meaningless unless you knew the code sequences, though under "identity" it said "head."

"We rigged it to say *head,*" said the engineer with the crazed look.

"Now move around the room," said the other one. I moved, and the readouts changed. "It's following you," he said.

I stepped behind Maggie and looked over her head. It was still following me, and when I came out from behind her, continued to follow.

"Your personal characteristics were read into the computer, so it followed only you. We have it programmed for a single target, or it would have picked up Ms. Kahn as a second target and started a separate reading on her, while registering that you were eclipsed behind her."

"Neat," I said. "Listen, what is this audio thing, and what use can you make of audio pick-ups if you've got two planes on diverging courses, each at, say, Mach 2?"

"Okay," said one of the engineers, slipping into a professorial tone. "You have to understand . . ."

Maggie and the director excused themselves after fifteen minutes of it. I stayed for another two hours looking at the machinery and talking about the software that would run the stuff. It was not my field at all, but I could see the concepts. If I started studying right away, it would only take six years to catch up with what they were doing. The AI and game-playing concepts were easier, and we got tangled in a complicated argument about gaming concepts.

We gave up at lunchtime, and I went looking for Maggie. She was in the director's office working with a business terminal. The director was hovering in the outer office, pretending to supervise a harassed-looking secretary.

"Ah. There you are," she said when I walked in. "All done?"

"Yeah. We ought to get a cheeseburger or something."

The director fussed over her as we went out, and shook my hand. As he turned back and Maggie went out through the door, his face flattened in a distinct look of relief.

"I think that guy was happy to see us go," I said.

"Yes," she said. "I scare him. Can't think why."

AT ANSHISER'S WE went through the wait-in-the-sitting-room routine again, and I spent some more time looking at the Whistler. When she came and got me, I thought I'd figured out how he did it.

"Maggie said you were a little worried that I might be nuts," Anshiser said cheerfully, when we walked into his office.

I glanced over at her and she grinned. "Yeah, a little."

"Good. If you didn't, we'd be worried about *your* stability. But we want you to understand how strongly we feel about this. I think about it constantly. I can't sleep, I can't do business. It might *be* crazy. But we've talked it out and we don't think so."

"So what do I do? Specifically?" I asked, dropping into his visitor's chair.

"First, we want your agreement that if you decide not to take the job, what we discuss never goes out of this office."

I wouldn't talk anyway. Talk wouldn't get me anything but a conspiracy indictment. I relaxed and crossed my legs. "Sure. If you want to take my word for it."

"Our research indicated that we could."

"I'd like to know about that research," I said. "How did you find me?"

"Dillon found you. Dillon is the best researcher in the United States. The Library of Congress calls *him*," Anshiser said. "When we found out what had happened, that String had been stolen, we knew we'd probably lose the competition for the contract. Oh, we wriggled and turned and twisted, and talked to lawyers and patent specialists, and the answer kept coming up the same. So I assigned Dillon to the problem. I told him to forget any parameters at all—just find a solution. As it happens, there is one. Maybe. It just isn't legal."

I glanced over at Dillon and the gray man smiled again. "That's true," he said.

Anshiser continued. "To save ourselves, we have to put their ass in a sling. Then, maybe, I can work some kind of deal."

"What kind of deal?"

"We'll have to see. An acquisition. Maybe we can buy them. Maybe a merger. I don't know. But I need an edge."

"I thought these guys were your blood enemies?"

"I can live with enemies. I just can't watch the company go down. If I can hustle them into a merger, I can take care of them later. Right now, there's no reason in the world they should talk to us. We need to give them a reason."

He turned back to the desk and picked up a black-bound typescript. "This is Dillon's report. In general, it says the best way to stop Whitemark is through their computer systems—design systems, accounting systems, information systems, scheduling, and materials. Altering them, destroying them, faking them out."

"This is a defense industry," I said. "If we're

caught, they'll drop us in Leavenworth for the rest of time."

"Ah. Now that's something Dillon's report covers quite thoroughly," said Anshiser. "I will give you a contract outlining the kind of attack I want. If you are arrested, you will present the authorities with a copy of the contract. I will voluntarily confirm that I hired you to do this work. You will instantly become a very small fry."

"And you join me at Leavenworth."

"No. I don't think so. I'm not absolutely sure, of course, but I don't think so. If I am arrested, or any of my people are arrested, I will publicly discuss the contributions I have given our president over the past ten years. He's exceptionally popular, you know, and intends to run for reelection. The contributions I made were quite illegal, but they kept his political career alive at several critical junctures. I am confident that any investigation will be quashed."

"Blackmail."

"Exactly. You've been around politicians enough to know that it happens every day."

"It's usually not quite so blunt."

"Oh, there won't be anything blunt about it. If they get to me at the end of the investigation, they'll punch me into their computers and a flag will pop up. Some flunky will run over to the White House, and the whole investigation will disappear."

I grunted and thought about it. It could work, but I didn't intend to commit myself without more thought. "It's shaky. I'd have to think about it."

"Think about the fee when you're thinking about the job," Anshiser said. He leaned back and tented his fingers. "If you take the job and it doesn't work out, one million dollars. If you take it and it does work, another million. I assume you would have to hire other people, buy equipment, whatever. When you sign the contract, Ms. Kahn will give you the first million in cash, plus one hundred thousand in expense money."

"Jesus," I said. Now I was thinking furiously. "Why so much? If I was willing to do it, it wouldn't take a million to convince me."

"Mr. Kidd," he said quietly, "I'm eighty-three years old and supposedly have a billion dollars. Maybe two billion. If I gave away a million a week for the rest of my life, I wouldn't keep up with accruing interest. I don't care what I pay you—but I suspect you do. With two million, you'll be free. Forever."

"Or in jail for eight to ten."

"Jail would protect you from distractions while you paint." He sat and looked at me, smiling. I thought about it . . . two million dollars.

"I might also mention that you seem to have precisely the right qualifications for the job. Not only are you able to do it, you have the will to do it. I had the most flattering report from our String engineers, by the way. They want to hire you to work on the AI software."

"That's nice," I said distractedly.

Two million. I had to be missing something.

"You need time to think," he offered.

"Yeah, I do. And the deal's not quite right," I said. "If I take the job, I'll want a second contract. Two million for computer consulting work. Security or something. So if I declare it with the IRS, it'll be clean."

"Agreed."

"And I want the Whistler."

"The what?" He seemed puzzled.

"The Whistler pastel down in the sitting room."

Anshiser glanced at Maggie, who said, "It's the one next to the mantel, to the right."

"Oh, that, the gray one," he said, the wrinkles disappearing from his forehead. "My wife bought it years ago. That was the last time I looked at it. Sure. Two million and the Whistler."

"I'll think about it," I said. "I have to do more research. On you, on Whitemark, on what we might do. I'll get back."

"How long?"

I shrugged. "A week."

He nodded. "A week, then. If you would go with Ms. Kahn, she will give you a copy of a report on Whitemark. And you can take this copy of Dillon's report." He pushed the black-bound typescript across the desk at me, stood, and rubbed his big wrinkled hands together. "Goddamn," he said. "I'm going to enjoy this."

Maggie said, "Follow me, please."

Dillon, who hadn't said a thing, followed us out of the office and turned the other way down the corridor, leaving Anshiser alone. Maggie led me to a smaller office and gestured at a chair as she settled behind her desk. There were two walls of bookshelves packed with texts and references, another window overlooking the lake, and a long oak table stacked with more books.

"You need a painting in here," I said.

"Send me one." She turned on her desk terminal, typed in a series of passwords, and punched a PRINT command. The Whitemark report churned out of a high-speed printer. In thirty seconds I had a sheaf of computer paper that ended with a list of names and job titles.

"That's as up-to-date as we can make it. It was good last week." She looked a bit haggard. For the first time I noticed the fine lines near the corners of her eyes, incipient crow's-feet.

"Frightened?" I asked.

"No, no. I'm a believer," she said, looking up at me. "But there will be problems. They're inevitable. We have a lot of complicated operations in our business. I've learned one thing about them: something will go wrong. Nothing ever works out quite the way you wanted it to. Nothing. With this operation, the consequences of error could be severe."

We talked for another minute, then she led the way back to the stairs and we circled down the staircase to the front entry. The chauffeur was waiting there with a package wrapped in brown paper.

"What's that?" Maggie asked.

"A painting from the waiting room," the chauffeur said. He handed it to me. "Mr. Anshiser said you should look at it while you think." He spread his hands in a gesture of incomprehension. "I don't know what it means. That's just what he said."

The picture, even with the thick fruitwood frame, was light in my hands. A Whistler.

Chapter 5

WITH THE WHISTLER under my arm, I decided against another night in Chicago and had the chauffeur drop me at O'Hare. On the flight back to St. Paul I thumbed through Dillon's report.

Whitemark headquarters, which included design and research facilities, were in Virginia, outside Washington. The company's main assembly plants were in North Carolina. If I took the job, we'd work out of a Washington suburb, so we'd be in the local call area of the Whitemark computer center. The report listed the names of the company's top officers, manufacturing personnel, and engineers. I made a note to call Bobby with the list.

Whitemark was founded by an eccentric electronics enthusiast named Harry Whitemark in the mid-twenties. Originally, the company manufactured radios. It barely survived the '29 crash, and in the thirties went into avionics. During World War II, the company rebuilt civilian planes as specialized light observation aircraft. When Korea came along, it refitted helicopters with special radio gear needed for medivacs and the increasingly complex ground-air networks.

Whitemark got into the fighter business almost by accident. In the seventies, the company found itself without a dominant stockholder, and Whitemark execs liked it that way. Nobody interfered with them, but there was one large fly in the soup.

The company was undervalued and cash-heavy, a sitting duck for a takeover. They looked for a way out and found a lowbrowed ne'er-do-well named Winton Woormly IV.

Woormly had inherited a majority holding in a medium-sized aviation company. The company specialized in jet trainers and small ground-support aircraft, marketing them in third world countries that couldn't afford the big stuff. Woormly was smart enough to understand that, if he tried to run the company himself, he'd screw up and lose it. Besides, he wasn't interested. He was interested in single-malt Scotch, ocean racers, polo, trout fishing, and young boys, in that order.

Whitemark offered him a deal; they'd give him a big lump of cash, a special issue of stock, and a place on the Whitemark board. In return, Woormly would turn over his controlling interest in the aviation company. Woormly jumped at the deal. He wound up with a title and more money than he could spend. Whitemark got a major stockholder who wasn't interested in running the company and whose stock holdings would scare off pirates. They'd also stripped themselves of excess cash, which made them a less inviting target.

The Woormly buyout was a success from the start. The two companies matched up well. There was always a demand for the ground-support planes. Then came the *Hellwolf* concept. Whitemark started lifting its eyes to the big leagues.

There was much more in the report: details on the *Hellwolf,* speculation about flight trials and cost overruns, arguments in the military press over the advantages and disadvantages of the *Hellwolf* versus the *Sunfire.*

I was still reading when the wheels came down. Out the window, the dark ribbon of the Mississippi curled through the lights of the cities, separating St. Paul from Minneapolis, the red-brick East from the chrome-and-glass West. I caught a cab into St. Paul, the Whistler on my lap.

The cat was out roaming the rooftops when I got home. I found a hammer, nails, and hangers, and hung the Whistler on the big interior wall of the studio, surrounded by the work of friends and personal heroes. The other work ranged from simple sketches in India ink to slashing Expressionist stuff in electric acrylics. The Whistler, simple as it was, dominated them. Age and power. The shamans are right.

I got a bottle of beer from the refrigerator and walked around and looked at it some more. I was still looking when Emily knocked at the door.

"You're back," she said. Emily has steel-gray hair pulled into a bun at the nape of her neck, like a nineteenth-century English schoolteacher. She's usually wrapped in a woolen shawl. If it weren't for the flinty sparkles in her dark eyes, you might take her for Whistler's aunt. "I thought you were gone until tomorrow. I heard the pounding and thought I should check."

"C'mere." I crooked a finger at her. She followed me into the studio and spotted the new piece immediately. From where she stood she recognized it, and said, "Holy shit! Is it real?"

"Yeah."

"What have you done?"

"Nothing, yet."

"It must be pretty extreme, whatever it is," she said. She grabbed my upper arm with a surprisingly strong hand. "I hope you don't get hurt."

"I'll be careful," I said. "You want a beer?"

"Sure."

When I came back from the kitchen with a longneck Leinenkugel, her nose was a quarter inch from the sketch. "Little Jimmy Whistler," she said. "You know he learned to draw at West Point? Flunked out. Couldn't pass chemistry.

Years later he said, 'If silicon was a gas, I'd be a general now.' He was probably right. He was at West Point just before the Civil War. West Pointers got quick promotions."

We looked at the picture some more, and then she went back to her apartment, and I went into the study to call Bobby.

What?

Need everything available on Whitemark Aerospace. Top execs with personal data. Access control to all internal computer systems. Any trouble with the law, political connections, business connections. Need soonest; will pay big bux.

Hundreds or thousands?

Stop for now at $5,000; could be much more later. May need major backup for big project. Also need information on Rudolph Anshiser, his secretary Maggie Kahn, assistant named Dillon, and other key Anshiser personnel. Also data on company.

Leave terminal on receive.

If I was going to do it, I'd need help.

A few minutes after midnight I walked into town for a snack. When the American fries and eggs were on the grill, I stepped across the street to the Greyhound station and called long distance to the Wee Blue Inn, a beer joint down by the Superior docks in Duluth. A man answered.

"Weenie?"

"This is him."

"This is the art guy from St. Paul. I came in that time with your girlfriend?"

"Yeah."

"I need to see her. I'm coming through town to-morrow at two o'clock. If you see her around, let her know?"

"Yeah. I don't know if I'll see her . . ."

"Sure. But if you do."

"Okay."

LUELLEN IS a thief. She steals only from the rich, for the excellent reason that they're the only people worth stealing from. Jewelry, coin and stamp collections, bearer bonds, cash. She's never ripped off a stereo in her life.

I met her one hot summer night when she was breaking into a neighboring apartment. I was lying in a hammock on the roof outside my living room window, lights out, looking at the stars. I was almost asleep when I heard a *clunk* at the opposite end of the building. It was an odd sound— distinct, but furtive. I crawled across the tarpaper roof and peered over the edge. A slight, dark fig-ure was climbing the wall opposite mine, a woman, moving like a professional gymnast. She'd thrown a muffled grappling hook over the balcony outside the third-floor apartment, and was swinging up the rope hand over hand.

I watched her slip over the balcony rail, pause, apparently listening, then pull the rope up behind her. A second later she was at work on the sliding glass doors. They were open in less than a minute, and I heard a telephone ringing. The woman went inside, and the ringing stopped.

The apartment belonged to a fat, unpleasant political hack with bad breath and size 15AAAA feet, who delighted in bragging about the strange things he does to hookers in Las Vegas, and sometimes to women who need his help in the City Hall turf wars. I didn't think I'd feel too bad if he was hit by a burglar.

In the next few seconds I went through a one-hand–other-hand sequence. On the one hand, I wouldn't mind seeing him hit, but on the other hand, it was a bad precedent to let my own apartment house get burglarized. The word could get around the crack houses that it was an easy target, although the woman who had just gone in the window seemed too smooth to be the typical smash-and-grab doper.

On occasion I had gone places uninvited, though not usually to steal so much as to look. I look at chips, plans, production schemes. The places I had gone were factories and offices, never homes or places where people might gather. And I always had inside help. Still, watching the thief go into the apartment, I felt a spark of collegiality. We weren't in quite the same business, but there were similarities.

A few seconds after she went through the sliding doors, I eased back across the roof and into my apartment. I found my auto-everything Nikon still loaded with a roll of Tri-X. I clipped on the strobe and went back out on the roof. Two minutes later she appeared. When she turned toward me, ready to go over the balcony rail, I hit her with the strobe. She froze, probably blinded. After the strobe recycled, I said "Hello," she looked up at me, and I hit her again, full in the face. Then her voice floated across, quiet but distinct.

"Who's that?"

"A neighbor."

"You alone?"

"At the moment. I'm thinking about calling the cops."

"Don't do that. Wait there a minute, and I'll be over. Will you buzz me in?"

I thought about it, thought about the fat fixer, and said, "Yeah."

She went over the balcony rail and down the wall. When she was on the ground, she did something to the rope, and it dropped to her feet. She coiled it and turned the corner, out of sight. It was a full half-minute before I started to feel foolish. She wasn't coming back, she'd be halfway to

Minneapolis. I was actually surprised when the doorbell rang.

A few minutes later she stood in the hall outside my apartment, trying to look earnest while I peered at her through the peephole. She was a small woman with an oval face and dark, close-cropped hair. She wore a bright red jacket and jeans.

"Are you going to let me in?" she asked through the door.

"Take off your clothes."

"What?"

"Take off your clothes. Everything. I don't want you bringing in a gun."

She didn't argue, just began peeling off clothes. When her underpants came off, I opened the door.

"Turn around," I said. She turned around. If she was carrying a gun, it was hidden under the butterfly tattoo on her left hip. I opened the door all the way.

"Ease on by, and keep your hands away from your clothes," I said. She walked past me, looking me over. I picked up the pile of clothes and carried them in behind her.

"Look," she said, as I shook them down. There was a pleading note in her voice. "I'm a former . . . friend of that asshole over there. He had some of my stuff and wouldn't give it back. I had to get in. Please don't tell him. He'll send his cop friends after me."

"What did you take?"

She cast her eyes down at the floor. With a heartbroken sign, she said, "Marijuana. I kept a stash over there. That's why you can't call the cops."

It was an impressive performance, especially done extemporaneously, bare-ass naked in a stranger's apartment. "Did you make that story up on the spot, or did you think it up days ago, just in case, or what?" I asked curiously.

"It's the truth."

"Bullshit. I told you to take off your clothes and you didn't hesitate. You stand there with your hands on your hips and don't even pretend to cover up. You wouldn't do that to protect a stash. Not unless you're crazy. And look at this jacket—bright red, reversible to black. I saw the way you went up that wall. You're some kind of pro."

She looked at me for a moment and frowned, unsure of herself. "What are we going to do about this?" she asked. There might have been an offer in the question, but it wasn't explicit. I caught myself staring.

"Take a good look, sucker," she snarled.

"Sorry," I mumbled. I tossed her clothes to her, feeling like a pervert. When she was dressed, we talked.

She had taken ten thousand in small bills out of the fat man's apartment. The money was intended by him as lubricant on a bar license question. She had no plans to visit the apartment complex again, unless, she admitted, somebody else showed up with ten thousand in untraceable cash.

"He can't even complain that it was stolen, because then he might have to tell somebody like the IRS where he got it," she said.

"Neat." I walked back to the kitchen, got the Nikon, rolled the film back, popped it out, and tossed her the cassette.

"For your scrapbook," I said. "Want a beer?"

She did. Several, in fact. I had several myself. Late at night we found ourselves laughing immoderately at some modest witticisms. Even later she shed her clothes again.

"How come you didn't hit on me when I had my clothes off before?" she asked, propping herself up on a pillow.

"We hadn't been properly introduced," I said.

"You were thinking about it."

"Maybe."

Since then she's visited me a few times, and one cold February we had a pleasant two-week trip to the Bahamas. I've visited her a couple of times in Duluth, which is her hometown, where she never steals. I've never been to her house, or apartment. I don't know where it is, or even that LuEllen is her real name. She's a pro, and she's cautious to the point of paranoia. She picks her targets carefully—never anything too big, never anything that will attract major attention. She takes down

$125,000 or $150,000 a year. Some fifty thousand goes into investments. She lives modestly on another forty thousand or so, and drops the rest on expenses, ponies, and cocaine. Every year she pays two thousand to the IRS on nonexistent wages from the Wee Blue Inn; Weenie declares her imaginary $15,000 salary as a business expense.

Weenie is her phone drop. If she was out of town, he'd have told me that he didn't know where she was. Since he didn't tell me that, she was in town, and he'd let her know I was coming. Whether or not she showed up was up to her.

DULUTH IS a seaport built around the grain and iron ore docks. There were two big Russian freighters taking on wheat at the docks, and a long, low ore carrier was headed out.

The Wee Blue Inn, which is neither wee nor blue, sits on the first bank level above the lake, at the base of the big hill that makes up the heart of the city. It's the kind of place where the bartender throws sawdust on the floor and calls it decor. Eggs and sausage float in scum-filled jars on the bar, sacks of garlic potato chips and cheese balls hang from wall racks, and the mirror was last cleaned in the fifties. Weenie is fat, chews a toothpick, and wears a boat-shaped, white paper hat. He was behind the bar when I arrived a few minutes after two.

"Back booth," he said. I got a bottle of beer

and headed toward the back. LuEllen was drinking a Perrier-and-lime.

"How's the painting business?" she asked as I slid into the booth.

"Okay. How's the burglary business?"

"Not bad. Nice and steady."

"Any scary moments?"

"Just one. Nothing serious."

"So tell me," I said. I tell her about my unconventional jobs, and she tells me about hers. Therapy, she called it.

She had been tracking a guy in Cleveland, the manager of three busy fast-food franchises on the Interstate. Every Saturday evening he picked up the collections from Friday and Saturday—all cash, no checks accepted. Most weekends he drove downtown and dropped the money—as much as twenty-five thousand—at his bank's night deposit. Sometimes, though, when he had a big date with his stewardess girlfriend, he'd take the Friday and Saturday receipts back to his apartment, where he lived alone, and leave it there overnight.

"So I'm talking to the stew—a friend called me about her—and she tells me about this guy. Doesn't like him. He's got money, all right, but he's a little rough and serious about his blowjobs, which she doesn't like so much. She's looking to dump him. So we talk about this and that, and she says she'll take twenty percent. I say okay and she lays a couple of keys on me."

"Just a little girl-talk," I said.

"Right. So on this one Saturday afternoon, the stew calls him up and he says, 'What's happenin', babes,' which is the way he talks. She hums a few bars from the 'Boogie-Woogie Bugle Boy from Company C,' and he says, 'Let's go.' "

LuEllen watched him take the money bag to his apartment.

"Ten minutes later, he's out of there, and I follow. I get him with the stew, watch them take off downtown, and then I head back to his place. There's no doorman, just the outside key and the apartment key. I go up and straight in. I get the door open and head for the kitchen—the stew tells me he puts the cash in the refrigerator when he's leaving it overnight. And there it is, in the freezer. I'm taking it out and all of a sudden there's this voice, a man's voice, from the back where the bedrooms are, saying, 'Is that you, Steve?' "

"Whoops."

"Yeah. Must've been a friend or something, staying over."

"What did you do?"

"Took the money and walked back out the front door, down the fire stairs and out."

"And?"

"Nothing. I walked out, got in my car, and drove away. Never saw the guy."

"Jesus. What do you do if he sees you?"

She shrugged. "Depends. Maybe I scream. I say, 'Don't hurt me, I'll call the police.' He says, 'Who the hell are you?' I say, 'Tina,' and come on like his friend's secret lover. But I act very nervous about being alone with this strange guy. Make him feel like a bully. Get out of there."

LuEllen had never been caught by the police or done jail time. There had been a few close calls, even a few actual encounters, like the one she'd had with me. But she'd always managed to talk her way out. So far.

We chatted a while longer, and finally she popped the question. Why was I in Duluth?

"How much more do you need to retire?" I asked.

"Maybe a quarter million."

"That's another four or five years?"

"Unless I get lucky. Or unlucky."

"Your coke bill still going up?"

"What am I going to do?" she asked sharply. "I need it to work. I can't do it cold anymore."

A customer walked past the booth toward the rest rooms in the back, and we both shut up until we heard the door close behind him.

"I've got a project," I said. "I haven't decided to do it, but I might be looking for help."

"Me?"

"I've got no one else who could do it."

"Jeez, Kidd. What are you into?"

"It's weird, but there's a big payroll. I get a million and change. You get half a million. There's another guy I'll talk to, he'll take a quarter. I pick up all expenses. It's illegal, but it's not stealing. Nobody gets hurt. And I'll cover you. When the guy pays me, I pay you. You might have to meet them, but they won't know where you come from or who you are."

She lifted her Perrier bottle toward the light and inspected the bubbles that streamed up through it, thinking it over. "That's an awful lot of money, Kidd," she said finally. "It couldn't be as clean as you say."

"I believe it will be. Like I said, it's weird."

"What do you need me for?"

"I'll want to get into some houses. General backup. Driving cars. Carrying stuff around. Maybe some computer stuff—I'd show you how. You'd have time to think about it. A week, anyway."

"Why don't you do it yourself? You've gone into some places."

"Never residences. I've always been set up from inside. I don't know the first thing about breaking into private homes."

She considered it for a full minute, and sighed. "I don't think I can take another four years," she said finally. "Okay. Tell me about it."

• • •

WE SPENT THE night in a Holiday Inn. The next morning I flew to Chicago and caught a noon flight to Washington. On the way, I rolled out the tarot cards. The Fool showed again. That's cool, I thought, that's okay.

I was at Washington National by three o'clock and took a cab down to a shabby, secondhand business district, a place called the Sugar Exchange. Judging from the lobby, the last white powder exchanged in the place hadn't been sugar. Dace Greeley was locking his third-floor office when I came up the stairs.

"Hey, Kidd," he said. He brought up the shaky remnant of a once-great smile. He had always been thin, even delicate, but now he was gaunt. In his twenties, he'd had an odd effect on young women: they wanted to take care of him. And those who were most likely to be burning their bras in the morning were most likely to be taking care of Dace in the evenings. It wasn't that he was hustling all the time. He'd go to a party, sit on a couch. Twenty minutes later the most interesting women in the place were hustling *him*. One told me it was his eyes, big dark pools under an unruly shock of black hair. His eyes were still dark, but now, against his starved face, they looked almost lemurlike. His hair had thinned and was shot through with streaks of gray.

The last time I heard about him, a mutual

friend said he was spending his days in out-of-the-way bars.

"Why don't you buy me a drink?" I suggested as we shook hands.

"Sure. If you want to crawl through a dive. I've got about four dollars on me. On the other hand, you could buy *me* a drink and we could go someplace decent."

"Okay," I said. "I'm buying."

We skipped the aging elevator and took the stairs down.

"You're looking good," he said. "Still training? Shotokan?"

"Yeah. How about you?"

"Shit, do I look like it?"

"Hey, you look like you're doing okay."

He grabbed my coat sleeve on the bottom landing before we went into the lobby.

"Kidd, my boy, we have had some interesting times together, so don't bullshit me. I look like a wreck. I can't get a reasonable job. My wife dumped me and moved to L.A., and I don't blame her. Let's go have a couple of drinks, but no bullshit." He was pleading.

"All right. But I need to know something right now. How bad is the booze? You a drunk, or what?"

Dace laughed, a high-pitched whinny that wasn't quite a giggle. "Jesus, if I was only a drunk, I'd be okay. But if I take a fourth drink, I puke all over myself. Can't keep it down. The doctor says it's an allergy. Says I'm lucky."

"Okay. So let's go have two or three."

Dace worked at the *Post* back in the Watergate days, when everybody there was young and hot and tough. He was an investigator specializing in the Pentagon. He had a nose for dirt. He did one story after another, probing the cozy relationship between the generals and the industrial complex. Then he found a big one. A group of ranking Army officers helped a defense contractor cover up critical faults in a particular run of artillery shells. Correcting the problem would cost a bundle. The Vietnam War was obviously winding down. If it had ended soon enough, the defective weapons could have been routinely retired and nobody would have known. But the war didn't end soon enough. A dozen grunts were killed by the friendly fire.

Dace had a leak, a disgruntled colonel with some combat ribbons of his own. The story was *big*. A brace of generals—a total of three stars' worth—and a half-dozen colonels found themselves looking for work. Dace was on his way. Or so he thought.

But the Pentagon was tired of Dace Greeley. When another story surfaced, even bigger than the first, Dace had it cold and had it exclusively. The *Post* ran it big, and it turned out to be a figment of someone's imagination. Supporting documents were fraudulent; sources denied their quotations.

Dace was held up as an overstepper, a reporter more intent on success than on the truth. Watergate had come along by then, with Nixon's attacks on the press. Everything had to be squeaky clean. The *Post* dropped Dace like a hot potato. Nobody wanted to hear about a conspiracy of military bureaucrats: who believes in that kind of fairy tale?

He went West for a year, worked on a solid, smaller paper, but he wanted Washington. There were no newspaper jobs, so he wound up in public relations. He was bad at it, but he was cheap and persistent, and eventually built a semipermanent relationship with a sportsmen's lobbyist group.

"I can live with myself," he told me over the first drink.

"You ever think about a book? A solid piece of work? You could do it."

"Who's got the time? I have to eat," he said. "I've got alimony. I'm four or five months behind, but it's out there. I'd need two years to do something right."

"I've got a project," I told him. "It's illegal. They could put you in jail if you were caught. I'll cover for you, but there aren't any guarantees."

"Doesn't sound so good," he said morosely, rattling his ice cubes.

"There are two good reasons to do it," I said.

"Tell me." He held a finger up to the waitress and pointed at our glasses.

"One: we fuck over some of those guys who tore you up with the *Post,* or guys just like them. Two: you get a quarter million in cash. Nobody knows where it comes from, nobody knows how much. You can spend the rest of your life in Mexico. Do six books."

"Jesus, who do we kill?"

"Nobody. You do research, take care of some logistics. Write some press releases and get them to people who'll read them. Figure out a way to cover us, so nobody will know where they're coming from. Do some light typing."

"What the hell are you into, Kidd?" His next drink was forgotten, and he was watching me closely.

"First, tell me what you think."

He ran his fingers through his thinning hair. "If it's like you make it sound—I know you haven't given me the details, but if it's morally like you make it sound—I'd buy it," he said. "I'd need to know the details."

The second round came, and when the waitress went away, I gave him a few.

Chapter 6

THE WHITEMARK JOB, if I took it, would be the first time I worked with a team. Teams are bad news; if a team is tracked and caught, there's always the possibility that a teammate will turn. The police have powerful persuaders; talk can get you a free ticket out of jail; silence can buy you five to ten, if another player talks first.

LuEllen was a solid choice. She was cool, action-oriented, decisive. A pro. She methodically calculated the possibilities and consequences of her work. She had rehearsed what she would do in virtually any situation. She didn't have to rationalize what she was doing. She knew she was a thief; she focused on being a good one.

Dace was a riskier proposition. He was good at what he did, but he lived on dreams. Dreamers lose track of what's going on around them; dreamers try to outrun bullets and outshoot cops. They move from one act to the next with no assessment of consequences. In the phony story that killed him at the *Post,* Dace never stopped to think, "What if these people are wrong? What if this is all bullshit?" He had fame at his fingertips. He was hot. He was on a roll. He *knew* he was right. A phone call might have saved him.

He had some problems, but I would take him anyway. He would not get a lot of pressure; he would mostly do paperwork. I also chose him for one of the oldest and least honored of reasons among thieves. He was available.

When I got back to St. Paul the computer was signaling that it had been accessed. Bobby. I dumped the file to the printer, and twenty feet of paper spewed out. With the exception of a few things pilfered from the Anshiser computers, it had all come from public databases. Most of it had been published in various magazines and newspapers.

Anshiser was a tough guy, Bobby's report said, but he'd gotten that way on his own. He'd never had to fight, never been on the streets, never been poor. His father was a German immigrant who started out at the turn of the century collecting scrap metal in a horse-drawn wagon. He wound up as the owner of the biggest junkyards in Chicago, a couple of steel reprocessing mills, and a small airplane company that he let his son play with. There was nothing about the way he'd jumped from wagon to steel mill, but it wasn't important. The old man had been dead for more than forty years.

World War II turned the airplane company, which he had given to his son, into a defense industry. Rudy Anshiser came out of the war with more money than the old man. When the war ended, Anshiser moved into the service fields, the hotels, the vending companies, the restaurant franchises. He made no movies, never bought a sports franchise.

His wife died in the early seventies, and he never remarried. In the past few years, as he became richer and richer, he grew more and more reclusive. Not a Howard Hughes exactly, but he seldom left his Chicago mansion.

There was more biography, including information on his wife and children. The wife had been a big benefactor of the Chicago Institute of Arts. The children kept every nickel they could lay their hands on, and spent most of their days in warmer climates.

Anshiser's company computers had routine defense industry security, Bobby said. He had gone in for a look around but had found nothing that interested him. It was all design work and perhaps a million pages of clerical records and correspondence. He did find references to Anshiser's accounting company, stumbling onto the records of traffic between the company's computer and that of the accountants.

Naturally, he followed up, tapping into the accountants' computer. Way down in the database Bobby found a private file that detailed Anshiser's cash gifts to the president and dozens of other working politicians. If you were given to *tsk-tsk*-ing, this would be an occasion. The president, as a Midwestern senator, had built an image as the plain-talking, square-dealing conscience of the Senate. So he took twenty thousand dollars in a brown paper bag in a Ramada Inn in Des Moines? *Tsk-tsk.* I carefully tucked away that portion of the printout.

There was also a report on Maggie. She was not quite as advertised. Before the hitch at the University of Chicago, she'd gone to a bad public high school in a Pennsylvania steel town. Her daddy worked at the mill before he disappeared altogether, leaving Maggie and her mother to get along as best they could. After high school, she worked for two years with an Indianapolis accounting firm, and then headed for the university. One of the partners in the accounting firm paid the ticket, at least for the first four years.

After that, she was hooked up with an economics professor, and then with Anshiser. She was not a secretary, except in the old-fashioned British sense. On two different occasions, she'd been dispatched to straighten out troubled companies. She had temporarily been the president of the vending subsidiary, and when she had it running right, interviewed and picked her own replacement. She also ran a trash-hauling company during an Arizona jurisdictional war, and won the war outright. She did it, if Bobby's reports were correct, in a little more than three months.

There were problems in that Arizona garbage gig, trucks burned, tires slashed, gas tanks blown up. Will see if can find more, but not much around except newspapers.

While Maggie was getting noticed in the business press, Dillon was the invisible man. There was nothing on him except credit reports and a few citations to articles he'd written for professional library magazines. The credit reports said he was a millionaire in his own right. There was a note that said he collected Japanese netsukes.

I READ BOBBY'S Anshiser material and reread Dillon's Whitemark report, sitting in a comfortable leather chair with a light over my shoulder, my feet on a hassock, looking out over the river in the darkness. I needed to think. It might be impossible to slow down Whitemark without attracting an awful lot of attention from the wrong kind of people. But the money . . .

I spent the rest of the week painting, fishing on the St. Croix River, and working out at the dojo. I read Dillon's report so often that I could recite it by heart. LuEllen called twice with questions, Dace twice more. They were ready to sign up.

At eight o'clock in the morning, six days after the flight to Chicago, I walked up the hill to the dojo. The first classes were at noon, but the sensei did office work in the morning. He came to the outer door when I knocked, raised his eyebrows when he saw who it was, and let me in without a word. I spent two hours on the vacant hardwood floor, working on a formal exercise called a kata. I know twenty of them, more or less. I had been working on this one, sochin, for six months.

A kata can really cool out the mind. When you do a kata right, the surface of the brain, the intellectual stuff, turns off. The action is all down in the lizard part, where reflexes and instincts are paramount.

The Anshiser job was intriguing. The money was a big factor, no denying it. It would buy a certain kind of freedom, a powerfully attractive freedom. But that wasn't the only motivating factor of the proposition.

Beyond the money was the game. This was a big target, with heavy players. Could I take Whitemark out? I didn't know. Maybe. If I won, I took a major prize. If I lost, it might be prison. Interesting stakes.

To tell the truth, I didn't much care what happened to Whitemark, any more than I'd been impressed with Anshiser's talk of people losing their jobs if Whitemark won the competition.

I had spent one and two-thirds military tours in Vietnam. I could remember running down a game trail on the border between South Vietnam and Laos. Two Hmong were up ahead of me, one of them, with a stomach wound, riding his buddy's back. An NVA hunter-killer team was on our ass, and I was screaming for help on the radio. The radio kept cutting out. I thought it might be the tape antenna I had twisted down my pack straps, but I was not inclined to stop and unfold the whip and try that one. The NVA team was too close and the whip rattles through the overhead when you run.

Because trees and ground contour and everything else can affect radio transmissions, I'd stop at high points and clearings to call. And since they were high points and clearings, I'd drop down on my belly to do it and the radio's transmitter would cut out. The radio worked earlier in the run, and I could receive. The choppers were calling, "Say again, Echo, say again" but everything I transmitted was broken up and unintelligible.

Things were looking so bad that I started calling on the run, and I found that, as long as I was bolt upright, the radio worked. It didn't make sense. With the NVAs maybe a half mile back, we climbed a small knoll beside a burned-out village, popped some smoke, and got a pickup. When the chopper was away, and a few minutes after the

Hmong died of his stomach wounds, I pried the back off the radio with a knife and looked inside.

Spare change. The asshole who did the final assembly left two dimes and a penny inside the protective box. Every time I went down, the penny skidded out on an electronics board and shorted it out. When I stood up, the penny fell into the bottom of the box, and the radio worked.

There are more stories like that, hundreds of them. Everybody in 'Nam had a story about the stuff we worked with, and the stuff we ate. The gear that rotted, the mortar rounds that fell short, the early M16s that jammed in firefights, the C-rations that included four cans of limas and ham and nothing else but a pack of Lucky Strike Greens, which had been manufactured in World War II. . . .

When I saw that loose change rattling around in the radio, I decided the whole damn defense industry could take a flying leap. I haven't changed my mind.

All this cooked down in the lizard brain while I worked through the kata, through the difficult stances, the slow pressing moves, and the impossible sidekicks. When I finished I was sweating hard. The sensei, who looked in from time to time, said with hard work I should have it under control in two or three more years. In another sport, the comment might have been sarcastic.

Not in Shotokan. He was absolutely sincere. It may have been the nicest thing he ever said to me.

After the workout, I hit the makiwara board fifty times with each hand, showered, walked back to the apartment. I called Weenie, he called LuEllen, and she called back five minutes later and signed up. I called Dace, and he was ready to go. Then I called Anshiser and told him I'd take the job.

"With one more condition."

"What?" he asked.

"I write the contract. You sign it and finger-print it, and I stash it. It will be straightforward and incriminating. No wherefores or parties of the second part. It might not be binding in court, but it will bind your ass if you leave us stranded out there."

"Agreed."

"I'll be there tomorrow. I'll want the first million. I'll want it early enough to get to a bank."

"Make it about one o'clock at the house. It'll take the morning to get it together," he said.

What?

I'm moving. Don't dump to apartment. I'll call. OK?

Ok. Got about 70 names/addresses/telephones for Whitemark execs who may use home terminals. Goes slow getting positives on addresses, confirming computers.

How long to finish?

Tomorrow.

Good. Money OK?

So far charged $2,250.

There's more if you need it.

OK/Goodbye.

It took a good part of the day to close the apartment down. I dumped the garbage, cleaned out the refrigerator, and put together a basic watercolor kit for road work. Emily agreed to take care of the cat and the Whistler and to pick up mail and pay utility bills. I gave her an envelope full of cash to cover it.

Before leaving, I spread the cards again. The Wheel of Fortune, reversed, was dominant. That told me nothing. *I knew that.*

Just after dark, I rolled onto Interstate 94 in my two-year-old Oldsmobile. It's a big, clumsy car with lots of power, comfortable seats, and a large trunk where eye-catching gear—terminals, printers, cameras, painting equipment—can be stashed out of sight. I tuned in WLS, and let the fifty thousand clear-channel watts of rock 'n' roll suck me down the highway toward Chicago.

Chapter 7

I SPENT THE early morning at the Art Institute. Rembrandt didn't paint *Young Girl at an Open Half-Door*, like the museum says he did, but I like it anyway. And even if you dislike pointillism, Georges Seurat's *Sunday Afternoon on the Île de la Grande Jatte* is a masterwork. When I see it, I tend to hyperventilate. It's like looking down that marvelous wall of Degas's paintings at the Met.

As usual, I overstayed my time and had to race across town to meet LuEllen at O'Hare. She was wearing a tan summer suit with slacks, a touch of lipstick, and a white panama hat that snapped down over her eyes. We picked up her bags and went downtown and rented safety deposit boxes at the Second Illinois. Afterward, I dropped her at my hotel while I went to Anshiser's. Maggie met me at the door and took me up. The money was in a small fake-leather suitcase on Anshiser's desk.

"The contract?" he asked. His voice trembled, and he cleared his throat. Dillon was back in his chair against the wall, still dressed in gray, still showing the small smile.

"Right here." I handed him a letter of employment. It clearly spelled out what I was to do. He read it and passed it to Maggie, who looked at it, nodded, and handed it back.

"That should do it," he said. He took a pen from his coat pocket and signed and dated our agreement.

"Now the fingerprints," I said. I took a stamp pad from my pocket and handed it to him.

"This will be messy," he said.

"A small price."

"Hmph." He rolled his fingers across the pad and onto the paper, leaving a row of neat, fat fingerprints below his signature.

"Both hands?"

"One is fine."

Maggie handed him a purse pack of Kleenex to clean his fingers.

"The money," he said. He pushed the case toward me. "It's all there. One million, one hundred thousand dollars. Twenties and fifties, nonsequential. It came right out of the cash box at one of our casinos. You can count it, if you wish."

I popped open the locks, peered in, and shut it again.

"I'll count it later," I said. "You want some kind of progress report?"

"Go ahead." He leaned back in his chair and crossed his arms over his stomach, now the executive listening to a subordinate. I told him I'd hired two associates and had begun processing names from Dillon's report. I outlined a couple of methods of attack, told him we'd be working out of the Washington area, and that I would call him every few days with reports. When I finished, he looked at Dillon, at Maggie, and back to me.

"We have a request," he said.

"What?"

"We want Maggie to work with you. To see what you're doing, how it's done. She won't interfere unless it looks like you're getting carried away. What I'm saying is—we'd like to keep some oversight."

I looked over at Maggie and thought about Bobby's report on her. She looked back, a level gaze, no smile.

"I run the show," I said to Anshiser. "It's my ass on the line. I don't care if she observes, but I'll give her only one option: she can pull the plug. If she says kill the program, we kill it. But she doesn't tell us how to run it."

"That's all we ask," Anshiser said. He pointed a finger at her. "If there's any sign of trouble, you get out."

"Right."

"Speaking of trouble," Anshiser said to me, a cold note in his voice, "let me say a few words to the wise. Do not try to steal this money from us, Mr. Kidd. We want performance. If you can't perform, say so. But you must try. I won't be stolen from. I'm not threatening to break your legs should you abscond, but a billion dollars can purchase a world of legal and financial trouble for anyone I'd choose to pick on. Understood?"

"Fine," I said. I picked up the money bag. A million dollars . . . It was lighter than I'd expected. "A friend and I are leaving for Washington tomorrow. I'll get back to you when we've got a place. Maggie can fly out then."

"Good luck," Anshiser said, standing and extending a hand. His hand felt cool and damp and mealy, like tightly wound wet tissue paper. I shook it, dropped it hastily, and left.

"Partners in crime," Maggie said in the hallway.

"I hope you're well paid," I said. "This will be a major event."

"I'm well taken care of," she said.

I opened my mouth, and quickly shut it.

"What were you going to say?"

"A wisecrack," I said.

"You're not deferential," she said, looking up at me with mild amusement. "Why'd you hold back?"

I shrugged. "My mouth sometimes gets me into

trouble with women I like. I'm trying to be friendly and it comes out wrong."

"You like me?"

I looked into her cool green eyes. "I could. You're bright and mean as a snake. Those are decent recommendations."

She laughed out loud, the first time I'd ever heard her do it. It sounded nice, unrehearsed.

"A MILLION BUCKS," LuEllen said in a reverent tone. "We could be in Brazil in eight hours."

The money was spread on the hotel bed, so we could look at it, count it, check serial numbers, and run our fingers through it. When we were satisfied that it was all there, we packed it into three bags. There was $600,000 for me, $250,000 for LuEllen, and $150,000 for Dace. We put the hundred thousand of expense money in with Dace's cash.

"A hundred thousand for expense money," LuEllen said. She looked at it, looked at me, and started giggling.

When she finally stopped, we checked out of the hotel, dropped our personal shares at the bank, and mailed the safety deposit keys back home—mine to Emily and hers to somebody in Duluth. I didn't ask who, and didn't tell her where mine went. The rest of the money, less a few thousand for pocket and purse, went into a small, hidden box just forward of the spare tire well in the trunk of the car.

Late in the afternoon, armed with the *Chicago Tribune*'s want ads, we drove around the suburbs and paid cash for two used Kaypro IBM-compatible computers and a Toshiba printer. Then we drove south, made the big turn at Gary, and headed for Washington.

"You sure about this friend of yours in Washington—Dace?" LuEllen asked.

"I'm sure."

"He's got a place for us?"

"Yes. Furnished, telephones, dishes, the whole works. We can move in the same day."

"How much?"

"Two thousand a week."

She whistled. "That's steep."

"It's a special deal. The landlord runs a call girl operation for the Pentagon brass, in Alexandria. The apartments are for the girls, but he let Dace have one. He's a crook himself, so he won't talk to anyone. There won't be any records, there won't be any receipts. He won't be around, won't see our faces; he stays out of sight himself."

PERSONAL CARS ARE invisible in America as long as you don't buy gas on credit cards or get traffic tickets. And if you drive off the main interstate highways, down into the midsized towns when you're looking for a motel, you can find one where all transactions are done in cash. They don't want to see a Visa card, they don't check your license plate to see if you wrote down the right number. Hand over forty dollars in advance, and they're satisfied.

There was a reason for our caution. Despite what Anshiser said about the powers of political protection, it was still possible that he didn't understand the magnitude of what we were doing. A computer attack on a major corporation is a technological-age nightmare. If word of a corporate war got out to the computer community, the reaction could be violent. Some very unpleasant people could come looking for us. Given that possibility, the whole job was best done with as few personal traces as possible.

WE TOOK OUR time getting to Washington, and talked about the attack.

"So if things started to get hairy," LuEllen said, "you might not even need me around at all? Especially toward the end?"

"Right. You could take off. You could probably take off anyway. Your job will be right up front, before the attack starts. I'd like you to hang around for a while, but you won't have to stay until the end."

"I'd like to know how it comes out."

"You'll know, one way or the other," I said.

"Either I'll call you and tell you or you'll read all about it in the newspapers."

"You fill me with confidence," she said.

LuEllen was pleasant company; she didn't feel pressure to talk all the time. In the evenings, after dinner, we would catch a movie on Home Box Office and afterward make love, a reasonably athletic event that made a nice transition into sleep. We were feeling almost domestic by the time we got to Washington.

We arrived in the late afternoon on a hot, damp Thursday. Our new headquarters was in a pretty neighborhood of narrow, green lawns, neatly trimmed hedges, and tastefully shabby private homes interspersed with well-kept apartments. The apartment buildings were mostly of dark brown or wheat-colored brick. Tenant parking was tucked discreetly behind screens of bridal wreath or in reproduction carriage-house garages with weathered wood siding. At the address Dace had given us we parked the car in a guest slot. The building was a long, two-story rectangle, with the narrow end toward the street. There were four separate entrances, each with eight apartment numbers above the outer door. We went to the door nearest the front of the building. A call phone hung on the wall of the entry. I dialed the apartment and Dace buzzed us in.

"Nice," LuEllen said as we stepped inside. "This is the kind of place I might do a job." A heavy, wine-red carpet covered the lobby floor, setting off the green-figured wallpaper. Four oak doors led off the hall. Between the two on the right was an elevator. Our apartment was on the second floor, on the right as we came out of the elevator. From the outside, it would be the second apartment in, on the back side of the building, away from the driveway. I rapped on the door and Dace answered.

"Hey, Kidd," he said. He was barefoot, in khaki shorts and a golf shirt. He stepped back and looked curiously at LuEllen as we shook hands. I'd told him other people were involved, but hadn't mentioned who.

"Dace, this is LuEllen, LuEllen, Dace." They said pleased-to-meet-yous and I said, "LuEllen is, uh, a spacial intrusion engineer."

"What?"

"A burglar," said LuEllen.

"Oh." Dace wiggled his eyebrows and looked interested. "Well, come on in and look around."

From where I was standing I could see a kitchen with a dining area, and a comfortable living room with overstuffed couches facing a console television. The fabric wallpaper was done in a discreet gold figure over beige, and nineteenth-century British sporting prints hung on the walls. A hallway led back to the bathrooms and bedrooms.

"Pretty nice," I said. "A little classier than I expected."

Dace shrugged. "He's got an upscale business. Can't have the place looking like a cathouse."

"You order the furniture?"

"Already here. In the big bedroom."

He led the way to the rear of the apartment. There were four bedrooms with a bath off each. The master bedroom had been converted to a neat and efficient office, with a big library table in the middle and four office chairs facing it. A telephone perched on one end.

"What happened to the bed?" I asked.

"He took it down the hall. He owns the whole building."

"Is there another phone?"

"Yeah. Four more. One in each bedroom, and one in the living room. There's a separate line for each."

"Jesus, you could run a book out of here," LuEllen said.

"I thought about getting somebody to move the phones, but then I figured maybe you would want to do it."

"Good. The fewer people who see this place, the better," I said.

In an hour, the whole thing was set up. I moved a second phone into the office, hooked both lines through the portables, and set up the printer. I tested it by calling Bobby.

What?

I gave him the new number.

Got a dump. Want now?

Sure.

Set to receive.

Two minutes later I had the files in the memory of one of the computers, and dumped them to the printer. The printer took another five minutes to print out two copies.

"I've never seen a computer working," LuEllen said, looking over my shoulder as I stripped paper off the printer. Dace was in the kitchen making coffee. "What is all that stuff?"

"Names, addresses, phone numbers, and background information on Whitemark executives, plus a few people who have home computer terminals we might want to get at. That's where you come in."

"We steal their computers?"

"No, no. We just steal the information they keep on their computer disks."

"I don't know what that means."

"A computer disk is like magnetic recording tape, except that it's flat, like a phonograph record. The information is stored on the disk in the form of magnetic markers. When we play the disk into the computer, the computer translates the markers into letters and puts them on the screen."

"So we're going to steal the disks."

"I hope not. We can use the computers to copy them. It takes a minute or two to make each copy. I'd rather copy the disks and leave the originals in place so nobody will know that we took anything."

Dace came back with the coffee. "So. What's next?" he asked.

"I want to look at this stuff and do some thinking," I said. "Why don't we call it a day? I'll brief both of you tomorrow morning. What we do first, where, all of that."

Dace nodded. "Nine?"

"Good."

"Think it would be all right if I went downtown and looked at the Washington Monument and the Capitol and everything?" LuEllen asked. "I've never seen them."

I shrugged. "Sure. Go ahead."

"I'll show you around," Dace offered.

When they were gone, I started working through the printout. It was neatly done, dozens of names with some personal background—appearance, credit ratings, marital status, type of automobile.

LuEllen got back about ten o'clock, yawned, and said she was going to bed. I went back a half hour later to get a copy of the Whitemark report I'd left on the chest of drawers, and found that we were no longer sleeping together. LuEllen had moved to another bedroom.

Curious, I poked my head into her room. The lump on the bed was too quiet to be asleep.

"Uh, do we have a problem?"

She half rolled toward me, so I could see a crescent of her face in the hallway light. "No, I just thought this would be better. As long as we're, like, going into combat."

"Does Dace have anything to do with this?"

There was a moment of silence.

"He's an awful nice guy," she said in a small voice. "He wants to go to Mexico and write."

"You're going with him?"

"I don't know. Nothing happened tonight, if that's what you're asking." She sounded a bit frosty, like she was about to claim she wasn't that kind of girl, but couldn't, since we both knew she was. "He's a nice guy. I like him."

"Okay, just asking," I said, turning away from the door.

"Kidd," she called.

I stepped back.

"I like you an awful lot, too," she said. Now she sounded sad. "But you're not a nice guy. I always wanted, you know, a nice guy."

"Gee, thanks."

"No, really. Do you think you're a nice guy?"

I had to think about that for a minute. Was I a nice guy? The question had never occurred to me.

"See?" LuEllen said in the lengthening silence.

SOMETIMES I'M SURE I don't relate well to women. There always seem to be a couple around, but they always leave. LuEllen, I thought, would be different. She was as self-contained as I was; we fit well together, we each thought the other was interesting. We didn't talk too much, didn't rub anything.

I went back to my bedroom, accepting the change of condition, but when my undershirt came off I found myself wadding it up and pitching it at the wall like a fastball.

THE NEXT MORNING Dace showed up at nine o'clock with a package under his arm and a look of mild embarrassment on his face. He walked casually through to the office bedroom and couldn't quite contain a look of satisfaction when he saw the rumpled blankets in LuEllen's bedroom.

"Ah, I see. . . ." he said, when he noticed me noticing him.

"Yeah, don't worry about it. You must have hit it off last night."

"A fascinating woman," he said. "We're talking about Mexico. Afterward."

"So I hear."

LuEllen came out of the kitchen with a cup of coffee. "Are my ears burning?"

"Just straightening out administrative details," I said.

"Details," repeated Dace. "Say, we got a box." He handed it to me.

The box had no return address, but the postmark indicated that it came from a California friend of mine who operates an electronics specialty business. He usually works from a rented garage, and his appliances are very, very expensive.

"Tools," I said. "Let's start sorting things out."

Chapter 8

hat?

Need fix on MURs.

Give me numbers.

Can't be simple patch.

Will do cutout.

OK. *How much?*

1K

OK

The phone company keeps computer records of local phone calls. Hackers call them "muthers," for Message Unit Records. If a hacker uses his home phone for illegal computer entries, and the law gets interested, the phone company can check his muthers to see when and to where he made calls.

Once Whitemark realized that their computer was under attack, they would call in federal investigators. The feds, with their Crays, could sweep the Washington muthers looking for a pattern of calls to Whitemark.

"If Bobby did a simple software patch, one that tells the muther computer to ignore calls from this number, the feds might find the patch and read the number right off it," I told LuEllen.

"So what's he going to do?"

"He'll rig a cutout. Every time we dial out, the call will be assigned to a random number. That's what muther will record."

"He can do that from wherever he is?"

"I don't know. He might hire a tech out here, but for the price, I doubt it. I think he does it from wherever he is."

MURs out w/ random bypass.

Thanx.

We ready for backup.

I'll get back.

We would attack Whitemark in two ways. We would enter the company's computer system and alter it. Some of the changes would be subtle, some crude. The damage would be extensive. As the computer breakdown got Whitemark into deeper and deeper trouble, we'd open the second front: Dace would leak word of the company's problems through the Pentagon rumor mills and the defense press. If it was done right, Whitemark's credibility would crumble, and with it, *Hellwolf*'s. But first we had to get into the Whitemark computers.

Defense industries like Whitemark have physical security ranging from adequate to pretty tight. Fortunately for the craft of industrial espionage, they do have weak points. One of them is greed. They like the idea of their engineers and key managers working at home. Those people inevitably have home terminals with phone links to the main computer center.

The existence of those outside terminals creates a paradoxical problem for the computer centers. On the one hand, if nonexperts, like engineers or accountants, are going to use the computers, the computers have to be friendly—easy to enter and easy to use. On the other hand, if they're too friendly, a bunch of hackers—or spies, if paranoia's your style—could get in and trash the system.

The usual answer is a tough, but thin, security screen. There are a number of different techniques for building the screens, but most are based on coded access. The home users of the system would have entry codes. To get into the Whitemark computers, we had to have the codes. We had to steal them.

The only way to do that was to get into the users' homes. We could copy the code-carrying software and leave behind a concealed bug that would relay computer traffic. If the whole business looked like an ordinary burglary, no one would suspect that computer security had been penetrated.

Once we had the codes, though, we had to start using them, because the damn things expire. And once we attacked the Whitemark computer, we had to keep the attack rolling. When Whitemark figured out what was happening, they would isolate the computer system and shut us out.

It was a matter of doing everything at once. It wasn't good, but there was no choice.

BOBBY'S RESEARCH TURNED up a long list of potential burglary targets. Dace knew Washington like only a local newsman can, and LuEllen cross-examined him on street layouts, crime rates, and landscaping styles. As we narrowed the list of prospects to a dozen, Bobby went into the credit companies and pulled out full reports on the primary targets.

Late in the afternoon, with the list down to a

handful of solid possibilities and their files in hand, we broke for dinner.

I drove, LuEllen in the front seat beside me, Dace in the back. As we stopped at the curb cut before entering the street, LuEllen reached over and touched my hand on the steering wheel, while turning to look at Dace.

"Okay, guys," she said, smiling, "I don't want anybody to look. But when we came out the door, there was a guy sitting in the driver's seat of that green van up the street. I think he was looking for us in his outside mirror, and when we came out he looked back at us. Now he's not in the driver's seat anymore. He's not around. I think he's in the back of the van."

"Watching us?" asked Dace, not looking at the van. It was thirty feet up the street, on the opposite side.

"I'm paranoid," said LuEllen. "I got a funny vibe when he looked at us. It was like our eyes met."

"We can't just sit here," I said. I looked both ways and turned down the street toward the van.

"Dace, you look," LuEllen said. "Like you're talking to me, but look past my head and see if there's anybody in the front seat."

We passed the van and Dace grunted, "Nobody."

"Shit," said LuEllen.

"Maybe the guy was just getting out when you

saw him and he left while we were walking to the car," Dace suggested.

"Nope," I said, looking in the rearview mirror. "The van just pulled out. He's coming after us." The van driver waited until there was another car between us, then fell in behind. LuEllen casually turned her head and watched for a few seconds and then turned back to me.

"What the fuck is this, Kidd?" she demanded.

"I don't know. We haven't made a move yet."

"You've been doing the computer stuff. Could the cops be monitoring already?"

"No. That's *too* paranoid," I said. "There are probably a half million data transmissions every day in this town."

She watched the van for another minute. "Well, then what?" she asked impatiently.

"I don't know, but he's breaking off, whoever he is," I said. The van had followed a few blocks, but as we approached a traffic light at a major intersection, it slowed, waited for two additional cars to get between us, then did a U-turn, and headed back toward the apartment.

I took a left, drove a block, took another left, and headed back after it.

"Go past the apartments and come back from the other side. They won't be looking in that direction," LuEllen said.

When we got back, the van was parked on the street directly in front of the building. A tall man

in green maintenance coveralls was just getting
out of the back and when he slammed the door,
the van pulled another half block up the street
and stopped.

"So there are two of them," LuEllen said. "The
outside guy is a lookout. The inside man has a
radio or maybe a beeper."

"So now what?" asked Dace.

LuEllen looked at me. "Our security must be
fucked," she said.

"It's not right," I repeated. "For somebody to
be onto us, it'd have to be the biggest coincidence
in the world."

"So what are we doing?" Dace asked.

"A million bucks," I said. I thought about it.
"We don't even know if we're the targets. If we
are, and we can take the guy inside, we might find
out what's going on. We haven't broken any serious laws yet. If we catch a guy in the place, and
talk to him, we might find out exactly where we
stand. And he might not be in there at all."

"We better move if we're gonna do it," LuEllen
said. "I'd be surprised if he's in there for more
than five minutes."

I shook my head. "That's if he's burglarizing
the place. If he's tossing it, looking for something
specific about us, or if he's putting in bugs, he'll
be a little longer. . . . Any ideas about that lookout?"

"Sure. I need a phone," LuEllen said.

There was a phone box on the side of a recreation center two blocks away. LuEllen called the cops and then came running back.

"I told them that the guy in the green van picked up a little girl outside the rec center and took her down the street," she said when she climbed back in the car. "They'll have a car here in a minute. That'd be a top priority call."

The squad car actually arrived less than a minute later. We waited on a side street. When the squad went by, I pulled around the block and went up an alley into the back entrance of the apartment parking lot. The cops had the van driver in the street.

"Dace, you wait here," I said over my shoulder. "If LuEllen doesn't come down in five minutes exactly, you get the cops up there."

"Why don't I come up?" he asked anxiously.

"I don't have time to argue," I said. LuEllen followed me into the building, and we took the steps to the second floor. At the door to the apartment, LuEllen put her finger to her lips, listened for a few seconds, then checked the door lock.

"Scratches," she said, pressing her lips close to my ear. "They weren't there before. They could come from an old-style automated lockpick."

"Can we get inside?" I whispered back.

"He'll hear us coming. If he's armed, we're in trouble."

"Will he take the elevator or the stairway?"

"Stairs."

"Let's go back there."

We walked back to the stairs and shut the steel fire door.

"You better go down and tell Dace we're okay," I said. "I'll wait here and try to take him when he comes through the door."

There was a small, mechanical sound from beyond the fire door. "Too late," LuEllen said. "He's coming."

"Shit. Get down the stairs, out of sight."

LuEllen scrambled down the concrete steps and stopped below the next landing. I stood behind the fire door and waited. If the person coming down the hall was one of the alleged hookers who frequented the place, or a Pentagon general, this would be embarrassing.

But it wasn't. The guy who came through the door was slender, anemic, with thin blond hair and pale, watery eyes. He was wearing coveralls and carrying the toolbox. He pushed the door open with his right hand and his body was into the doorway before he saw me. His eyes widened and his mouth dropped open, and I pivoted and kicked the door as hard as I could, a good solid karate-style thrust kick that smashed the steel door into his body and the side of his head.

His tool case fell. Its contents spilled over the landing as the door rebounded off him, and he half stumbled. I kicked a leg out from under him and rode him down to the concrete. He put out his hands to break his fall and I got a knee in his back and an arm around his throat.

"Fight and I'll break your fuckin' neck," I said. LuEllen had come back up the stairs, and I said, "Tell Dace." She turned to go, and froze: a rat-faced guy was on the landing. He had eyes like ball bearings and was pointing a small, black pistol at my forehead.

"Let him go, motherfucker," Ratface said. He had a high-pitched, ragged-edged voice like a chalk squeak, but there was nothing ragged or shaky about the black hole at the end of the pistol's barrel. It was cold and round and absolutely steady. I stood up and the guy beneath me got to his hands and knees, sobbing, saying, "Jesus Christ," scooping his gear back into his toolbox. Except for a few pairs of pliers, screwdrivers, and some black plastic tape, the equipment was all electrical, and mostly illegal.

"Who the fuck are you?" I asked Ratface. LuEllen looked like she was ready to make a move, but I put out a hand, and she relaxed.

"Shut up." The hole at the end of the barrel never wavered.

When the tech's box was packed, he stood up, shot me a fearful look, and scurried down the stairs past Ratface. The gunman backed down after him, the gun steady on my face.

"We're walking out," he said. "Don't come after us."

We heard the door slam below, then the fire door opened above us. Dace.

"What happened to you?" I asked him. "The second guy came in right on top of us with a gun."

"Christ, the cops talked to him for a couple seconds, and then they left. I mean, they just got in their car and drove away. About one second later this guy was running over here. I never had a chance to get in front of him; I was too far away. I took the elevator up; I was hoping that if you were inside, he'd stop in the stairwell and wait or something."

"How'd he get in the door?"

"Key," Dace said.

"Probably had keys to the outer door, but not to the apartment. That's how they got into the stairwell, too," LuEllen said. She looked at me. "We all fucked up, it's not Dace's fault."

I said, "Something's really fouled up. This guy wasn't a burglar, he was a wire man. And I can't believe that somebody's already on us. It must come out of Chicago."

In the apartment we packed, and I took the phones apart. They were bugged. The bugs were crude and so was the installation.

"He wasn't in here long enough to do much

more," I said. "We could probably sweep the place and we'd be okay."

"Let's check Chicago," LuEllen said. She had packed everything she brought with her. She wasn't planning to come back.

We moved into a Holiday Inn for the night. When I called Chicago, Maggie was vehement about her security.

"There's no possibility of a leak here," she said flatly. "Three people know about your team—me, Rudy, and Dillon. Period. And none of us would talk. It's more likely this guy Dace is the problem."

"I don't think so. We go back too far," I said.

"You don't know, though."

"No, I don't, but he's a friend. My instinct tells me he's okay. He was scared today. And surprised."

"I tell you, the problem isn't here," she insisted.

"I still can't believe they just stumbled over us," I said. "If we can't figure this out, we'll have to call it off."

"Christ, just hold on for a couple of days. I'll get Dillon checking. . . ." There was a longish pause, and then she said, thoughtfully, "Say, do you suppose this might be some kind of leakage from the previous tenants? Didn't you say it was some kind of whorehouse?"

"Something like that," I said. I thought about

it. It made some sense, at least, better sense than the other possibilities.

"What's the landlord's name?"

I gave it to her, and she told me she would get back to us.

THAT NIGHT I worked the tarot. LuEllen and Dace came to argue, huddle together, and watch me turn cards.

"That tarot shit is spooky," Dace said after a while.

"It's okay," LuEllen said. She looked at me. "Tell him about it."

"I use it to game," I said shortly.

"What the hell does that mean?"

I looked at a spread of cards dominated by minor swords. Distress, tension. They got that right. I turned to Dace.

"Back in seventy-nine I was hired by an astrologer to put together an astrology program. Preparing an astrology chart is all mechanical. Figuring moon rises and stuff."

"I thought it took years to learn how to do it," Dace said.

"That's the interpretation of the chart. The chart itself is fixed. Anyway, a computer can do the mechanical part as well as a human—better, really, because it doesn't make computational errors—and save a lot of time.

"So I had to build a scanner to scan the

ephemeris—that's the book with the actual astronomical information in it, when the planets rise and set and all that. Then I had to work out another program to scan it in again with a second method, so we could compare the two bunches of data to cross-check for errors. It was a hell of a job. It took weeks. Anyway, this astrologer fooled around with the tarot, and I got interested."

"You tell the future?"

"No. Almost everything you read about the tarot is bullshit. But if you take the cards as archetypes for different kinds of human motives and behaviors, it becomes a kind of war-gaming system," I said.

"So what does that do?" Dace asked.

"When a person looks at a problem, it's always in a particular context. Most of the time, he's blinded to possible answers by his own prejudices and by the environment around him. By gaming a problem, you're forced outside your prejudices. So our question is, why do we have a security problem? I'd never think that LuEllen was the problem. I trust her. But maybe LuEllen got caught in that apartment back in Cleveland, and maybe she has a federal indictment that I don't know about, and when I got in touch with her and explained what I wanted to do, maybe she went to the U.S. Attorney and cut a deal.

"Or could be Bobby's got a legal problem and he cut a deal. The cards throw out random possibilities, and then you lay back and think about them."

"I didn't cut a deal," LuEllen said.

"I know."

"How do you know?" Dace asked. "I mean, just as an example."

"I've seen LuEllen do her act. She wasn't acting today. She was about to take on that gun."

We all thought about that for a minute.

"That's weird," Dace said finally. "Do you ever do just an old-fashioned magic reading?"

"I can. I don't do it often."

"Doesn't work?" he asked curiously.

"No. Just the opposite. It does seem to work. And that worries me."

"Why?"

"Because I don't believe in that shit," I said.

MAGGIE CALLED JUST before midnight. "You said the man with the gun was short and rat-faced, with a brush cut?"

"Yeah."

"What about the other man? Was he kind of tall and wimpy, kind of thin and nervous?"

"Yeah. Where'd you get that from?"

"They're private detectives from Washington, at least the rat-faced one is. The blond guy works for him. They do divorce work."

"What do they want with us?"

"Nothing. The landlord says he had another

run-in with these guys a couple of months ago. They're chasing after some general who used to meet a woman in the apartment you're using."

"That's a pretty pat answer," I said after a minute.

"That's what the guy said, the landlord. You can go on over and meet him tomorrow. He's pissed; he'll talk to Ratface tomorrow. He says he'll get them off your back. He's going to tell them the apartment is leased to a private computer-security group working out of the Pentagon, and that you want to go after them with the FBI. He says that'll take them out. This detective supposedly has a bad reputation with the feds, and he won't mess with anything that smells like government security."

"I don't know," I said. But it sounded reasonable. It would account for the archaic bugging equipment and what LuEllen said was an old-fashioned lockpick. "I'll have to talk to the other two. They're pretty spooked."

"Look. Find another place if you want, but get on the job. This was just a bizarre coincidence. Talk to the landlord."

That night, with Dace's suggestive questioning in the back of my head, I did a "magic" layout with the tarot. I got the Seven of Swords overlaying the Emperor in a crucial position. Later, I knew what it meant. But then it was too late.

• • •

DACE AGREED TO talk to the landlord the next morning while I went out and bought a commercial bug detector. You can buy them across the counter—just another necessary appliance in Washington, like VCRs and compact-disc players.

"I'm pretty shaky about this," LuEllen said as we went back in the building.

"No reason," I said. "We haven't done anything detectably criminal yet. If we see any problem at all up here, we walk away."

We didn't find anything. I took the bugs out of the phones, checked the lines, then went over the rest of the place inch by inch with the scanner. Nothing.

"We're clean," I said finally. "He wasn't up here long enough to do more than the phone. Certainly nothing so sophisticated that it would be completely invisible and wouldn't show up on this." I waved the scanner at her.

LuEllen was skeptical, but when Dace came back from meeting the landlord, he seemed convinced.

"I'm pretty sure he was telling the truth. Ratface's name is Frank Morelli. The other guy is a phone technician he brings in on some of his cases. They tried to get in once before, nine weeks ago, chasing this Pentagon guy. The Pentagon guy drops his mistress like a hot rock, but he was back here last week for a party. Morelli must have been watching him and figured it started up again."

"So he talked to them?"

"Yeah. He says Morelli used to be a cop. That's how he got around those cops we sicced on him. He pulled out his private eye card and mentioned a few names, and told them he was on a job. They said okay and took off."

"So what do you want to do?" I asked, looking at LuEllen. "You're the skeptical one. If you don't want to do it, we'll call it off."

She chewed on a thumbnail.

"A half million bucks," she said.

"Yeah."

"All right," she said. She pointed a finger at me. "But one more problem and I'm outa here."

"WE HAVEN'T DONE enough research on these guys," LuEllen said. It was the next day, and she was draped over an easy chair, looking at the final list of Whitemark burglary targets. All of them, Bobby thought, had access to Whitemark computers from their homes. "We're going in semi-blind. It bothers me."

"We don't have time for more," I said.

"If you get caught, the whole job goes up in smoke," said Dace from his perch on the arm of a couch. He had a tin can of Prince Albert in one hand and a pinch of tobacco between the thumb and forefinger of the other.

"That's why LuEllen's here. To keep risks to a minimum."

"But you're not taking her advice," Dace argued. "She said we need more research. You're pushing to go in now."

He was right, but there was no help for it. Every day that passed brought Whitemark's version of String closer to completion. If we didn't move quickly, there wouldn't be any point in doing it at all.

"Look, couldn't we spend a week scouting all of them, and then pick the best two or three?" Dace asked.

"We don't have a week," I said. "We have to take our best shot and go into the computers and see where we are. Maybe we'll only need one or two, and all the other scouting would be a waste of time."

"But . . ."

"Wait a minute, wait a minute," LuEllen said, waving us down. "It makes me nervous, but I didn't say we couldn't do it. We have to be careful, that's all."

"I don't like it," Dace said. "I hate sitting around here. I wish I could come along and drive. Or something. Anything."

"We already talked about that. Having you along wouldn't help, it'd only make things worse," LuEllen snapped. "Let's just work on this list, okay?"

We wanted to do three specific things inside the Whitemark computers. We wanted to interfere with the programs used to design the *Hellwolf*. We wanted to destroy Whitemark administrative systems. And we wanted to attack the computer itself, to fundamentally bollix up the way it operated.

The best way to do that was to get the entry codes of the top systems programmer. With those codes we would be able to move through the whole system. But going after a systems man was dangerous. Computer experts are paranoically sensitive about security: if we broke into the top man's house he might change his codes as a matter of routine. It would take only a few minutes, and he could do it himself, so why not?

Instead of going after the systems programmer first, I decided to go after an engineer and a manager and hope we could get into the programming levels through their terminals.

"We want a suburban neighborhood of single-family houses, not an apartment complex, because there are fewer people around. We don't want kids, because kids get sick and stay home from school, or come home at odd times. And if there aren't any kids, both the husband and wife are probably out during the day, at work," LuEllen said, ticking off the points on her fingers. "If the neighborhood and the house are right, the Ebberly woman ought to be our top target. Bobby's credit report says her husband is an executive with the Postal Service, which is a nine-to-five job. The other ones, where the husband works for Whitemark and the wife works somewhere else, it's hard to tell how important they are. They could be working late shifts or early shifts."

"So we go for the woman, the personnel evaluator. Samantha Ebberly. Samantha and Frank," I said.

LuEllen nodded. "We'll give them first look, anyway."

That night I did a few spreads with the tarot, but couldn't find anything significant. The Fool was in hiding.

WE LEFT THE apartment at nine o'clock the next morning. The day was already thick and sultry, with thin, morose clouds sliding off to the south. We were dressed in tennis whites and court shoes. We carried tennis bags with racket handles sticking out of the side pockets.

"White folks think burglars are these big black dudes with panty hose on their heads, who come in the middle of the night. They won't look twice at a white couple walking around at ten o'clock in the morning with tennis rackets," LuEllen said while we were buying the equipment. "We put the crowbar and the bolt cutters, the gloves and your tools and the electronic stuff in the bottom of the bags. If there's a problem, we ditch the bags and jog back to the car. Jogging is one way you can run in the 'burbs without a single soul paying attention to you."

The Ebberlys lived in Falls Church, Virginia, in a neighborhood of upper-middle-class ranch homes and bungalows. The streets had names like Willow Lane and Crabapple Court, and twisted endlessly back on each other like a ball of twine. There were sailboats in the side yards, basketball hoops on garages, heavy, black barbecue grills on brick and stone patios. The houses were separated by tall hedges and lines of weeping willows.

We drove by the Ebberlys' home and LuEllen looked it over.

"It feels empty," she said. The house was a two-story, split-entry design with evergreen bushes on either side of the front door. She was pleased by the layout.

"I like those shrubs. They cut off the view from the side. These streets are good, too, with the curves. There's nobody right across the street looking at the target's front door. Gives you some extra privacy to work."

We went by a second time. She took out a pair of compact Leitz binoculars and scanned the place.

"You look for lumps of dark green grass in the backyard, especially along the fences," LuEllen said idly. "If they have a dog, and he does his business in the yard, there'll be dark clumps of grass, like pimples. It's not a sure thing, but it can warn you off."

There was nothing. Satisfied by the house, we drove six blocks out to a convenience store, where we had seen a drive-up phone. Checking the list from Bobby, she called the Ebberlys at their separate offices. Samantha came on, and LuEllen rattled the receiver a few times and hung up. Frank wasn't in his office, but had been just a minute ago. He was probably down the hall for coffee, according to the woman who answered the phone, but he had an appointment coming up so he should be right back. LuEllen promised to call in fifteen minutes.

"Get my bag," she said. I reached into the backseat for her bag, as she dropped another coin into the phone. "Who now?" I asked.

"The house." She listened while the Ebberlys' house phone rang thirty times, then glanced around the parking lot. Sure that nobody was watching, she took a pair of compact bolt cutters from the tennis bag and nipped off the phone receiver.

"Let's go," she said, tossing the receiver in the backseat. "Let's do it."

"You're sure?"

"Goddamnit, let's do it," she snarled. LuEllen carries no excess fat, and now her face muscles stood out in bundles. She slipped a packet of white powder out of her purse, carefully tipped some on a matchbook, and snorted it up.

"You want some?"

"No."

"Good stuff," she said. "It'll give you an edge."

"I've got an edge," I said.

"Then drive."

As I pulled out of the parking lot, she retrieved the amputated receiver from the backseat and stuffed it out of sight in the glove compartment.

"If you cut the receiver off, nobody will try to use the pay phone," she explained. "That means nobody will hang it up, so the phone should still be ringing at the Ebberlys' when we get there."

"If there's nobody home."

"Right."

We stopped at a neighborhood park two blocks from the target. Both tennis courts were occupied. We did some stretches, got the bags, and walked down the street toward the Ebberlys'.

"When we get there, we turn right in. I knock. If somebody comes to the door, we ask where the park is. If we hear the phone, and nobody answers the knock, you back up so I can get at the door. I pop it, and we go in. Keep everything slow," she said quietly. As she talked, her head turned from the street up to me, and back to the street. Her smile switched on and off, the perfect rhythm for a friendly husband-wife talk on the way home from a tennis game. The streets were eerily quiet for a nice summer day. No kids, no cars.

"It's an older suburb, one of my favorite situations," LuEllen said. "Young families can't afford it. The people who moved here when the houses were cheap are in their forties and fifties. Their kids are growing up. There's nothing to do here during the day, so the teenagers take off for work, or go into the city or out to the beaches. It's empty, nobody home."

She glanced up at me and grinned. "You're twitching."

"I'll be okay," I said, irritably. The words were strangled in my own ears.

"It's a trip," she said. She put her hand up to her face as though she were coughing and took another hit on the cocaine.

Nothing moved along the street as we came up to the house. LuEllen looked casually around. "Let's do it," she said hoarsely. Halfway up the drive, we could hear the phone ringing. On the front step. LuEllen pushed the doorbell with a knuckle, and then knocked. Nothing. She took a silent dog whistle from her pocket and blew on it, hard. There was no answering bark.

"Probably okay," she said, looking around again. We'd been at the door for fifteen seconds. She took a short, curved bar from the tennis bag, and I stepped back to cover her with my body. She shoved one end of the bar in the crack between the door and the jamb, and threw her full weight against it. There was a loud crack, and the door popped open.

"Goddamn. That was loud," I muttered.

"Nobody ever looks," she said. She pushed the door open with the back of her hand, and we stepped inside. We were in a short hall off the living room. The kitchen was to the left, with coffee cups and cereal bowls still on the table. The living room was furnished with a couch and easy chair, a piano, a couple of tables. There was a cheap Art Barn–type oil painting over the couch.

"Let's move. Get the gloves on," LuEllen said. She handed me a pair of latex surgeon's gloves from the tennis bag.

"The computer's probably upstairs in this kind of house," she said. "You go up there. Check all the bedrooms before you do anything. I'll check the basement." As I headed up the stairs, she picked up the phone in the kitchen to kill the ringing.

The computer was in a converted bedroom. I checked the rest of the rooms, found nobody, and went back to the computer. It was a standard IBM-AT with a Hayes modem. An inexpensive plastic disk box sat next to it. I brought the computer up and started flipping through the disks. All but three were neatly labeled—Word Perfect, Lotus 1-2-3, Files, and so on. The three unlabeled disks were from different manufacturers, so Ebberly

probably kept track of the contents simply by remembering the brand names. I took a box of
blank disks and a special disk-cracking program
of my own out of the tennis bag. When the computer came up, I loaded my cracker disk, and
stripped the directory out of the first unnamed
disk. Games.

I loaded one to make sure, and a popular baseball game flashed on the screen. Pirated, of
course. I killed it and shoved in a second disk. It
was a custom communications program. After a
little manipulation it coughed up a short list of
seven-letter words. Code words.

"That's the baby," I muttered to the machine. It
took two minutes to duplicate the disk on one of
my blanks.

As I made the copy, LuEllen was working in the
other parts of the house. From the sound of it, she
was trashing the place, but there was no time to
look.

When the code disk was copied, I dropped it in
my bag and pushed in the third disk. More
games. I put in another disk, labeled as Files. I
opened one and found personal letters. I opened
another, and an accounting program showed a list
of personal accounts. The Ebberlys were doing
well, according to the accounts—and I was pretty
sure that they weren't being clever with mislabeled disks. As I put the original disks back in the

storage box, LuEllen came to the door. She was panting.

"How's it going?"

"Halfway there," I said. She nodded and disappeared, and I looked at the phone outlet where the modem was plugged in. It was a standard AT&T connection. I got a screwdriver from the tennis bag, removed the wall plate, and pulled out the tangle of wires behind it. It took a minute to find the right wires, isolate them, and strip a half-inch length off each. The bug, a piece of exotic hardware about the size of a beer bottle cap, clipped onto the bare wires. The work was not difficult, but it was delicate. Every move took an eternity.

When it was done, I put the wall plate back in place and screwed it in tight. If a knowledgeable phone tech took the plate off, the bug was hanging there like a great, fat leech. With any luck, it wouldn't happen for years.

"We've been in ten minutes. That's my personal record," LuEllen said from the door. Her face was screwed tighter than I'd ever seen it.

"Right. I'm done." I threw all the tools back in the tennis bag and wiped my forehead on a shirt-sleeve. "Christ. I'm falling out."

"Let me in there," LuEllen said. She pulled open the drawers in the file cabinets and dumped the papers on the floor.

"Like we were looking for money," she said. "Let's go."

We walked back to the front door, where she picked up her tennis bag. "Carry mine," she said. "It's heavy." I stripped off my gloves and took her bag. It felt like an anchor was stuffed inside.

"What's in here?" I asked.

"Guns."

"What?"

"Pistols. Heaters. Rods. Gats. You know. Guns. One of the Ebberlys is a collector."

"Why take them? If we get stopped . . ."

"Because this is supposed to be a horseshit smash-and-grab burglary, looking for money, dope, jewelry. One inch up from a stereo thief," she said as we stepped out on the porch. She carefully pulled the door shut behind us. From ten feet away, it would look intact. "Nobody but a real specialist will leave guns behind. On the street, pistols are as good as cash. If we left them, the cops would know something was wrong. We had to take them."

"So what do we do with them?" I asked as we walked out of the Ebberlys' driveway.

"Throw them in the river," she said. "Drop them in a sewer. I don't care. We couldn't leave them."

Our walk back to the car seemed to take twice as long as the walk to the house. A mailman came down the street in his red, white, and blue jeep, and nodded at us as we went by. LuEllen told me twice to slow down and talk. "You look like one of those long-distance race-walkers," she said with a practiced smile. "Slow the fuck down." At the car, I dropped the tennis bag in the back and buckled up before we pulled away.

"Jesus Christ," I said after a couple of blocks, as my stomach uncoiled.

"It does get intense," LuEllen giggled. She went into her purse for the cocaine again and took two hard hits.

I'd never been caught inside a factory during one of my midnight research excursions. With a couple of exceptions, I walked inside with a regular employee, a paid guide. If somebody had stopped us to question my presence, the employee was supposed to claim I was a friend waiting for him to get off, that we didn't think it would hurt if I hung around for a while, sorry about that, etc.

On the few occasions I went into a hostile plant, cold, the pre-entry research had been so thorough and the objectives so limited, that I had been more interested than excited, and not particularly worried.

This entry had been different. More free-form. Like jazz, say, compared to Bach. If you're an anonymous guy in a huge defense plant and a security guard comes by, that's one thing; there's a ninety-nine percent chance you can talk your way out of any problems. If you're in somebody's house and they walk in the door, that's something else altogether.

I was still buzzing from the entry and LuEllen started backseat driving. She kept me three miles an hour under the speed limit, and called out every street and stop sign. When we got back, Dace met us at the door with an anxious look.

"What happened?" he demanded.

"What does it look like?" asked LuEllen.

"We went in," I said, grinning. "It was perfect."

"Get the computer stuff?"

"Yeah. We're wired in."

LuEllen walked across the room and grabbed him by the ears. "C'mere, you," she said, and tugged him into the bedroom and slammed the door. I was left by myself in the front room. A few minutes later, when I realized the apartment wasn't quite as soundproof as I had thought, I got the watercolor kit and drove down to the Potomac. It was hot and humid; the buildings across the river shimmered like white silk scarves, and I tried to get them down just like that.

I GOT BACK to the apartment late in the afternoon, arriving just behind a metallic-blue Corvette. The 'Vette took the first available slot and I pulled in three spaces down. The 'Vette's driver was already striding down the lot when I got out of the car. It was an entrancing sight. She was small, dark-haired, and perfectly built. She moved like a dancer.

She used her key at the entry door and let it close behind her. I used my own key and caught her waiting for the elevator. She looked me over with a careful eye.

"You must be one of the people in two-A," she said, with a touch of a French accent.

"Yes. And you're . . ."

"Two-D," she said. "Are you . . . a business?"

"Consultants," I said.

"Ah, consultants," she said brightly, as though it explained everything. In Washington, of course, it probably did. "To tell you the truth, I was happy to see Louis and his little friends move out."

"Louis?"

"The landlord."

"Oh, sure. I've never met him. One of my associates actually rented the place."

"Ah." The elevator came and she got in and pushed the button for the second floor.

"What, uh . . ." I gave her my best, most open smile. "I can't resist gossip, I'm afraid. That's why I'm a consultant. What about Louis's friends?"

She shrugged, and her eyes evaded mine. "If one is heterosexual . . ." She shrugged.

"There's an uneasy feeling. I know what you mean."

"You are heterosexual?"

"Yes."

"I saw the woman, your associate. She is very attractive."

"Yes. She looks not unlike you. Very attractive."

She dimpled and was about to say something when the elevator arrived at the second floor. "I do not mind homosexuals," she said, pronouncing the word with care. "But there were . . . so many of them. Five or six living there at once. In the evenings, sometimes, it sounded like they were all in one pile. . . . And then one hears about AIDS."

"Now you've got me worried. Were they living there for long?"

"Two years?" she said.

"God, I'll have to spray the place."

"Oh, that's not . . . you are joking me."

"I'd never joke you," I said. We were at my door; she continued down the short hallway and turned when she got to her door.

"Could I buy you a drink sometime?" I asked.

She considered for a moment, then shook her head in what looked like genuine regret. "I have a friend," she said. "If I did not, I would like it." She pushed her door open, gave me a final smile, and was gone.

LuEllen WAS STANDING just inside the door when I opened it, with Dace a few steps behind her. A half-finished microwave pizza sat on the kitchen table.

"We heard you talking," she said, a question in her voice.

"Another tenant. She told me something . . . odd."

"What?"

"She said the landlord's gay and that he used to keep a bunch of male friends in here. Several of them. For maybe two years."

"Aw, shit," said LuEllen, nibbling her lip.

Dace looked puzzled. "What difference does it make?"

LuEllen turned to him and asked the question that was bothering both of us. "If there were a bunch of gays living here, how come Ratface was bugging the place to catch a general and his mistress?"

"Jeez . . ."

"Somebody's lying to us," LuEllen said.

We hashed it over without reaching any conclusion.

"I'll sweep the place again and make sure Bobby is sterilizing the phone lines," I said. "And I'll see if Bobby can get a line on Ratface—Morelli—whatever his name is. Maybe Bobby can do something with his phones."

"Should we be talking about this?" Dace asked, looking at the walls.

I went over the apartment inch by inch and

again found nothing. Bobby said our lines were clean. Guaranteed.

"Maybe we're worrying about bullshit," I said. "There's no way anybody could know about us, not unless Anshiser has sprung a major leak. And if anybody did know—the law—they would have moved."

Dace shook his head. "Paranoia," he said. "Shadows."

LuEllen was looking doubtful. "I don't know," she said. She took a couple of slow turns around the front room, then plopped on the couch. "I can't figure it."

"Let it go for now," said Dace.

"Maybe Bobby will come up with something," I said.

"It's worth a try," LuEllen agreed. "Okay. We let it go. For now."

"Good." Dace turned to me. "Wanna look at the loot?"

We dumped LuEllen's tennis bag on the front-room floor. There were a half-dozen pistols, two hundred dollars in cash, three credit cards, and several good pieces of gold jewelry, including a gold and diamond stickpin. Total value, she said, would be about two thousand on the street.

"It'd be a good haul for a junkie," she said. "They usually get a transistor radio and a bottle of picante sauce."

Late that night, she and Dace dropped everything but the cash and guns in the alley in one of the harder districts of Washington. They'd be picked up and get about the use that the cops would expect. The guns they dropped in the Potomac; the cash we kept.

While they were out, I dialed the Ebberlys' number. Before the phone rang, I blew into the receiver with a pitch pipe. The whistle activated the intercept, which linked their line to ours. I flipped the open line over to one of our computers and left it.

When the bug detected a computer's electronic sound packets, it would relay them to our computer. It would also pass them through to the Ebberlys' machine. Ebberly would get her work done as usual. We would have a complete record of it.

Nothing happened the first night, or early the next morning. We left the apartment a little after nine o'clock to scout more targets. When we got back, the computer showed a transmission from the Ebberlys' home to Whitemark.

"That's what we wanted?" Dace asked.

"That's what we wanted," I said. "She must have been working at home this afternoon. Good thing she wasn't there yesterday."

"She's probably home because of the burglary," LuEllen said. "Talking to cops."

A computer work session, printed out, soaks up an enormous amount of paper. Every time Samantha Ebberly even glanced at a personnel form, the computer printed the whole form. I ran the session back across the screen, did some quick editing, and printed it. It was seventy pages long, and I handed it to Dace.

"We need to extract procedures," I said. "We want to do things just the way she did, get in and out without being noticed. Map these things for us. Every time she gets on, map them again. By the time we're ready to go in, we should know how to operate as well as she does."

"All right. But it'll bore my brains out."

"Think about the money."

"I've been doing that."

"Didn't work?" asked LuEllen.

"No, no, it worked. I'll sit here and watch the computer. But don't tell John Wayne."

Chapter 9

SAMANTHA EBBERLY WAS a manager, so her codes would get us into the administrative side of the Whitemark computers, but we also had to get into the engineering side. We scouted four of the five engineering targets, and all were marginal prospects. The morning after the Ebberly entry we went to check out the fifth engineer.

From the moment we turned the corner the target looked bad. Aside from the dying brown grass, the front yard was devoid of plant life. A battered ten-speed bike was lying at one side of the driveway, next to a green-and-cream '57 Chevy set up on concrete blocks. The driveway was stained black by a tear-shaped oil slick that was creeping out from under the car.

The backyard was surrounded by a shoulder-high, chain-link fence. There were no clumps of extra-dark-green grass, because there wasn't much grass, but subtle signs were unnecessary.

Two old-fashioned doghouses squatted against the house, and an evil-looking, white-eyed hound crouched beside one of them. The chain around his neck looked as if it might once have been used to haul logs. As we drove by, a blonde in a tight, black T-shirt banged out the front door, followed by a teenage boy who swatted her on the butt as they cut across the moribund grass toward his Harley, which was curled up to the curb.

"Just keep on rolling," LuEllen said. "Don't bother to look back."

"Christ, it's the Jukes."

"Nice Harley, though."

"Wonderful."

"Softtail," she said.

"I'd rather eat worms than ride a Harley-Davidson," I said, remembering a bumper sticker I once saw on a Honda.

"Riding a Honda's like fuckin' a faggot; it feels sorta good, but you wouldn't want your friends to see you doin' it," LuEllen said. "I thought this Bobby guy was finding us people without kids."

"He's doing it from databases. There aren't any guarantees."

"So now what?"

"The Durenbargers are probably the best bet," I said. "You've seen the other choices."

"Durenbarger, Jason and Ellen," she said, reading from the list. "They make a lot of money between them. Goddamn, I hate apartments."

The Durenbargers lived in an apartment called the Summit Rock, not far from our own.

"There are too many people around," LuEllen said as we sat on a bench across the street from the Summit Rock. "If you crack the door with a crowbar, somebody will hear you. It's only a short walk down the hall to check. Then they see the door and call the cops.

"And there are too many eyes around, even where there shouldn't be. Look how you caught me, outside your place. You were on the fuckin' roof. In the middle of the night. Asshole."

"Always be alert; America needs more lerts."

"Right. Then, with apartments, there's a hassle getting through the outer door. In some towns, like Des Moines or Lincoln, you can walk up to the front door as one of the tenants goes through and catch the door as it closes. You say 'Thanks' and go on in. Most of the time, you get away with it. Here, there's too much crime. Everybody's suspicious. You try that trick in a big city, and they'll ask to see your key."

"What do we do?"

"We get a key," she said. "Do we know what they look like? What their cars look like?"

"Yeah, we know the cars. His is a dark-brown Thunderbird. She's driving a red Toyota Celica." I thumbed through the report Bobby had sent us and found the license numbers.

"Okay. We wait. We see if there's any chance to get a key."

"That could take forever."

"No. You said time is getting tight. We'll give it a couple of days, and then we'll try cracking the place."

The street in front of the apartment was one-way. The paired street was on the other side of a narrow public boulevard six blocks long, dotted with oak trees and green, metal benches. We found a place to park across the boulevard and waited.

LuEllen waited well. I didn't. I was looking at the story of my life, as represented by the folded and bent bits of paper in my billfold, when LuEllen cleared her throat.

"Ah," she said.

"What, ah?"

"You think it's Dace? The leak?"

"I don't know if we've got a leak. We had a problem, and it seemed to go away. We get some information that doesn't fit with other information, but nothing happens. I don't know."

"If we have a leak . . ."

"I still don't think it's Dace," I said. "He doesn't lie well enough."

"Look at it this way," LuEllen said. "You talk to him. He's nodding his head, but inside, he's saying, 'What a story. Giant companies raiding each other.' It could be the story of his life."

"I thought about it," I admitted. "But it doesn't feel right. He's just too . . . innocent."

She looked out the window and sighed. It sounded like relief. "I think the same thing. But I had to ask. You've got one of the great poker faces in the Western world. But I kind of trust your instincts."

"You in love?"

She pushed out her lower lip and squinted at me, thinking.

"Maybe," she said.

Jason Durenbarger showed up at six o'clock, his wife a half hour later. They parked in back of the Summit Rock, their cars side by side in a fenced compound.

"Too bad they don't have garages," LuEllen said. "Most people hide spare house keys in garages. We could shake down the garage and find it."

"If pigs had wings . . ."

"Yeah."

We waited four more hours. For the first twenty minutes, we talked. Then LuEllen turned the radio on, and we discovered that it's impossible to listen to a radio in a parked car. Something about the ambience. After she turned the radio off, it was like driving across North Dakota, except we didn't get to stop for gas.

"They aren't gonna move," LuEllen said finally.

"Now what?"

"Home."

• • •

"MAYBE WE OUGHT to rent an apartment there, if they've got vacancies," Dace suggested, when we told him what had happened. "We've got the money. Once we're inside, we could take a chance on popping the door."

"It's an idea," I said, looking at LuEllen.

"Two problems: The manager gets a good look at us and knows we're guilty as sin if we pay for the place, then split the day after the burglary," LuEllen said. "So we'd have to stay on for a while. That's the second thing. We can't stay. If there's a burglary a day or two days after we move in, the cops'll look at us. Just routine. I don't want to be looked at."

"Hmph."

"If you watch people long enough, something happens. They go to a restaurant, she goes into the can, leaves her purse on the sink. I only need a minute with the keys to make an impression."

LuEllen had three or four metal Sucrets boxes filled with damp clay. She could open them, press both sides of three keys in each, and shut the lid to protect the impressions. The process took two seconds per key.

The next day we looked at another prospect in the suburbs. The husband was an engineer who specialized in fiber optics as they applied to airframe control. The wife was a real estate agent who sometimes came home at odd hours in the middle of the day. The neighbors on one side had a half dozen kids, and there were more kids in the house across the street. It was possible, but dangerous.

We got back to the Durenbargers' at five o'clock. Jason Durenbarger arrived promptly at six, as he had the night before. His wife was only a minute behind him.

"They're young; they ought to go out," LuEllen said. "They won't stay in two nights in a row."

The day before we'd picked out what we thought was their apartment. The lights went on a minute after Jason went inside, confirming it.

"Here we go," LuEllen said half an hour later. The Durenbargers walked out the front door of the building, around to the side toward the parking lot. We were on the opposite side of the block. I hurried around the boulevard to get behind them, and moved too fast. They still hadn't come out of the driveway as we approached. LuEllen ordered me over to the curb.

"Fuck it. Just wait," she said.

There's a technique for following another car. You never get too close, you stay in an adjacent lane rather than directly behind the car you're following, and you memorize the other car's taillights. A good surveillance man will risk losing the car before he risks being spotted.

And here we were, illegally parked fifty feet from their drive, in plain sight. A good surveillance man would have been weeping in disgust. It didn't matter, because they pulled out with barely a glance up the street. We memorized the taillights, gave them some distance, and followed them onto Interstate 295 and across the river to Georgetown. As they got off the main streets, we were forced to close up, but I managed to keep a car or two between us. Finally they slowed and turned through a curb cut beside a nice-looking, redwood-and-fieldstone restaurant.

"Oh, God, get in behind them. Quick. Right now," LuEllen said, almost shouting. "Look at the valet. Oh, shit." I didn't know what she was talking about, but her tone was clear enough, and I eased in behind the Durenbargers. Jason walked around the front of the car, took a tag from the valet, and they went inside. The valet put a flat hand out to us, telling us to wait, and drove the Durenbargers' car back into the lot.

"Get out and stand by the car and wait for the valet. I'm going to get out and go over to his hutch. I'll call him over to talk before he gets to you," LuEllen said in a rush, slipping out the passenger side. I got out on the driver's side and waited there. The valet was back in fifteen seconds and swerved toward his hutch when he saw LuEllen standing beside it.

She said something about the little girls' room, and he smiled and pointed at the door and motioned sharply around to the left. At the same time, he casually reached into the hutch and hung the Durenbargers' keys on a peg. LuEllen thanked him and started away. He handed me a tag and slid into the car. As soon as he was out of sight, LuEllen was back. With a quick look around, she reached into the hutch, took the Durenbargers' keys, and led me into the restaurant.

"The bar," she said. We got a booth and ordered cocktails. When the waitress had gone, LuEllen opened her hand to show me the key ring. There were five keys—two car keys, two that might be apartment keys, and one that looked like it might fit a suitcase. She took out the Sucrets tin, made her impressions, and wrote down the code for each key. We finished the drinks and left.

"Make it?" the valet asked with a grin.

"Just barely," LuEllen said. I gave him the tag and as he went after the car, LuEllen hung the Durenbargers' keys back on the hook.

"We're in," she said, a light in her eyes.

Dace was at his own apartment when we returned. LuEllen phoned him and asked where we could get some key blanks with no questions asked. He called around, and ten minutes later we had the name and address of a locksmith. The voice on the other end of the phone said he'd be around for an hour yet.

It took almost an hour to find the place. It was a dingy dump in a shopping center, sandwiched between a brightly lit but empty Laundromat and a vacant storefront that had last housed a used-clothing store called One More Time. A guy in a sleeveless jeans jacket was sitting on a trash can outside the Laundromat, watching the fat white moths circle the parking lot lights.

As we got out of the car and walked across the cracked pavement, the guy on the garbage can shifted his weight. For a moment, it looked like he might say something. He had shoulder-length black hair, chin whiskers, and a DEATH BEFORE DIS-HONOR tattoo on one skinny upper arm. When we went to the lockshop instead of the Laundromat, he settled back on the can and watched us. The front of the shop was dark, and the door was locked, but a light was shining in the back. LuEllen banged on the door until somebody yelled "Yeah, yeah, yeah." A minute later the locksmith walked through the gloom to the door.

"We're the people who called for the keys," LuEllen said through the glass.

He nodded and unlocked the door, and locked it again behind us. We followed him toward the light at the back of the shop. He stepped around the counter, fished under it for a moment, and came up with three blank keys.

"Elwin four-oh-twos," he said. "That'll be ten bucks. Each."

"Jesus Christ, what are you talking about?

That's forty-five cents apiece if . . ." LuEllen squealed. The locksmith cut her off.

"Tell it to somebody else, lady. Somebody asks me for a bunch of key blanks for Elwin four-oh-twos, the kind of locks you find on rich guys' apartments, and I sell the four-oh-twos, blank, no questions asked, for ten bucks. That's the price."

LuEllen looked at him for a minute, then cracked a tiny, tight smile. "I'll remember you," she said. It was a promise of future business. She turned to me and said, "Pay him."

I gave him a twenty and a ten.

"Thanks," he said. "For another hundred I'll cut them off impressions."

"No thanks," LuEllen said. "We don't consort with crooks."

The locksmith laughed, showing crooked, yellow teeth. "Come back anytime," he said.

Outside, the guy in the sleeveless jeans jacket was waiting. As we stepped outside the door, he came up close behind and said, "Give me your wallet." He had one hand in his jacket pocket.

LuEllen looked him over. "You gotta be kidding."

"Hey, lady . . ."

"Hey yourself, asshole. If you had a gun in your hand it'd make a bigger lump. There's nothing in there but your fist. Why don't you take it home and fuck it?"

The guy looked at her, mouth half open. Then

he did something with his hand in his pocket. There was a pop, and LuEllen said, "Oh, shit, he shot me."

When the gun went pop, I kicked the guy on the inside ball of his knee. His leg went out from under him and he lurched forward, and I hit him with a right hand on the bridge of the nose. His nose crunched, and he went down like a sack of sand.

LuEllen was looking at her arm. "Maybe I'm not shot. No, I think I am."

The guy was face down on the blacktop with both hands covering his face, trying to figure out what happened. Broken noses do that to you. For the first few minutes, it's impossible to think about anything else.

LuEllen pulled up the sleeve of her blouse. An inch above the elbow was a red streak where a small-caliber bullet had grazed her, pushing holes through the shirtsleeve both coming and going.

"He could have hurt me," LuEllen said.

The locksmith had seen the commotion. He came out and looked at the guy lying on the blacktop.

"Tried to rob you, huh?"

"Yeah. Thanks for the warning."

The locksmith shrugged. "I ain't the Sisters of Mercy."

"He shot me," LuEllen said. The guy tried to get up on his knees, one hand still cradling his face. LuEllen moved behind him and kicked him in the crotch, a full-footed punt. The guy gurgled and knotted up, his hands in his crotch now. Blood streamed down his chin into his little black beard. LuEllen dipped into his jacket pocket and came up with a single-shot .22 built into a stainless steel Zippo cigarette lighter.

The locksmith reached out for it. "A .22 short. Effective range, about the length of his dick. What a dipshit."

"Let's go," said LuEllen.

"Ain't you going to take his money?" asked the locksmith.

"You can have it," LuEllen said. As we drove away, the locksmith was going through the guy's pockets.

LuEllen didn't say much for a while, just kept looking at her arm, and finally giggled. "Wish I had some coke."

"Probably good that you don't."

"You should have felt his nuts squish."

"Yeah, right, a real treat, and I missed it."

"How come you didn't go for his nuts in the first place?"

"Too chancy a target. If you miss and kick a thigh instead of the balls, he'll be inside your shirt. There's no reflex to protect the knee, and that's crippling if you get it. And nothing hurts as bad as the first two minutes of a broken nose."

"It really sounded ugly when his nose broke," LuEllen said. "It gives me the shivers thinking about it."

"Yeah, well." I touched my own nose, which has been broken twice. I can remember each time with painful clarity. "You ought to hear it from the inside."

THAT WAS ON a Friday. We couldn't risk going into the Durenbargers' place over the weekend, so Dace and LuEllen drove out to a cabin he owned in the hills of West Virginia. "The shack," he called it. "My wife hated the place. She called it Chigger City."

On Sunday afternoon, while they were gone, Bobby called. I'd given him Ratface's real name— Frank Morelli—and with the help of a Washington phone phreak, he'd been watching Morelli's phones. No activity.

I look up gas stations near Morelli apartment and check data banks for most likely credit cards. Morelli makes five charges in past week Atlantic City area.

He's out of town?

Yes/week. Also check consumer credit reports, shows personal loan secured by Chevrolet, year unknown, but bluebook value at $4,500 so must be old. Also estimated pretax earnings last year $52,000.

Thanx. Keep tabs.

Yes/Bye

LuEllen and Dace got back at midnight, and I told them about Bobby's call.

"So it's unlikely that he's watching us," LuEllen concluded.

"And he's a small-timer. Fifty-two thousand in billings wouldn't keep a church mouse alive in D.C., not if he pays for an answering service and an office in addition to an apartment," Dace said.

"I feel better about it," LuEllen said. "That's still weird about the gays, though. I wish I knew about that."

WE WENT INTO the Durenbargers' first thing Monday morning. I made my copies, set the bug, and we were out of there like a cool breeze. LuEllen didn't touch a thing.

Chapter 10

MONDAY NIGHT, WHILE Dace and LuEllen went to play in the District, I broke down the disks we'd taken from Ebberly and Durenbarger. The Whitemark code system was simple. When the central computer was called from the outside, it asked for a name and account number. After receiving those, it sent a code word back, directly to the home computer, and asked for a matching word from the code disk. The home computer scanned the list of words on the disk, found the match, and returned it. If the code was correct, you were in.

When I understood the code operation, I reviewed Dace's outline of Samantha Ebberly's sessions on the Whitemark computer. She had gone directly to a number of administrative files, and also called up a letter form. The format was standard. When I was sure that I knew what I was doing, I dialed one of our computers into the Ebberlys' to make sure she wasn't talking to the

Whitemark system. She wasn't. I left the line open, in case she came on, then I dialed our second terminal into Whitemark.

Entry was routine. Inside, I found a typical mainframe administrative system, stuffed with files and forms. Using common techniques worked out by hackers over the past couple of decades, I spent four hours wandering through the system, opening files, reading, and moving on. There were no surprises, and there were some disappointments.

Security was a notch tighter than I hoped it would be. Key files were protected with personal passwords, and I had no way around them except laborious trial and error. I let that go for the time being. Whitemark programmers had also constructed programming barriers between the various sectors of the computer. Using Ebberly's codes I could wander at will through the open administrative sector, but I couldn't get down to the underlying programs. I couldn't get into the system itself.

I next checked the Durenbarger codes. Once again, entry was easy. On the engineering side, the computer was jammed with numbers and designs and ongoing work, with key files protected by personal passwords, just like the administrative side. And, as on the administrative side, access to the programming level was thoroughly blocked.

LuEllen and Dace came in late, saw me work-

ing, and tiptoed away. Much later, I went to bed
and lay staring at the ceiling. By four in the morning, I'd decided there were no options. We had to
get into the programming level of the computer.
We had to crack another house.

AT BREAKFAST, LUELLEN rambled on, sore,
about the play they'd seen the night before. It
concerned a street gang. The single scene was set
in a basement, where the gang was waiting for a
shipment of pistols.

"It was like one of those World War Two
movies, where there's a Jew and a black guy and
an Italian and the coward and this cool, white
guy who's the hero. You know, one of everything," LuEllen said. "That's what this gang was
like. But I know gang punks. I went to school
with them. You don't find any Jews and blacks
and whites together. You hang out with a white
gang and it's nigger-this and nigger-that. If a Jew
comes along it's fuckin' kike. In real life, these
guys are assholes."

"It was supposed to be allegorical," Dace said
dryly.

"Right. What really happened was, the guy
who wrote it had his head up his ass." LuEllen
trailed off and peered at me. "Why so glum?
Something we should know about?"

"We have to hit the systems programmer's

place," I said. "The head man's. There's no way around it."

"You knew we might." She was leaning on the refrigerator, munching a bowl of dry Honey-Nut Cheerios. The play was forgotten. "When do you want to do it?"

"We can cruise by this afternoon, see how it looks."

"Is this the last one?" Dace asked.

"Yeah. If he's got the codes. And he should."

"We're pushing our luck."

"I know. I sweat blood every time," I said.

While LuEllen and I had been scouting the homes of Whitemark employees, and hit the first two, Dace had worked out the tactics of the propaganda attack. After breakfast he produced a yellow legal pad with a list of notes, and outlined the plan.

"When you get the computer operation going, we'll start leaking stories about their production and design troubles. We'll get that out to the technical press. It'll scare the brass over at the Pentagon. They've been burned too often—they're gun-shy about design problems.

"But most newspaper and TV reporters don't care about that stuff. Whitemark might be able to sweep the whole thing under the rug. If we really want to nail them, we need raw meat. Corruption. If you tell a *Post* reporter that there's a ten-million-dollar cost overrun on a control circuit for a fighter plane, and anyway, the circuit doesn't even work, he'll say, 'So what's new?' But if you tell him the company president spent ten thousand on broads and booze for a couple of generals and you've got the pictures to prove it, he'll camp out on your doorstep."

"So where do we get the pictures?" LuEllen asked.

"We could make them up," Dace said mildly.

"Frame them?"

He nodded. "Yeah. Frame them." He looked sanguine about the prospect, sipping tea and watching us.

"Sounds risky," I said.

"There are advantages, too. If we frame them we can make the corruption as spectacular as we want, and we don't have to waste time looking for it. We can go in and out fast. Plant the documents, create the backup and supporting material, and call the papers. The biggest problem we'll have is getting somebody to listen to us."

Washington is overrun with crazies. The city desk receptionists at the major newspapers and television stations dealt with a dozen screwballs a day, by telephone and in person. There were letters from a dozen more. Some threatened to wipe out the Zionists, some the Arabs. Some reported the deleterious effects of fluoride on the nation's testicles. Others could prove that AIDS was a deliberate plot by the Russians, the Chinese, the gays, the blacks, the CIA, or the League of Women Voters, take your pick. Several hundred people knew of the island where a brain-damaged JFK was still living, sometimes with Elvis.

"If we can find or create something good enough, I can handle it. I can get us in, but it has to be good," he said. "Once we get in, the media will stay with it, especially if they get the credit. A big defense contractor paying off the generals, and caught in the act by a vigilant press? That's good stuff."

"What about the poor assholes who supposedly took the bribes? I mean, we could be killing these people," LuEllen said. "Look what happened to you."

Dace nodded. "That's not the only thing. If you frame someone, everything must be precisely right. If we say General Jones was getting laid on Bimini on March 4, and he can produce fifty witnesses who say he was in Boise speaking to the Mothers for Righteousness, the whole effort goes down the drain. If we frame them we'll have to make it a loose frame—slush funds, women, cash payoffs, but no names."

"Will that take?" I asked.

"We could rig something," Dace said. "But see where I'm headed? It would be better to find the real thing, if it's spectacular enough. The real thing always has a special flavor. You *know* it's real. And I'm sure it's in there, somewhere. All of these big companies do favors for the brass. Maybe it's not money or sex, but it's something. If you could get me into their general files, I could find something. But it might take time."

"I've already been in, so entry is no problem," I said. "And it seems like the payoff potential would be bigger."

"Yeah, it would be. I'll outline a frame, just in case. But we should take a run at their files and see what we can find," Dace said.

LuEllen and I looked at each other, and LuEllen said, "I don't like the frame."

I nodded. "Okay. We can't take more than two or three days to look, but let's try it. And first we hit the systems programmer's place, so I can get into the system."

"When are you going to Chicago?" LuEllen asked. I wanted one last talk with Anshiser, to get the final go-ahead.

"If I can get into the system soon—like tonight— I'll go tomorrow or the next day."

"Are you still planning to bring this Maggie back?"

"If she wants to come."

"It makes me nervous, another outsider knowing our faces. My face," LuEllen said. "I hope she's all right."

I shrugged. "No guarantees. There's not much choice, either, if we want to get paid."

Chapter 11

MAGGIE SOUNDED GOOD on the phone, her voice low and husky. She laughed once, and it brought back the memory of her scent, the iris and vanilla, and the feel of the day we met on the sandbar.

"We have to make one more entry," I said. "We'll try it this afternoon. How's Anshiser?"

"He's worse. We're going ahead, but he's not so good."

"Can I talk to him when I come in?"

"Sure. He's functional, if that's what you're asking. When are you coming?"

"Day after tomorrow, if everything works out. If we get in this afternoon."

"Be careful."

"Always."

THE LAST TARGET was in an exclusive suburb in the Virginia countryside. The sprawling lawns were shaded by full-sized trees. Swimming pools were standard equipment and a few yards had tennis courts, screened by lilacs and honeysuckle. Most of the houses had small signs posted by the driveways: THIS HOUSE PROTECTED BY ACME ALARMS. LuEllen scanned the target, looking especially at the phone line coming out.

She was spooked. "What is it?" I asked. "The security?"

"No. We can get past that, if they have it. But something's not right," she said. "These people aren't important enough for this house. You say this guy makes seventy-five or eighty thousand? These places must start at three hundred and fifty and go up from there."

"Maybe Papa had money."

"Maybe," she said, but she wasn't happy about it. The neighborhood was quiet. We rolled through it three times, from different directions, without seeing anything obviously threatening.

"Let's go make the calls," LuEllen said finally. "But if we can't get them at work, I want to wait."

We got them, though, virtually on the first rings. LuEllen dug some coke out of her purse, and took a hit while I called the house, cut the line, tossed the phone receiver in the backseat, and drove back to a neighborhood park.

We ambled down to the house in three or four minutes, taking our time, LuEllen miming a cough to cover a couple of additional hits on the cocaine. We could hear the faint ringing of the phone as we walked up the driveway. There was no security sign outside, but that meant nothing.

"When I pop it, you step right inside the door behind me, and stand there. Don't do anything until I tell you," she said as we walked up to the front door. She took a pair of wire cutters out of her tennis bag and slipped them into the pocket of her shorts. "I'm going to be running around like a rat for a couple of minutes."

At the door, she rang the bell and blew hard on the dog whistle. There was no response. She dipped into the bag for the bar, and I covered her with my body while she cracked the door. We stepped into a dark-paneled entry hall; the kitchen was to the left, the living room straight ahead. Hanging on the entry wall was an eye-popping Egon Schiele drawing of two women, nude except for calf-length silk stockings, making love. It was worth a good fraction of the house's value. I began to understand LuEllen's misgivings. That drawing belonged in a museum, or a millionaire's bedroom, not in a suburban house in Virginia.

LuEllen launched herself into the house, literally running, ripping open the front hall closet, pivoting, going into the kitchen, pulling open the cabinets one after another.

The Doberman pinscher caught her on her knees halfway down the kitchen. He came around the corner from the dining room—black and brown and rippling with muscle, running like a leopard.

I was looking at the Schiele drawing when I heard the dog's toenails on the kitchen floor, and LuEllen screamed "No" and I turned, and the dog was coming. He must not have seen me behind LuEllen, because he leaped toward her snarling, and she half stood, her hands in front of her. I took two steps toward them, and as he hit her upper arms and she started to go down, I kicked him in the throat. LuEllen's arm pulled out of his mouth as he tumbled over and down, then he scrabbled his legs under him, recovering, and I took another step and he was almost on his way again, and I kicked him in the head and he went down again.

He was still alive and still trying, and I kicked him again in the ribs without doing much damage except to roll him over, and then LuEllen pushed by me, lifting the crowbar over her head and bringing it down like a baseball bat. The dog rolled his head, and the bar bounced off; she flailed at him again, and this time connected squarely. Blood spattered across the floor, and the dog's legs started to run in a death kick, and she hit him again, and again, and I grabbed her and pulled her off.

"Let go," she said. "I'm okay." She dropped the bar and began flinging open the doors of the kitchen cabinets and raced into the dining room and looked down the stairs, and then went out through the garage door.

The phone was still ringing in the background. I hunted it down and pulled it off the hook, and rehung it. In the sudden silence I could hear the dog's bubbling breath as he died.

"Get that fuckin' dog and stuff it in the hall closet," LuEllen snarled as she came back in the house.

I went back to the kitchen and dragged the dog by its collar into the hallway, and pushed it into the closet. "What happened with the whistle?"

"Some dogs are trained to ignore them. In fact, they go on alert when they hear one. I don't think there's an alarm, by the way. The dog was it." She was examining her upper arm, and there was blood on her shirt. "There's no entry alarm. There's no motion or sound detectors I can see. I thought maybe they had a direct-call alarm, but I couldn't see anything on the phone lines. I cut them anyway. Let's get this done in a hurry."

"How bad are you?"

"He got me, but it doesn't look too bad."

"Let me see." I pulled the neck of her shirt down over her shoulder, and found four gashes, each an inch long, ragged and deep. They were bleeding profusely.

"Hurts like hell," she said. "I have to find a different shirt and something to soak up this blood."

We went down the hall, and she suddenly stopped and said, "Whoa." The living room had been done by the Marquis de Sade. Scarlet flocked wallpaper set off a two-inch-deep wool pile carpet as black as India ink. The furniture included a walnut-colored baby grand piano and an inky-blue overstuffed living room suite of velvet. A candelabra mounting six black candles sat on the piano. The room smelled of incense and marijuana, and something else, something from the locker room or the bedroom. Sweat. Human juices. Something.

On the walls, at eye level, were groupings of small, high-quality art photographs and engravings, all expensively framed, all pornographic.

"I don't believe these things," LuEllen said, as she examined one of the engravings.

"Everybody needs a hobby," I muttered, looking around. "Let's find that fucking computer."

"Fucking computer is right," LuEllen said, walking from one picture frame to the next. "You could hurt yourself doing some of this stuff."

"Think it's up or down?"

"What?"

"The computer, for Christ's sake."

"Up," she said. She peered closely at me. "You okay? You looked cranked."

"It's okay. It was that dog."

The computer was in the first room at the top of the stairs, an efficient little office with an IBM, two big lockable disk boxes, both unlocked, and a desk made of a Formica countertop set on a half dozen two-drawer filing cabinets. The only odd element was the clock on the wall. The face of the clock portrayed a nude woman seen end-on, her legs representing the clock's hands. The view was unblushingly gynecological.

I brought the IBM up and was shuffling through the disks when LuEllen called.

"Hey Kidd, take a look at this."

"Just a second." I popped my cracker disk into the machine and started it loading. When I stepped out of the office, I found LuEllen in the hall, holding a wad of Kleenex against her bleeding shoulder, and gazing into a bedroom.

"Look." She pointed into the bedroom. There was a waterbed with black candles on the headboard, and a mirrored wall. The main attraction was a photo mural of a woman's face as she performed oral sex on a man who was mostly, but not entirely, out of the picture.

"Look at the size of that thing," LuEllen said.

"Shoot, I've seen donkeys bigger than that," I said.

"I meant the picture, not the guy," she said, coloring a bit. "But I'll tell you what, Kidd. These people aren't a *little* weird. They're a *lot* weird. There's a picture like this in every bedroom. This might be some kind of whorehouse. Maybe that's how they could afford to buy the place. Maybe that's why they don't have any alarms. They don't want the cops coming in, no matter what."

"I got to get back," I said. I returned to the office, and LuEllen started trashing the bedrooms. I loaded and reloaded the disks, looking for the communications program. The boxes were full of disks identified only by number. I was on the fourth or fifth one, all files, when LuEllen went past the door, stuck her head in, said, "Found two grand in cash, three guns, and six dildos," and kept going. A second later, she went down the stairs to the living-room level.

The communications program was on the seventh disk. I had pulled off the phone plate and was ready to wire in the bug, but took a minute to run through the program. There was a list of code words, but they looked too similar to the words used by Ebberly and Durenbarger. They might get me into all the system files, but I wasn't sure they would give me access to the programming level.

As the disk was being copied, I finished wiring the bug into the phone box, and put the plate back on. When the communications disk was copied, I dropped the copy into the tennis bag, and looked quickly at the rest of the disks. They were all files, mostly long lists of names and addresses. The files were protected by a commercial security program that wasn't quite worthless: it slowed me down by about five seconds per disk.

When I finished, I pulled out the file drawers under the counter and went through the paper files. Nothing of immediate interest. I was closing the bottom drawer when a flash of white on the inside front panel caught my eye. I pulled it all the way out, and found a piece of masking tape. Seven ten-digit numbers were written on the tape. That looked promising. I copied them out in the order they were written in.

"Kidd!" LuEllen was shouting up the stairs. "C'mere, quick."

I pushed the drawer shut, shoved the copied disks and the list of numbers into the tennis bag, and headed down the stairs. There was no one in the living or dining rooms.

"Where are you?" I called.

"Down in the basement."

The windowless basement was divided lengthwise down the middle. In one half was the utility room, with a washing machine and drier, a tool bench, storage, and what looked like a small bathroom. With the exception of one room, the other half was nothing like the upstairs. It was a warehouse, a paradigm of efficiency, with fluorescent overhead lights and flat white tile floors.

The exception was the neat little photo studio. It had a velvet couch, a pile of red and black velvet drapes, and a cardboard box full of sexual implements: dildos, handcuffs, a whip, masks. And dolls. The Army dolls that boys play with, and two old-fashioned fat, plastic baby dolls that cry when they sit up. There were three lights with umbrella reflectors, pulldown seamless paper, and a pair of Hasselblad cameras, each with its own tripod. Next to it was a professional color darkroom.

The rest of the basement was stacked with cartons and envelopes. LuEllen had opened the cartons and held a sheaf of slender, full-color magazines.

"Take a look at these," she said.

The magazines ran the gamut of the sexual activities usually portrayed by porno magazines, with one significant difference. In each picture, one of the participants was a child. And the shots had been taken in the neat little photo studio.

"These are those child-porn assholes you hear about," LuEllen said. She was wearing a pink blouse, not her own, holding her shoulder, and shouting. "I'm going to burn this fucking place down."

"No, you're not," I said, grabbing her around the waist and pulling her tight. "We can use this. You get everything you'd normally take—guns, money, jewelry, and grab those Hasselblads and all the lenses you see; those are worth a bundle. Let's hurry. Take one copy of each magazine, but don't mess them up. And for Christ's sake, don't get prints on them."

I ran back up the stairs and started making

copies of all the file disks. If they were what I thought, I'd have a complete mailing list for the child-porn ring. It took fifteen minutes to copy the files. While I did it, LuEllen went through the place with a vengeance. She came into the office once, to get my tennis bag, and when I finished, I found her with two fat garbage bags in the kitchen.

"We'll take twenty grand out of here," she said with satisfaction.

"Jesus, if a cop sees us carrying those bags, he'll stop us for sure," I said. "There's way too much stuff."

"I know. So we leave them here in the kitchen, except for your disks, and go get the car, come back, load them up, and take off," she said.

"Oh, man, I don't know."

"It's what a doper would do with a load this size," she said defiantly. "He'd take the risk."

So did we. We brought the car back, and I jumped out, while LuEllen waited with the car running in the driveway. I walked up to the front door, knocked, pushed through, got the bags, brought them out, tossed them in the backseat. On an impulse I walked back to the house, took the Schiele off the wall, carried it out to the car, and handed it across the seat to her.

"That was stupid," she said fiercely as we drove away. She was hurting.

"Yeah."

A few minutes later she said, "I feel bad about the dog. He was doing his job." A minute later, she punched me on the arm. "Saved my ass, Kidd."

LuEllen went up to the apartment ahead of me, and when I came in, carrying the bags, Dace had her wrapped up in his arms.

"We've got to get a doctor," he said.

"Can you handle that?" I asked. "Somebody who'll keep his mouth shut?"

"Yeah. I know a guy."

"Tell him the dog was a neighbor's, and we'll make sure it's quarantined, and not to sweat it, we don't want any trouble, no reports," I said.

"I knew something was going to happen," he said. "Sooner or later."

"What are you going to do about those freaks?" LuEllen asked.

"If the number codes get me into the system, I can make some changes that will give me the same status as the systems programmer," I said. "I'll be able to go anywhere in the system. After the operation is running, we'll write to the cops. Tell them the truth. That we broke in, what we found. I got a copy of their whole subscription list, we'll print it out and include that, say we found it with the magazines. Child pornography is not appreciated in the state of Virginia. They'll be looking at ten years in the joint."

"What if the burglary scares them so much that they dump all the stuff?" LuEllen asked.

"They'll freak out, but they won't dump it," I said. "There's too much money involved. Especially if they think they were hit by a crackhead who wouldn't be any further threat."

"What about the kids who get fucked between now and then?"

I shook my head. "It's not a perfect world. If you want to nail these people, put them out of business, this is the way to do it."

She wasn't happy. Dace, on the other hand, was pleased in a grim sort of way.

"This is a major story," he said. "Major-major! We'll drop this thing on Whitemark like an atomic bomb. We've got to do it right and wait until they're already in trouble, and then boom. This could sink them."

Dace took LuEllen to see his doctor while I sorted through the stuff we'd taken in the burglary. There wasn't much we could save, but I would keep the Schiele drawing—he was among the best draftsmen of the twentieth century, and his erotic pieces are stunning. This was a good one. It could tie me to a burglary, but I looked at it, and looked at it, and knew I'd keep it.

THAT NIGHT DACE and LuEllen dumped the rest of the loot, and I went into the Whitemark computer using the system programmer's codes.

The word codes got me through the first line of protection. The number codes got me into the programming level. It was there that I found the complete list of passwords for every file in the computer, no matter how confidential.

When LuEllen and Dace returned, LuEllen was laughing. "We're going to get a crowd if we dump any more stuff in that alley," she said. Her shoulder had been bandaged, and the doctor gave her a small envelope of pain pills. She took them all and was looking very relaxed.

"I'm in, and I've got to stay with this," I told them, nodding at the terminal. "I'm going to build my own back door into the computer, so I won't have to use the operator's codes. I'll have my own."

I picked up the second telephone, looked Whitemark up in the phone book, and called. When the operator answered, I asked for the computer room.

"Systems."

"Hey, I heard a rumor that you're shutting down early tonight. Is that right?"

"Nope, I don't think so. Let me check." The receiver on the other end clattered onto a desk, and lay there for a minute. Then the voice returned. "Nope. Regular time."

"So how late can I stay on? If I push it?"

"All the way to four o'clock. If you want to stay for another hour, give us a ring and we'll leave it on. But we have to shut down by five for system maintenance."

"Thanks."

"No problem."

I WORKED THROUGH the night, setting up my own back door. The next day we started breaking into the key files, Dace looking over my shoulder as I worked. Letters, memos, plans, and budgets rolled up the screen and into oblivion. By six o'clock, we were getting tired. A long, white snake of computer paper twisted across the table. Two wastebaskets in the corner were crammed with more jumbled printouts and with empty Coke cans.

"What's next?" I asked. So far we had rifled the confidential, personal, and private files of a half dozen top Whitemark officials. There was some interesting paper, but nothing incriminating.

"Vice president for materials," Dace said. He yawned and shuffled through a Whitemark phone book we'd printed out early in the process. "His name is Bell, I think." Dace ran a finger through the Bs, and I started looking through the filing lists for a Bell.

"Hold it," Dace said suddenly. He was looking into the phone book with a frown wrinkle across his forehead. "Heywood Beltrami?"

"Say what?"

"They've got a guy here named Heywood Beltrami."

"So what? You know him?"

"Yeah. He's a hairball. I had no idea he was working for Whitemark."

"With that name, there sure as shit couldn't be two of them," I said. "What's he do?"

"It says here he's in corporate relations," Dace said.

It took two minutes to find Beltrami's files. It took another five minutes with the master list to figure out which code words were his, and another minute to run them. Beltrami wasn't a technical man, and there was nothing technical about his files. They were all letters and memos.

"Let me in there," Dace said. I gave up the seat at the computer and went to get a beer. LuEllen was watching television in the front room.

"Got anything yet?"

"Dace found somebody he knew. Says he's a sleaze," I said. I went into the kitchen, got a beer, and stopped to watch the game show for a minute.

"I couldn't do computers," LuEllen said after a while. "I mean, it sounds neat, but it's really just sitting in front of a TV tube and pushing buttons, isn't it?"

"Yes and no. You could say that reading a newspaper is looking at long lists of letters, but it's obviously more than that. Same thing with computers."

I was about to go on, but Dace interrupted.

"Got 'em," he yelled from the office.

LuEllen got off the couch and followed me back. Dace was grinning at the computer screen.

"An old dirtbag never changes his grease spots," Dace said. "I knew we could count on Heywood."

He tapped the computer screen with a finger-nail.

"This is a letter to a very heavy Air Force acquisitions guy at the Pentagon. Two stars. There's a whole series of letters in here. They talk in circles, but when you see them all at once, it's pretty clear. Some of them talk about employment, and some of them talk about problems with specs on the *Hellwolf.* You have to look at the dates, and what's going on, before you realize that White-mark is promising to take care of this guy and his buddies when they retire. Consultant jobs. Big bucks. Big offices. Cars. Goddamn. All White-mark wants is some *help* with spec changes. It restores your faith in mankind to know that people like Heywood are still out there oozing around after all these years."

Dace was happy. He looked, in fact, about ten years younger. LuEllen squeezed his shoulder, and I said, "Right. Let's get it printed out."

We dumped everything in Beltrami's files into

our memory. As it came chugging out of the printer, we decided on the next step.

"We can work through the stuff tomorrow, decide the best way to leak it to the media," Dace said. "And we'll get a package together on our pornographer friends, so we can hand it to the cops."

"I'm going to Chicago," I said. "I'll be back the next day."

"We start the day after you get back?" asked LuEllen.

"Yes. The fuckin' Rubicon."

Chapter 12

MAGGIE WAS WAITING at the O'Hare arrival gate. She wore shades of blue this time, and low business heels. The outfit was subtly chic and must have set her back a thousand or more. She wore no makeup except a touch of pearl-pink lipstick. When she saw me, she smiled briefly and lifted a hand in greeting.

"Did you check any bags?" she asked, as I came through the gate.

"Nope. Just this." I held up the canvas carry-on.

"I've got a car." She led the way toward the exit, and I tagged along behind like a friendly basset. The first two times I'd seen her, her hair had been loose on her shoulders. Now it was swept up in a knot. Her bare neck made her seem more vulnerable. Her carriage had also changed. She seemed softer. Tired. Crumpled.

"You look down. Worn out," I said, struggling for the right words.

She glanced back. "It's Rudy," she said. "There's been a lot of pressure."

"How sick is he?"

"I don't know," she said. "He's been having headaches, pretty bad ones. He had migraines when he was young. He's afraid they've come back."

"You called in a doctor?"

She gave me the brief smile again. "Oh, sure. Billionaires aren't allowed to suffer. He's had all kinds of scans and probes. They can't find anything organic. They've given him tranquilizers. They seem to help."

I grabbed her arm and stopped her. She pivoted to face me.

"What are you telling me? That he's out of control?"

"No. He still has control, but sometimes the pain . . . affects him." We started walking again, and I held onto her arm. "He gets angry, out of all proportion to whatever set him off. And when it goes away, the relief is so strong that he gets almost maniacally happy. Overconfident. The swings are hard to deal with."

"How is he now?"

"He's in pretty good shape. He had a bad headache yesterday, but it was gone this morning."

"Are you still planning to come to Washington?"

"Yes. He insists on it. The worse the headaches get, the more determined he is to follow this through."

We passed all the usual exits to the parking ramps and approached an unmarked desk manned by an elderly guard. He saw us coming and nodded at Maggie. She walked past him to a door labeled FIRE and bumped it open with her hip. We were in a reserved section of the parking ramp, separated from the rest of it by a concrete wall. It was the kind of place whose existence I never would have suspected, though it made sense. The average car was probably worth sixty or seventy thousand. There were a half dozen Rolls-Royces and a few sleek Italian jobs that made Maggie's Porsche look Puritan-plain. She dropped neatly into the driver's seat, opened the passenger door, and I climbed inside.

During the ride to Anshiser's she was friendlier than she had been in the past. LuEllen fascinated her, and she asked a dozen questions about the burglaries as we loafed along. When I mentioned that LuEllen and Dace were sleeping together, she half turned toward me in the dark.

"Isn't that a major change?"

"Um."

"You're not distraught?"

"LuEllen and I like to roll around together. Our relationship is important, but not serious. If you know what I mean."

"This Dace. From what you've told me, he seems very . . . likeable."

"LuEllen says he's a nice guy. She says I'm not. She wants to try nice for a while."

She thought about that, and it occurred to me that I was feeling some electricity. I wrote it off as fantasy, a product of unrequited hormones. In any case, she stopped talking about LuEllen, and I brought her up-to-date on the Whitemark project.

"So you're ready," she said when I finished.

"Yeah. If Anshiser says *go*."

"He will," she said. She glanced at me. "Dillon was doing more research, you know, just because he's Dillon. Anyway, he found a reference to a paper you wrote about the tarot. He went out and bought a deck."

I grinned in the dark. "Where did he find it? The paper?"

"That was the strange thing. It was at the War College."

"Yeah. I knew they were using it."

She wanted more, but we were in the twisting streets, and a moment later she turned in at Anshiser's wrought-iron gate. It rolled smoothly out of the way and she gunned the car up to the house.

Anshiser was a shock. He'd been thin when I last saw him, and he'd lost another ten pounds. The lines in his face had deepened and his short hair seemed to stand on end. His nose appeared redder and larger.

"Mr. Kidd," he said hoarsely, as Maggie ushered me into the office. Dillon was nowhere to be seen. "I understand we're ready to go."

I gave him the report I'd given Maggie on the way in. He was pleased. When I told him what we planned to do with the child pornographers, he said, "Goddamned right," and laughed. "That ought to open up some sinuses over there." He whacked the top of his desk with sudden energy.

"You don't look so good," I said. "Maggie said you're having migraines."

"Something like it. Not quite, but close," he said somberly. "To tell you the truth, I think I'm dying."

"My God, Rudy," Maggie protested. "The doctors say it's tension. It could be Kidd's project doing this. Who knows? You're not dying."

Anshiser laughed again, the laugh trailing off to a cough. "The doctors are full of horseshit," he said. "I know what I feel like." He looked at me and held his hand to his head. "I can't explain it, but when I have one of these headaches, my whole body feels empty. I don't know what it is; I've never had it before. And it's bad."

"Look," I said, "you're making me nervous. If you're about to lose it, either mentally or physically, we could have serious problems. You're our backup, if anything goes wrong."

He hacked again, covering his mouth with his fist, his eyes never leaving mine. "I'll last," he said. "I'm too damn mean to die before that's done." He reached under his desk and produced a nylon handbag and pushed it toward me.

"Half of the remaining money," he said. "A half million dollars. I'm extremely pleased with your progress."

I looked at the bag for a minute and then back up at Anshiser.

"The real thing starts the day after tomorrow," I said. "Maggie and I will get out of here tomorrow, we'll show her where we're at, and then we do it. I need you to say right now to go ahead."

"Do it. I wish you luck, I do," Anshiser said. He pushed himself slowly out of the chair, and I picked up the bag and leaned forward to shake his hand.

"You take good care of Maggie," he said. "She's the daughter I should have had. Or the wife." He grinned, and for another instant, the vitality was back.

Maggie led the way to the door, and just outside, put a hand on my arm. "I wasn't expecting this," I said, holding up the money bag.

"That's Rudy's way of telling you he's happy," she said. "Do you have reservations in town?"

"No. I thought it would be better to show up somewhere and pay in cash. I sure as hell have enough of it."

"Why don't you stay at my place? I have an extra room, and you're welcome to it. It would be untraceable."

"That's nice of you. Thanks."

"I have to talk to Rudy privately for a moment. I'll be right back." I waited in the hallway, heard the sound of their voices, then Anshiser laughed again, and a moment later she came out.

"His sense of humor seems to be intact," I said as we headed down the stairs.

"You seem . . . not exactly to amuse him, but to make him laugh," she said. "It's good for him."

"What'd I say?"

She glanced back at me, the smile extending to her eyes this time.

"I told him I'd offered to let you stay at my place, in the spare bedroom. And how you said, 'That's nice of you.' And he said, 'God Almighty, Maggie, why don't you take that boy home and let him screw your brains loose?' "

"That's when he laughed?"

"No, he laughed on my line. He never laughs on his own." She was ahead of me going down the stairs, so all I could see was that tantalizing neck, and not her face.

"What was your line?"

She'd reached the bottom of the stairs and crossed the short hall to the outside door. She turned at just the right moment, with one hand on the knob. "I said I planned to do exactly that."

I said "Oh" to an empty doorway.

AS A TOP-LEVEL manager, and a large, athletic woman, she was surprisingly soft and yielding in the bedroom. While LuEllen went after sex with the enthusiasm of a beer-drinking cowgirl, Maggie was slower and looser and almost submissive. When we broke apart after making love the first time, she rolled onto her back. The skin of her stomach and breasts was shiny-damp in the dim bedside light, and she said, sounding satisfied with herself, "There."

"There, what?"

She propped herself on one elbow and looked down at me. "There are some men . . . getting them in bed is a challenge, you know? You were such an arrogant asshole the first time we met, out on the sandbar, with your brushes and your paintings and your torn shirt and your tan. I was sweating like a pig, my nylons were full of holes, my hair was a mess, and when I try to make conversation about the hole you cut in your painting, you cut me off at the knees. What a jerk."

"Jesus," I muttered.

"What?"

"Nothing. I'd just . . . heard something similar."

"Well, you're the type who would."

"Not about me. About someone else," I said. Time to change the subject. "Are you worried about the raid? We could call it off right now, and nobody would ever know."

She dropped flat on her back again. "Sure I'm worried. I'm paid to worry. I'm worried about Rudy, too. The way he talks about dying."

"Don't ignore that," I said. "Sometimes people know what the doctors don't."

"That's what worries me. That he might somehow talk himself right into the grave." She looked sideways at me. "Tell me why this attack is going to work."

I thought for a moment. "Because it's set up right," I said. "We took some time, and we know what we're doing. There's a possibility that we'll be nailed right away, that there's some kind of invisible monitoring system in Whitemark's software, but I've been careful and I haven't seen it; and I've been deep enough into their system to know that they depend on it. When we corrupt that system, they'll be effectively frozen."

"People will be hurt."

"Not physically. Like Anshiser said the first time I saw him, it's either his company or Whitemark. Somebody's got to lose. Whitemark cheated. That makes it a little more okay."

"But not completely okay."

"Nothing is completely okay."

"What about this problem with what's-his-name, Ratface?" she asked. She knew about the incident with the woman from down the hall, and that we thought the landlord had been lying about Ratface.

"I still don't know what that was about," I said. "Bobby's watching him, but nothing's happened. I have it in the back of my head that maybe it wasn't a divorce thing, that maybe Ratface and the landlord were involved in some kind of blackmail business. You know, we're not even sure that the technician was putting those bugs *on* the phones. Maybe he was taking them off. Maybe the landlord called them and said, 'Hey, these guys are some kind of computer freaks, maybe you better get those bugs out of there.' I don't know. That doesn't feel right either."

Maggie laughed softly. "It all sounds nuts. You know, whacky. Like something one of those right-wing fascist weirdo groups would fantasize about."

"Yeah, but they'd do it in tree-bark camo," I said. "The main thing is, nothing has happened. Ratface is still off in Jersey."

Maggie snuggled up on my shoulder and I looked at the ceiling, feeling her there, and neither one of us said anything for a few minutes. Then her hand crept down my stomach and she said, "Hmm."

•   •   •

"IT'S GOING TO work," she said a half hour later. I was a little confused and wondered for a second if that was a personal comment. I thought it *did* work. "Dillon did a risk evaluation on this job. We had a hard time evaluating the first phase, the burglaries, because we didn't know what kind of personnel you'd have. That's why Rudy kept me out of it until now."

I'd caught up with her. "How about the second phase, going into the company?"

"That was easier to evaluate. We know you and your work, and there have been studies of this kind of attack by the National Security Agency and the FBI. Dillon thinks this will be the least risky phase. But after we hit, and the news reports start coming out, the risks escalate. The key is picking the time to get out. If you wait too long . . . zut." She drew a finger across my throat.

"And if we get caught? What happens then?"

"That depends. It's absolutely critical to keep your name and face, everybody's name and face, out of the media. The biggest danger is that you would be arrested, and processed, before we could interfere. Once something is on paper, it gets much harder," she said. "If you can keep things private and give Rudy time to operate, we should be okay."

"So we keep things informal."

"Absolutely."

"Jesus, I wish I still smoked."

"Why?"

"I could use a cigarette."

THE NEXT DAY, while Maggie took care of last-minute business at Anshiser's, I went into Chicago and stashed my share of the extra money in a second safety-deposit box. I mailed the key to Emily in St. Paul, along with a note telling her that everything was fine.

We flew out of Chicago in the early afternoon and got to Washington in time to catch the evening crush on I-395. When we arrived at the apartment, I unlocked the door and pushed through, carrying my own overnight case and Maggie's three-suiter. Dace and LuEllen were working in the office. LuEllen was wearing jeans and her white, tassled cowboy boots; Maggie was in one of her blue power suits.

"Dace and LuEllen, this is Maggie Kahn, and Maggie . . ." I gestured at the other two.

"Pleased to meet you," LuEllen said cheerfully, sticking out a hand. Maggie shook it, smiling, and said, "My pleasure. I've heard something about your work from Kidd. I'd like to hear more."

LuEllen glanced sideways at me, then back at Maggie. "What did he say?" Her tone was light, but her eyes were dark and serious.

"Well, he told me that LuEllen might not be your real name, that he doesn't know your last name or where you live, and he doesn't know what you do when you're not working, but that he does know you're good when you are work-ing."

LuEllen relaxed. Her security was sound. Dace shook Maggie's hand and offered to show her around. She looked at the office, tapped on the keyboard of one computer, and glanced through the letters between Whitemark and the generals. "I'd like to look at those administrative formats you worked out. Maybe I could help run through their files," she said in her executive voice.

"Any time you want to see them," Dace said. "We can take you through the sign-on routine to-morrow."

"Thanks," Maggie said. She glanced around the office again, then stepped outside and looked down the hall.

"Where's our room?" she asked. "I want to get out of this suit."

"Uh, right over here." I pointed at the door. "I'll bring your suitcase."

She disappeared into the bedroom, and as I picked up the heavy case in the living room, a grinning LuEllen slapped me on the butt and whispered, "Way to go, José."

I may have blushed.

Chapter 13

COMPUTER PROGRAMMING CAN be as beautiful and complicated as a tree, as compelling as the best painting. Programmers admire each other's code. They talk like rock climbers: that was a very difficult pitch, and look how he did it—with *style*. A good programmer uses a computer's potential to create worlds where other people will live. Or, in some cases, where they will fight.

The attack on Whitemark began after breakfast on a beautiful August morning. Maggie and I split a bag of bagels and a pot of coffee, chatted and laughed, cleaned up the kitchen, and went to war. The attack lasted precisely four weeks: twenty-eight days to the hour.

The first moves were invisible to Whitemark. We infested their system with a virus. A virus is a chunk of computer code, compact and deadly. Once a virus has infected a computer's system software, it makes copies of itself and inserts them into the working programs being run through the system. The working program, in turn, infects other operating systems. Unless the virus is detected, it will eventually infect every program that passes through the system. And those programs will infect every other program they encounter.

Besides replicating itself, the virus usually does damage. Not always. There are Christmas card viruses, for example, that insert graphic Christmas cards in every text file they find. When somebody opens the computer file, the first thing that appears is the Christmas card.

The disease viruses are a different story. They are killer bugs. They erase information, jumble it, destroy expensive, one-of-a-kind custom programs. There are some viruses, more complicated than the straight-out bombs, that may change a system's programming in more subtle ways.

Our first virus was not subtle. It was a bomb, pure and simple. Forty-five days after being inserted in the Whitemark computer system (viruses can count), it would explode. Any Whitemark program containing a virus would be thoroughly and irretrievably jumbled. Nothing would come out of the company's computers but garbage.

"Why forty-five days?" Maggie asked, when I explained the virus to her. We were in the Whitemark computer using the special entry codes I had created for us.

"The Whitemark programmers will eventually

catch on to what we're doing. We've got three or four weeks at the most. If their top systems man is busted on the porno charge, we may get a few more days out of the confusion. Anyway, when the trouble starts, they'll do the routine system checks. That will take a couple of days. When nothing works, they'll start sweating. Eventually, they'll figure it out. They'll realize they're under attack, and they'll shut down outside access. There are some ways around that, but only for a day or two. At that point, we'll be fifteen or twenty days out, and they'll call in the FBI, or somebody like that, to look for us. They'll be worried about sabotage.

"Once they get everything shut down, there'll be a couple of weeks of confusion. They'll be paranoid about the system. They'll run all kinds of tests. Then they'll start repairs, bringing in new software. Checking it. That should get us five or six weeks down the road. So then, at six and a half weeks, the bomb explodes. It'll be the finishing touch. They won't recover before the contract deadlines."

She thought about it for a minute, nibbling on her lower lip. "So what's the first move after you get the viruses in? The first thing that will affect them? If we don't hurt them soon, it'll be too late."

"I'll start on that tonight," I said. "Most of their design work is done at individual work stations, but all the stations are tied into the central computer. I can get to them when they're not being used. I'll start by hacking up the math programs. Engineers run a million numbers through their computers. I'll stick in a program that will add or subtract various small percentages on certain calculations. It won't be quite random. Identical calculations will come out the same way every time, so if they check their work, it'll be confirmed. But it'll all be wrong."

She didn't understand. "What's the practical effect?" she asked. "Tell me a practical effect."

"Okay. Say you were designing a screw-in gas cap for your Porsche. There's a male part and a female part. The threading has to be the same on both parts. Say the twist on the male part is altered just slightly—the pitch is changed a few degrees. The cap becomes worthless. You can't look at the plans and tell that it's worthless; you can't tell it's worthless when you're making it. It looks fine right up to the time you try to screw the parts together. Then they don't work. And the whole problem is in a calculation somewhere.

"Or say that you want to design the kind of round gas-cap cover that goes on the outside of some cars, on the fender. Say you make the round metal cover a quarter inch too big in diameter. It won't fit; it's useless. You can't make it fit any more than you can push a nickel through a pop-bottle top. But it looks fine, right up to the moment you try to put it on the car."

She considered it for a moment, staring dead into the eye of an onion bagel.

"That sounds pretty crude," she said finally.

"Those examples are," I agreed. "But if you do analogous things in electronics, it gets more complicated. You can't see which parts are wrong; it can take days to figure out a mistake. Every individual part works, and every part is just as specified, but the system won't work. Anytime you build a complicated electronic machine there are always mistakes, pure accidents. They're nightmares. Sometimes it takes days to find them. You don't know if you're dealing with a basic design flaw, or if there's a bad electrical connection somewhere. If mistakes are generated on a large scale, by design . . . I don't know of a cure."

She thought that over as she got into the onion bagel. "How do you know that they just won't check the computer and fix it?" she asked as she chewed.

"They will, sooner or later. But probably later. Computers are the water engineers swim in. They don't question the answers they get from computers any more than a fish questions water. They *know* the computer is correct: the problem must be somewhere else."

That seemed to satisfy her, although she was more thoughtful than pleased. Later in the morn-

ing, I injected the first of the viruses into the
Whitemark system. When it was done, I wandered into the kitchen and heard her talking on
an extension phone, relaying what I'd told her.
When she got off the phone, she came in and sat
down.

"I was talking to our systems man," she said.
"I didn't tell him what we're doing, of course, but
I did say that I'd talked to a guy about computer
security. He says you're right. But he says the
chances of a good enough programmer ever getting into *our* system are slim and none."

"That's why it could be done."

I was tempted to tell her that Bobby had already been in the Anshiser system, but some
things are best left untold. "If I were you, I might
have another little chat with him."

"I made a note," she said. She smiled, and the
skin crinkled at the corners of her eyes.

WHILE I WAS working on the attack programs
that we'd insert into the Whitemark system, Dace
was working on the publicity angle. His first
product was a package on the systems director,
the pornographer.

"I put it together with words cut out of the
Post," he said. He was wearing surgeon's latex
gloves and holding the paper by the corners. It
was an ugly jumble of clipped-out news type
Scotch-taped to a piece of spiral notebook paper.

"The hardest part was getting the words right. Nothing too big, but nothing too small, either. Something just right for a half-bright crackhead."

The text was three paragraphs long and explained:

we needed the MONEY from

the Robbery for medicine. so

we started robbing Houses.

found these Porno magazines

FUll of little children, which

was not Cool. which is a

Hundred Times more cruel than

ANYTHING we Ever done.

It specified names, the address, and the day and time of the burglary.

Maybe They HID it BY now.

But If you watch Them

you Catch Them.

little kids ARE getting Fucked.

A sample magazine was enclosed, along with the list of subscribers.

"One thing that strikes me as phony is that we're sending it to the right police jurisdiction. A junkie would probably send it to the Washington cops," Dace said as he sealed the envelope. "I don't want to take a chance that the whole thing would get lost in the bureaucracy, so I'm going to send it to the right place, to the chief. Even if they're a little suspicious, they'll check. Especially with the magazine and the subscriber list."

"What do you think they'll do? The cops?" Maggie asked.

"When I was working a police beat years ago, they'd pass it off to the vice squad. The vice cops would go over to the house, see if the door looks like it had been broken in recently. I'm assuming that the break-in wasn't reported. Then they might look in the windows and see if we described the place right. Or knock on the door with some phony excuse, to see if it looks right. If everything jibes, they'll watch the place, see who comes and goes. Maybe have a quiet talk with a neighbor or two. They'll do a computer search and see if these people have ever been involved in a sex thing in the past. If they find anything, they may do a discreet black-bag job themselves, to check the place out. Then, depending on what they find, they'll go to a pet judge and get a search warrant. They won't have a real good case, but it should be enough for a warrant."

"What if they did report the break-in? For insurance?"

Dace shrugged. "In that case, they probably moved the porn out, at least during the investigation. If they did report it, the cops would have corroboration in their own files that the burglary took place. They'll still watch the place. Sooner or later, they'll bust them."

"It better be sooner," Maggie said. "If it happens two months from now, it won't help."

"It's not a sure thing," Dace said. "But I'd be willing to bet it'll happen in a week."

"How'll we know if it happened?"

"We'll give the cops a couple of days to work. Then we tip off the papers and the TV stations that they're about to bust the biggest kiddie-porn ring in the country. It's hyperbole, but the TV people love that kind of thing. A new record for kiddie porn. They'll get in touch with the cops, and that'll goose the cops along. We'll see it on the evening news."

THE NIGHT AFTER the first attack, Maggie lay on her back in bed, the lights out. The code was still running through my head.

"It's weird," she said, reaching over to pat me on the stomach. "When Rudy and Dillon and I talked about hiring you, I had this picture of somebody climbing a barbwire fence with plastic explosive in his teeth. Instead, we sit in an air-conditioned apartment and eat donuts, and you type on a computer."

"You never carry plastic explosive in your teeth," I said.

"Have you ever seen the Whitemark building?"

"Nope. Should I?"

"I guess not. There's not much to see. Just a big glass cube with a funny pyramid thing for the roof. I thought you might be curious."

"Nah. You can tell more sitting here than you can from looking at the outside of the building."

She shook her head. "That doesn't seem right, somehow. It's like . . ." She groped for an analogy. "It's like dropping bombs on Vietnamese peasants. You know, you push a button and people die, but you go home to lunch. If you're going to have a war, you should have the courtesy to kill your enemies in person. And maybe suffer a little bit."

"You're rambling," I said.

"I know. I don't even know what I'm trying to say. But it seems . . . wrong . . . to be able to attack somebody you've never seen, don't know, and probably won't ever meet."

"You mean I should find the president of Whitemark and personally rip his heart out."

"Oh, bullshit, Kidd. You know what I'm getting at. This seems so . . . sterile. I mean, it's scary.

It's little electronic lights ruining a huge company."

"Welcome to the big city," I said.

"That's an ugly attitude," she said.

"Yeah, but that's the way it is. You wanted this done, and I can do it. We're both consenting adults. It's the new reality. The little electronic lights are more real than that glass building with the pyramid on top."

She shivered.

THE LETTER ABOUT the porn merchants went in the mail the first day. Over the next two days, as I jimmied the Whitemark computer system, Dace and Maggie worked and reworked the approaches to the media on the public attack.

Dace suggested that the Whitemark letters to the generals be leaked first, anonymously, to a weekly defense newsletter called *From the Turret.*

"A lot of people read it, a lot of reporters. *Turret*'s not too scrupulous about what they use or where they get it. If we drop them a note, say we have been unfairly demoted in the company, and send along the letters, they'll use them," he said.

"It doesn't sound public enough," Maggie said with a frown. "I mean, frankly, every company in the defense industry hires retired generals to lobby for them. We do. You put that story in a defense newsletter, there might be a few raised eyebrows, but nothing much will happen."

"Ah. But this isn't hiring a few generals. This involves a quid pro quo. They're saying, 'If our airplane is picked, there'll be jobs in procurement for those who helped us.' That's not recruiting, that's bribery. As soon as *Turret* publishes, we call the *Post, The New York Times*, and Knight-Ridder bureau, and so on, and tip them off. Just being in print gives the story cachet. They'll be interested, because it's the kind of thing they expect to find in a newsletter. Then the next day, we send along copies of the letters to the papers' defense specialist writers."

"Think that will break it out?"

"I think so. It won't be the biggest story of the year, but it will be a nice one. The front pages of the *Post*, probably a good inside spot in the *Times*."

"After we get that going," Maggie said, "we should get in touch with the business magazines about the problems they're having meeting the *Hellwolf* schedules. That will have a nasty effect on their stock prices."

DACE AND LUELLEN usually went out at night, and often spent the night at his apartment. I worked evenings. Maggie talked with Chicago or worked with the other computer terminal, via telephone, with her Chicago office. One night, simultaneously overcome with office fatigue and horniness, we staggered into our bedroom, pulling off clothes, and fell on the bed in a frenzy. Afterward, Maggie showered and dropped into the bed, naked, and was instantly asleep.

The next morning, I woke first, yawned, slid out of bed, and half-opened the narrow venetian blinds that covered the bedroom window. Light flooded across the bed, illuminating the long valley of her spine and the turn of her hip and shoulders. Her face was turned away, her blond hair spread over the pillow. She was still sleeping soundly. I looked at her a moment, then tiptoed out and got the big pad of parchment paper I use for sketching. When she woke, I'd done a half dozen preliminaries.

"What are you doing?" she said sleepily.

"Drawing."

She was suddenly awake, alarmed. "Let me see those." She crawled across the bed and I showed her the pad. She looked at the drawings, and lay back. "Can't see my face," she said.

"I can always put it in," I joked.

"Just what I need. A nude picture of myself hanging over the bar. What are you going to do with them?"

"Probably do a painting—if I can convince you to lie in the light for a few mornings, so I can get your skin."

"I don't know; I'd feel silly. I'm no model," she said, and seemed genuinely shy.

That afternoon, by chance, I saw an old-fashioned red-white-and-blue-checked comforter in a shop window, and went in and bought it. Dace and LuEllen were gone again the next morning, and I got her to lie on it, nude, face down, her head turned away, the light streaming in over her shoulders and butt. I spent an hour doing color studies before she put a stop to it.

"How much do models get paid?" she asked.

"Depends on how good they are," I said. "Anything between nine and fifteen dollars an hour."

"You owe me fifteen bucks," she said, pulling up her underpants.

"'Fraid not. You're awful. Five bucks at the most. You kept scratching your back, and you'd move around on that checked background. Drove me nuts."

"Awful, huh? So it's not a fallback if I get fired?"

DACE SAW THE beginnings of the painting that afternoon and whistled.

"Nice ass, huh?" Maggie said.

"Nice painting," he said seriously.

Maggie looked at me as if she had never seen me before.

• • •

THE CHANGES I sneaked into the Whitemark computers were worked out on editing programs at the apartment. I wrote the code on our machines, tested it, developed the sequence for inserting it at Whitemark, and put it in. I was on-line with Whitemark for only a few minutes—sometimes a matter of seconds.

As the work progressed I drifted into the traditional programming schedule. The programming and debugging were done at night, and I slept late. Once I even ordered out for a pizza with everything, the only official programmer food.

The attack programs were inserted into the Whitemark software during the heavy computer-working hours in the morning, when we'd be less likely to be noticed.

In the afternoons, I'd paint. I'd never worked in Washington, but it was an exceptional place, with its heavy subtropical flora, the water, the varied stone and brick buildings going back two hundred years. The light was almost Italianate, but bluer and clearer. When I went out to paint, often along the Mall, Maggie would come along, bring a book and a blanket, and lie in the sun and read and doze.

Dace and LuEllen were making plans for Mexico. With the burglaries done, LuEllen had almost nothing to do, and spent the days touring Washington. Scouting possible burglary targets, I suspected. Twice she flew back to Duluth, alone,

to make arrangements for a longer absence. Dace
had decided on the west coast of Mexico, a semi-
modern fishing village in Baja with American-
owned villas on the hillside. "Just the right
combination of ambience and convenience," he
said. His first novel would involve Pentagon
power politics with a dash of sexual intrigue.
"Like it really is."

Maggie and Dace sent the material on the generals off to *Turret*. Dace, playing the part of a demoted and treacherous executive, called the
newsletter to make sure they had gotten the package, and that they understood it. They had, and
they did. The television stations were tipped on
the pornographers and promised to make in-
quiries. Dace also spent some time hanging
around the Pentagon, talking with reporter
friends, listening for rumors about Whitemark.
There was nothing at first. Then, slowly, they
began to come. . . . Trouble with plans; trouble
with production; disputes between lower-level
managers over a series of brutal snafus . . .

On the ninth day of the attack, I found something interesting in the Whitemark system. I had
noticed a data-exchange line that ran out of the
main computer to a satellite computer elsewhere.
I paid no attention to it, until one day I saw an
exchange that involved a remote terminal beyond
the satellite. That meant that somebody was tele-
phoning the satellite computer, and from there,

was getting into the main computer. If I could learn how to access the satellite from the outside, I could avoid the phone lines that went directly into the main computers. For practical purposes, I would be working from inside the Whitemark building. Toward the end of the attack, it might buy me a few more days of work.

Unfortunately, the computers accessed each other with special codes, and I couldn't find the code listings inside the main system. It was all done inside the satellite.

What I could see were incoming codes. Each five-numeral code group was unique—the same one was never used twice. All the codes were handtyped, so they weren't coming off a master list on a disk. Eventually I fed a list of once-used codes to Bobby, explained the problem, and asked if he had an analysis. He called back three hours later.

The code is the 17th Mersenne Prime, 13,395 digits in 2,679 groups of five, starting with 85450. Your code sample starts 875 groups in and continues in sequence. I am sending you the next 500 sequence groups. Enough?

Plenty. How much?

My pleasure. No charge.

Bobby is not a person to bother with unimportant matters, so I never asked him directly how he figured it out. That he did is bizarre beyond words.

Once I had the codes, I got inside the satellite. It turned out to be a small computer in the accounting department. I got its phone number from its files.

On the tenth day of the attack, Maggie flew out to Chicago. She was back two days later.

"How was Anshiser?" I asked.

She sat at a dressing table with her back to me, peering into a dark mirror as she took down her hair.

"Worse," she said tersely. "I hate to look at him. He's losing more weight. His skin looks like crepe paper."

"The doctors still don't know what's wrong?"

"They keep saying stress, but some of them are nervous about the diagnosis. He may go out to the Mayo."

"He should have gone a month ago."

I was lying on the bed in my shorts, all the lights out except the small pink-shaded lamp on the dressing table. The apartment was quiet. Dace was at his apartment, closing it down, and LuEllen was in Duluth.

"How has it been here?" Maggie asked, unscrewing an earring.

"Whitemark will figure it out soon now," I

said. "The engineering system is falling apart. Things must be chaotic. The office mail system will stop working tomorrow. That's the main way they route assignments and schedules, so that'll be shot. On Friday the paychecks all come up short."

Maggie dropped a second earring on the table-top and turned on the cushioned bench, so she was facing me. "*Turret* comes out tomorrow," she said. "I called Dace this morning before I left Chicago. He had solid word that the generals' story would be in it."

"He didn't mention it to me," I said. "I didn't see him today, just the note on the table saying he would be at his place tonight."

She stood up and stepped toward the bed, wearing a brassiere and panties and slip. She pulled the slip over her head and tossed it negligently on a side chair. "You were on the computer, and he didn't want to bother you," she said. "He said you were in a fugue state. Undo me?"

She sat on the edge of the bed; I propped myself up and unsnapped the brassiere, and kissed her between the shoulder blades. She arched her shoulders and pivoted on her butt and lay back on her pillow, her hair spreading out.

"Haven't heard anything about the kiddie porn yet," I said.

"Ah. Dace said something was happening. He

attached his video recorder to the TV and set the timer for the news programs. It's running now," she said.

"Jesus, I didn't even see it. I've been out of it."

She rolled on her side facing me and slid her hand down inside my shorts. "Aw, has you been aw wonesome and sulking since mama's been gone?"

I groaned. "God save me from women who talk baby talk to my dick."

"Oh yeah?" she said.

Later that night we were lying in spoons, my arm over her hip, her butt against my stomach. When she had been breathing deep and steady for ten minutes, I got up and padded out of the room and quietly closed the door behind me. I had the computer up a minute later, and I was out on the phone lines, looking around. Sometimes, nothing will stop the code in your head.

THE NEXT DAY was the peak of the programming. I sat on the computer for nine straight hours, working out one piece after another, checking, debugging, rechecking. When I got out of the chair I could barely walk.

"You need a Fuji," Dace said as I hobbled out of the office.

"What's that?"

Fuji's Water-Gate was a thoroughly westernized Japanese bathhouse not far from the Pentagon—

westernized because the patrons wore tank suits
and bathed in private groups. The bathing pools
were not much bigger than good-sized hot tubs,
but the water was infinitely hotter. Dace and
Maggie dropped into it, moaned for a few seconds, then relaxed, and watched LuEllen and me
test the water.

"C'mon, you'll live," Maggie said. "No guts?"
With that, LuEllen dropped in like a stone, went
completely under, gasped, and tried to crawl back
out. Dace, laughing, grabbed her around the
waist and held her squealing until she settled
down. "Get your ass in here, Kidd," she said.

The water was hot enough to boil lobsters. I
slipped in, an inch at a time, to my hips, supporting my weight with my hands.

"That's the worst way," Dace said snidely.
"You get ten minutes of pain instead of ten seconds."

"I'll do it my way," I said.

"You'll boil your balls, is what you'll do,"
Maggie snorted. LuEllen and Dace looked at her
strangely, and she blushed, then all three burst out
laughing.

"All right, all right." I took a breath and
dropped the rest of the way in, up to my chin.
LuEllen, who is as strong as an ox, reached over
and pushed my head under. For a moment, I
thought my heart had stopped. When it started

again, I huddled up next to Maggie until all the nerve endings died and I could straighten out.

"Jesus. How long do we have to stay in here?"

"An hour or so," Maggie said, grinning.

"We'll be dead in an hour."

"Nonsense. In two minutes, you'll feel fine."

She was right. Two minutes later I felt fine. We floated around the pool, talking, not touching, never mentioning Whitemark or the attack. LuEllen had been to the Smithsonian and—Dace laughed—had been looking at the display of locks. Dace, LuEllen said, had been closing down his apartment, and she had been helping. When she cleaned out the front room, she found a sack lunch behind the couch. Dace admitted that it was probably two years old, from a tough time when he was making his own lunch. There was a little plastic container of green grapes, LuEllen said, that had gone past raisinhood and had reached petrification.

Maggie told the other two that when I thought she was asleep, I snuck out of the bedroom and went back to the computer. "I can't compete, I guess."

"Of course you can," Dace said, ogling her thinly concealed breasts.

"Down, boy," said LuEllen.

Maggie threw back her head and laughed and lay back in the water, and she looked like a medieval swan queen come to life. Sometime during the forty-five minutes we spent in the pool, the code stopped running through my head.

THE HEAD OF the Whitemark systems department, his wife, and twenty-three-year-old son were arrested at seven o'clock the next morning on a variety of pornography charges, all of them felonies. It was midmorning, and I was already on the machine, working, when the phone rang and Maggie answered. She listened for a moment, said, "Great" and "What channel?" and "Goodbye."

"That was Dace," she reported, leaning in the doorway. "He said to look at the 'Morning Break' news on Channel Three. He said the cops picked up our pornographer friends. There was a 'Live Eye' report right from the house."

We went into the living room and backed up the video recorder until we found the "Morning Break" segment, and watched the three people coming out of the house in handcuffs.

"I feel kind of sorry for them," Maggie said. The wife, a weighty, gray-haired matron, was weeping. She tried to cover her face with her hands, but the cameras tracked her right to the car.

"Think about what they were doing," I said. But it wasn't pretty.

After the unhappy family was bundled off in a squad car, the camera cut to a half dozen uniformed cops filing in and out of the garage door, carrying boxes full of magazines. We watched until the end of the segment, and then Maggie called Channel Three.

"Listen," she said when she got the news department, "if you hadn't heard, this man they arrested on the child pornography is a very important executive at Whitemark Aerospace. I work there, and I know. He runs all their computers. I think some of the other guys in that department may be working with him on this porn thing. They're pretty close."

She listened for a minute. "No, I can't. If I told you my name I could get fired. But he's really a bigshot."

She dropped the phone on the hook, and it rang again almost before she had taken her hand away. She listened for a moment, said "Thanks," and hung up. "Dace again," she said. "*Turret* is out. The generals are on the front. They reprinted the critical letters word for word."

"Ah. We're rolling."

"Yes." She got the phone book and methodically called the rest of the television stations about the tie between the pornographer and Whitemark. Then she started calling the newspapers and wire services, urging them to look at the *Turret* article.

On day 16, *The Wall Street Journal* ran an expanded version of the *Turret* story. *The New York Times*, the *Post*, and the Associated Press followed the next day, although the AP story was so hedged against libel that it was hard to tell what was happening.

The *Post* is not nearly as good a paper as the *Times*, but it can bleed a story like an eighteenth-century barber-surgeon squeezing every exquisite moment of agony out of a public death. After reporting the generals' relationship with Whitemark, it followed the next day with a complicated explanation by Whitemark. The day after that, there was an even more complicated explanation from the generals, paired with a *Post* editorial deploring military corruption. The day after that, there was an analysis, and the day after that, more of the letters—Dace had saved a few to use as fresheners after the story started to age. Dace also called the *Post* metro desk and reminded them of the pornographers' arrest. He hinted that the release of letters was revenge taken by somebody in the computer department on the company that was currently blackguarding their former systems director. That produced a masterpiece of analysis that ran on day 23.

In the meantime, the paychecks failed on day 18, and Maggie planted rumors that swept through Wall Street on the following Monday, containing the killer phrase, "inadequate cash flow." Whitemark stock, which had drifted higher during the year, on favorable rumors about the *Hellwolf*, plummeted from seventy-one to fifty-nine on Monday, rebounded to sixty on Tuesday, and dropped to fifty-four on Wednesday.

"Is that good enough?" I asked.

She snorted. "Anytime you take twenty-five percent of value off your target in two days, you're doing okay," she said.

"You've done this before?"

She had one computer hooked into a market bank, and she looked up from the numbers and smiled. "Not exactly like this. But we've taken down a few in our time."

ON DAY 21, Dace overheard a rumor about a fistfight at Whitemark. He chased it, and over a couple of drinks an old friend told him that an engineer had attacked a computer tech on the production floor. Another computer tech jumped in, and a couple other engineers tried to break it up and wound up in the fight themselves.

"Something weird is happening out there," Dace's friend told him. "The security guys hauled everybody down to the lounge area to cool them off. One of the computer techs told one of these security guys that the computers were possessed."

"Possessed?"

"Yeah. You know, by the Devil."

ALL THROUGH THE attack, when I was alone, I looked at tarot spreads. I did two dozen spreads on day 22. The Emperor, the Empress, the Wheel, the Moon, the Hanged Man. The Fool. I worried it, I assigned identities and reassigned them. I went to bed dreaming of Anshiser and the Hermit.

ON DAY 23, Maggie had a long talk with Dillon. LuEllen and Dace and I were in the kitchen drinking coffee when she got off the line.

"Dillon's freaked out," she said. "Whitemark is shaking right down to the roots. They're paralyzed, their String copy is failing, they're running into new problems with *Hellwolf*. Dillon said they're completely out of control. He sounded scared. He said we're making history. He said this was like Pearl Harbor, but nobody recognizes it except us."

"So it's working," said LuEllen.

"Look what happened to the Japs," Dace said.

"How's Anshiser?" I asked.

Maggie shook her head. "Dillon says he's about the same. He's not losing much, but he's not gaining, either."

"So?"

"So we just go on."

AT ONE O'CLOCK on the morning of day 24, a few hours after Maggie talked with Dillon, the phone rang. I picked it up and got a 2400-baud carrier tone. I punched the modem up, and there was a quick squirt of data and the line shut down.

Something happens with Whitemark phone lines. Cutouts. Watching incoming calls at Whitemark, set to trace. From now on call me at special line number only. Call now.

I dialed a special number Bobby had arranged that couldn't be traced out to him. The techniques were unremarkable, he said, but if a trace were made, it would end at an Afghanistan banana stand, which he'd found while paging through a Kabul phone directory in the Kremlin.

When he came up this time, there was no *What?*

Tried to trace the tracers. Not go to FBI, go to NSA. Scary shit. Recommend stay off wires, use back door only.

Okay. Recommend that you change your main number, leave me only special line.

Will do now.

Need more money?

You got more?

Sure. Will send $10K.

'Bye.

Frankly, what I did in Vietnam—it sounds silly now, when I think about it—was run up and down the Ho Chi Minh trail and bug VC telephone lines. Most people don't think about the VC having phone lines and operators and all that, but they did, of course. I'd find a good place, tap into a line, lead it out to a battery-operated radio disguised to look like a lump of mud or a pollywog or whatever the backroom boys at the CIA thought was good that month, and sneak away. For the next couple of weeks, we'd listen to their phone calls, which, I was told, went mostly like this: "Hey Vang, you see the knockers on that PFC came down with that load of bike tires yesterday? Honest to Ho, I wanted to crawl right in between them and play motorboat, you know what I mean?"

In the course of gathering this intelligence, I met dozens of people from the CIA. Most of them were okay, a few were stone killers, and one or two were terminally stupid. I met only two guys from the National Security Agency. Both were frighteningly smart. Somewhere at the back of my head, I tucked away a personal memo that said, "If you get your ass out of this, don't fuck with the NSA."

AFTER BOBBY'S WARNING, I began entering the Whitemark computer through the satellite, the computer that used the codes from the Mersenne

Prime. It was an old machine, a minicomputer with its own phone lines. It wasn't used much, but it did have that direct line into the main system. I would call into the satellite, and from there, plug into the main system. If the NSA was watching only the incoming phone lines for the main computer, I could still get in without being noticed. If my presence in the main machine was detected, it would seem that I was working from inside the system itself.

On the morning of day 26, I put in several minor bombs calculated to alter some critical bits of software in a way that would not be immediately detectable, but which would thoroughly screw selected work output.

On day 27, on the same day the Justice Department announced a special task force to investigate the Whitemark relationship with Defense Department officials, I changed the code that did Whitemark's floating-point mathematics. The change would be virtually undetectable, and the resulting design problems would be almost impossible to pinpoint.

At one o'clock on the morning of day 28, as I was working on a couple of final items, Bobby called again.

More phone changes. Believe monitoring entire exchange for data transmissions. Recommend shutdown.

Can I get in one last time?

There was a pause, and then:

If you call special number, can piggyback on me. I call Whitemark, when get in, you put in code, I watch lines. One time only.

Okay.

Tomorrow 10 a.m. your time.

LuEllen was back the next morning, and she and Dace came in with Maggie to watch over my shoulder as we put the last program in. Or tried to.

"Is there any possibility that they could trace us here?" LuEllen asked.

"I don't think so. But with the NSA, you can't be sure. If they do, Bobby will know. We'll get out."

LuEllen looked around the room. "What about fingerprints and everything? We're all over this place."

"If they're good enough to trace us through Bobby's intercepts, we're cooked," I admitted. "All we can do is run for it and hope Anshiser's interference will pay off. Even if they pick up prints, we'd have a day or two. You guys can get out to Mexico, Maggie can get back to Chicago, and I'll take off in my car."

"Shit. That doesn't sound so good," LuEllen said.

"What's the risk, what's the benefit?" Maggie asked.

"I've got a nice finishing touch to put in. And to tell you the truth, I think Bobby's at least as good with phones as anybody at NSA. Besides, they're not expecting him. They don't know we can see the traces coming out."

She thought about it for a minute, pulling at her lip. "Let's do it," she said.

You on line with code?

Yes. 9-second squirt.

Be ready.

Bobby dialed us into Whitemark through the satellite. When it came up, I punched it in, and our modem started transmitting. Two seconds into it, the transmission shut down as though cut with an ax.

"Holy shit," I muttered.

"What?" LuEllen said anxiously.

"Bobby shut us down. I hope."

"You hope?"

"Yeah. I hope it was Bobby."

A second later the phone rang, and we all looked at it like it was a cobra. After a couple of rings, I picked it up and heard the familiar carrier tone. I turned on the modem again.

Those suckers fast. They on line, followed me at least to Rome. Maybe all the way to banana stand.

You okay? We okay?

Yes. But you must shut down now. No more entries or they get us.

Yes. Will call later, still special line.

'Bye.

"What's the special number?" Maggie asked.

"It's a cutout. I don't know the details, but it signals him that I'm trying to reach him. He's changed the main number, the one I used to have, and I don't have it anymore. We don't know exactly what NSA might do if they caught us, but just in case . . . I mean, if they use chemicals, it's better if I don't know how to get him. If they get the special number out of me, and try to use it, he'll see the trace and get out."

"Good luck on that," LuEllen said.

We all sat and looked at the monitor for a moment. There was nothing on it.

"That's it," I said, feeling suddenly tired. "We're all done."

"Jesus," said Dace.

I looked over at Maggie. "Satisfied?"

"I'm going in to Chicago," she said. "Dillon will be doing a final analysis."

"We'll shut down here. Are you coming back, or should we come there?"

"You wait here. There might be something else Dillon thinks we should do—I don't know what. But maybe something. I'll bring the rest of the money."

She looked pinched, taut. If the job wasn't done now, it would never be done.

Dillon would know.

Chapter 14

THE FIGURE OF Maggie was the best paint-ing I'd ever done. She looked at it when it was finished and said, "It's mine." The day after the end of the attack, I rolled it and slid it into a shipping tube as she packed her clothes.

"This has been a strange experience," she said on the way to National. She had the window down and her hair blew out behind her. "A team like yours opens up all kinds of possibilities. When I get back to Chicago, I'm going to ask Dillon for a crash study of corporate aggression. To work out the limits and the consequences."

"Tell him to call me," I said. "I have some thoughts about it."

"Yes." She turned and stared out the window, lost in thought. "This attack on Whitemark . . . there's a temptation to write it out, document it, then stash it somewhere. It could be a classic someday. Like Clausewitz's *On War*."

"Don't use my name," I said. "Call me Ann Smith. Or something equally innovative."

At the airport, I waited until her plane was called and kissed her goodbye. She walked out through the gate with the painting tube under her arm. She looked back once and smiled.

Dace and LuEllen finished packing his apartment. The few things he wanted to keep were put in storage, and the rest of it was sent to a Goodwill store. I spent the afternoon working at the apartment, disassembling the office and cleaning up. A little portable computer with a built-in modem watched the phone, in case Bobby called.

The attack programs we used against Whitemark had been written in a deliberately structured, functional, but inelegant programming style. If NSA or the FBI had a textual analysis capability for computer code, the structured programs wouldn't match any examples of my usual programming style. It was a small piece of security, probably unnecessary, but who knows?

The computers and printer had to go for the same security reasons. If there were tapes of incoming data from our terminals, a sophisticated analysis of transmission peculiarities might identify them. Same with the printer type, should they compare samples with the printout sent to the cops with the pornography package. I hated the thought of dropping the equipment in the river, so I packed it with newspapers in three big cardboard boxes, hauled the boxes to a delivery service, and had them sent to an elementary school in a slum area. The note said the equipment was from a friend.

Dace and LuEllen showed up just before dark and we all went out to eat. Later that evening, I put the phones back where they were when we rented the place. We would leave the working table. The landlord could get rid of it.

The next morning, Dace and LuEllen took care of financial matters and shopped. I called Bobby at the special number, told him we'd be out of touch for a few days, and took the portable and the rest of our personal stuff down to the car. When the apartment was empty, I started wiping the place down. It was another piece of security that would probably be unnecessary, but Maggie, before she left for Chicago, had insisted on it.

"We know the place is used by prostitutes. If there should be any trouble here in the next few weeks, and they find fingerprints from a computer expert and an executive from Anshiser Aviation and a Washington publicity expert and a burglar . . ."

"I'm not on record as a burglar anywhere," LuEllen said.

"You see my point, though?" Maggie had said. "Somebody smart could reach the right conclusion."

"The chances of a problem are almost nonexistent," I said.

"Exactly. Almost. But not quite. It'll take two hours, and it'll eliminate the possibility." She stuck out her lower lip. "For me?"

I WAS NEARLY finished wiping the apartment when the phone rang. It was Maggie, calling from Chicago.

"It's done," she said crisply. "I'll be back tonight with the cash."

Dillon's analysis indicated that Whitemark was reeling. Its stock had dropped into the forties, then started drifting back up, but only because of takeover rumors. The *Hellwolf* project was dead in the water, due to massive problems with their design system computers. Work on their copy of the String system had stopped. Manufacturing had problems with supply coordination, and couldn't straighten them out. Routine administrative work was completely tangled. The company would again fail to meet the payroll at the end of the week. The unions threatened to walk out unless the paychecks were validated.

The press was still pushing the corruption stories, and procurement people at the Pentagon were afraid to talk to anybody at Whitemark. The Whitemark systems director had been fired after his arraignment on child pornography charges. To make everything worse, the FBI was crawling all over the place, questioning employees about a possible source of the attack, which they suspected was internal. The interrogations further disrupted the process of straightening out the company.

"Rudy is very pleased—also a little frightened. He hired the biggest computer security people in the country to revamp our system," she said. Her voice sounded oddly tight.

"Who have they got?" I asked.

She mentioned three names, and I recognized all of them. One was a charlatan, but the other two were good. They were all expensive, and not likely to miss much.

"How soon will they finish?" I asked.

She hesitated for a moment and then said, "Yesterday."

"Yesterday?"

"Rudy hired them right after we started the attack on Whitemark. My reports scared everybody out here, so he hired these people and gave them three weeks and a big bunch of money. Most of what they did was rearranging phone lines and moving furniture, and they changed some procedures. There wasn't much new equipment involved. Anyway, they finished yesterday. Rudy was talking about hiring you, in a year or so, to see if you could crack it."

"You know where to find me," I said.

"Right. On a sandbar," she said. "Have you got the apartment cleaned up?"

"You mean wiped? Just about. I'm just finishing the kitchen now. We could meet downtown somewhere to split the cash, but we thought this was convenient to the airport."

"No, no, I'll see you there. I should be in about seven o'clock."

DACE AND LUELLEN got back in the early afternoon, and Dace had shed another five years. He was wearing an expensive tweed coat, a dark blue shirt with silk knit tie, whipcord pants, and leather boat shoes. He was pleased with his appearance.

"For Christ's sake, don't touch anything," I said, as they came in.

"What do you think?" he said, spreading his arms. LuEllen stood behind him, grinning.

"Straight out of *Esquire*," I said.

"And look at this," he said. He pulled out a bundle of traveler's checks, twenty-five thousand in tens and twenties.

"I made him go to ten different banks," LuEllen laughed.

"This ought to take care of us for six months or a year," Dace said, thumbing through the stack of checks. "If it doesn't, we can always come back for more."

With the new clothes and the money burning in

his pocket, Dace wanted to run around to newspaper and public relations offices and buy drinks for a few friends and contacts.

"It wouldn't be a good idea if I just disappeared," he said. "Besides, I like some of these guys. I'll be back in time to eat."

I got my painting gear, and LuEllen and I went down to the banks of the Potomac, where I did a watercolor as good as anything I'd ever done. The Whitemark attack sat on the surface of my mind, but the painting took care of itself. It was all eye and hand, and the pigment seemed to flow without effort. By the time I finished, I was beginning to hyperventilate. LuEllen had gone off across the park, and as I was looking at it, wondering about one more touch, one last touch—it's always the last ones that ruin paintings—she walked up and looked.

"Jesus Christ, Kidd, that's good," she said.

I swirled the brush through the ice-cream bucket I used as my main water container. When it was clean, I dropped it back in its box, and tossed the bucket of water out on the grass. It *was* good, by God.

September is beautiful in Washington, one of the best months of the year. The sky was a perfect china blue, and there was just a hint of leaf smoke in the air. LuEllen was chatting along as we walked back to the car, and I kept sneaking looks at the painting. The nude of Maggie was the best figure I'd ever done. This was the best landscape, and it had come out in two hours. Was it luck? Or was it a breakthrough?

I put the painting in the trunk, carefully braced between two suitcases, on top of the portable, so it wouldn't rattle around.

On the way back to the apartment, I stopped at a grocery and bought a pack of kitchen gloves. Having wiped the entire place, I didn't intend to leave any isolated prints during the final clean-up.

At the apartment, there was an odd moment before we went inside. A car was parked across the street, a red Buick with tinted windows. Dark glass wasn't uncommon in Washington, and I paid no attention. But as we walked up to the apartment door, I happened to glance back at it and caught the white crescent of face close to the glass in the car's back window. Maggie?

If you work in figurative art, you quickly become aware of the strange qualities of human perception. A mother can walk up to a playground and immediately spot her kid among dozens of others, all of whom are about the same size and color and wearing similar clothing. You can see a friend from a block away, too far to pick out details of face or color or dress, and recognize him instantly.

I saw the flash of white, and thought, *Maggie*. But nobody got out of the car, and she wasn't due for two hours. I let it go and followed LuEllen into the apartment and up the stairs.

Dace was sitting in the kitchen, drinking a cup of coffee and reading the *Post*. He looked up when we came in and said, "Haven't touched a thing except this coffee cup!"

"You ready?" LuEllen asked, kissing him on the forehead.

"Anytime," he said.

"I want to go through this place literally on our hands and knees, to make sure we're not leaving anything behind," I said.

"Let me finish the sports," Dace said. "I don't think they write about the 'Skins down in Mexico."

LuEllen and I pulled on the plastic gloves, and she followed me to the first bedroom. I got down on my knees and looked under the bed. She pulled open the drawers in the bureau.

"There's not going to be anything," she said.

"Look under the shelf paper, too," I said. She rolled her eyes and started pulling the shelf paper out of the drawers. We were about finished with the first room when the doorbell rang. LuEllen looked at me, and I stood up.

"Maggie," I said. "I thought I saw her . . ."

"Could be the landlord," Dace said, coming out of the kitchen with the paper in one hand and the coffee cup in the other. "I told him we'd be pulling out." He crossed to the door and opened it.

Two men stood in the hallway. The one in back was mostly out of sight, but he was big. The one in front was wearing a neat red-and-white striped golf shirt, tan slacks, and tennis shoes. Ratface. He pulled a long, skinny gun from under his shirt and raised it toward Dace. Dace said "Wait" and held up the newspaper, and Ratface shot him three times in the head.

The shots went phut-phut-phut. LuEllen, who had gone into the hallway before I did, spun and started toward me and we both surged back into the bedroom, and I slammed the door and flipped the lock. Since it was a whorehouse, the door was heavy wood and the locks were solid, but I picked up the rosewood dressing table and literally threw it against the door. LuEllen didn't stop to look. She dashed across the bedroom to the old-fashioned, double-hung windows, frantically turned the crescent lock on the top of one and slid it up, and slapped at the hooks holding the screen outside.

"Go—go—go," she screamed; she had her feet out the window, and I ran across the room toward her. The guy in the hallway outside kicked the bedroom door at the lock, but it held, and he kicked it again, but by then I was at the window, watching LuEllen drop into the alley behind the apartment. She landed like a cat and turned to run toward the back of the building. I slid through, hung for a second, heard the door splinter, and dropped.

LuEllen was thirty feet in front of me when I landed; I yelled, "Car, car," and she cut behind the apartment. When I turned the corner she was squatting, gasping for breath, next to the passenger door. I unlocked the driver's side, slid in, pulled the lock, and cranked the engine. We left the back end of the lot in a hurry, and LuEllen, looking back, said, "There he is!" Looking in the rearview mirror as we turned the corner, I saw Ratface limp around the building, stop, and then hobble back out of sight.

"They killed Dace," LuEllen moaned.

"Yeah." There was nothing else to say.

I took a left at the next corner, drove a block, took another left, and headed west toward a big commercial street. There was no sign of a chase.

"What the fuck happened?" LuEllen demanded. "Who were those guys?"

"I don't know," I said. "But they've got Maggie, too."

"What?" LuEllen was stricken, her face white and drawn, but she was functioning. "What makes you think that?"

"When we were going into the building, I thought I saw her face in a car across the street. I didn't think it could be her, because she's not due for a couple hours. But I got a bad feeling. . . ."

"They're not coming after us," LuEllen said.

"Let's get on another street somewhere, find a phone, and call Chicago. They'll know if she left early. If she didn't, they should know her flight number, and we can catch her at the airport."

I drove another two miles and spotted a phone booth outside a convenience store. I pulled around to the side of the store where the car couldn't be seen from the street, and called Chicago, collect.

Maggie had not left early. She'd taken a three o'clock flight out of O'Hare, just as she had planned, and was still in the air. Dillon was stunned by the shooting. "I don't know what to tell you," he said. "This is far out of bounds from anything I've ever heard of."

"Who would they be? Whitemark? They can't just be some fuckin' private eyes like you guys said," I said.

"That's what we got from people in Washington—good people. That they're just private detectives. I don't know, it doesn't add up." There was another long silence and finally he said, "I can't imagine it would be Whitemark. Big corporations can be ruthless, but we don't have gunmen hanging around. I'm afraid it might be the federal people. When we checked on these private detectives, we heard they'd had some trouble with the government in the past. Remember?"

"Yeah, I remember something like that."

"So maybe somebody's got them on a string. It

would be a way of . . . killing somebody without official involvement."

"But why would they come after us?"

There was another moment of silence, and he said, in a cooler voice, "It's very hard to think. Very hard. But suppose they figured out what happened at Whitemark and talked to each other, and said, 'If we arrest these people, the publicity could set off a whole rash of these things. Like a rash of jet hijackings.' If there is some kind of murder squad in the CIA or the NSA, they might have decided that this was the most expedient way to solve the problem."

"Jesus," I said. I thought about the people I'd known in the Strategic Operations Group. A few were killers, plain and simple. They were career military men, Special Forces, and some held rank, but at heart, they were gunmen. If an intelligence agency needed a couple of shooters, they'd know where to find them. And private investigation was just the kind of job that attracted former company cowboys.

"Where are you?" Dillon asked. I looked around, but there were no street signs. "I don't know. Standing at a 7-Eleven on a street corner. We have to stay out of sight for a while and then head out to the airport in time to find Maggie."

"No. Don't do that. They may very well be looking for you at the airport. I'll call Maggie in the air. We have a business code we use for open phones, when we're negotiating deals, and I can warn her off. She'll call me from National, and I'll tell her what happened and turn her right back around. There won't be anything you can do for her. I'll arrange for extra security and talk to Mr. Anshiser about what to do next."

"So what about us?"

"If we can get a line on who it is, we might be able to work some kind of a deal. Can you call back here later?"

"Yeah. We'll get out of town. Find someplace we can hide out for a couple of days until we figure out what's happened."

"What about your friend? The one who was shot?"

"There's nothing we can do about that," I said. "There's no way he could still be alive."

"All right, we can leave that for now. Had you finished wiping the apartment?"

"Yes."

"Good. And you still have your car?"

"Yes."

"If they're federal or have federal sponsors they may put out a watch for your car. They won't have done it yet, though, if they thought they would catch you at the apartment. And if they're an assassination team, they're illegal; it might take them a while to get everything set. Can you hold on there just a minute?"

"Yes."

His phone receiver hit the desktop, and I scanned the street for the red Buick with the dark windows. Nothing. Cars coming and going, some of them red, but nothing that looked like the Buick.

"Okay, are you still there?"

"Yes."

"I'm looking at a road atlas. I would recommend that you take Highway Fifty east through Annapolis, cross the bay, then head north through Wilmington and into New Jersey. I'm not up-to-speed on police procedure, but as I understand it, watch bulletins usually go out on a state-by-state basis. That's the shortest distance that will get you out of all the states surrounding Maryland-Virginia. You can be in New Jersey in less than three hours."

"That sounds good," I said. "We'll call you when we find a place." Dillon had pulled himself together. He sounded like an intelligence officer giving a briefing: calm, detached, certain. But then, he wasn't being hunted. And he hadn't known Dace.

"Get as far away as you can. The closer you get to New York, the less attention the local police should pay to routine watch bulletins. They've got other problems."

"Okay."

"Call back here in six hours. I should know something then."

LuEllen was lying in the backseat of the car. She wasn't weeping; she was absolutely still, her arm thrown across her eyes, her breathing shallow and quick, as though she had been injured.

"You okay?"

"I'm fucked," she said. "Just drive."

I went back into the 7-Eleven, bought a map, a pack of donuts, and a Styrofoam cooler that I stocked with ice and two six-packs of Coke. In the car, I traced out the course Dillon had recommended, and five minutes later we were on the way.

We caught the evening rush going out of town; the trip was a nightmare of stop-and-go. We saw state troopers twice; both times they were involved in clearing fender-benders. LuEllen lay in the backseat for an hour before climbing into the front. Her eyes were red and sunken, but there were no tears.

"There's no chance he's alive, is there?"

"No. They shot him three times going in. If he was still alive, they would have shot him again before they left."

"Who were they?"

"We don't know. Dillon's trying to figure it out. We'll call him from Camden."

"Think they'll come after us?" she asked.

"Probably. I'll be the main target, but you've seen their faces. We'd better stick together until we find out. If they haven't made you, you'd best get on a plane to Duluth and lie low for a while."

We stopped once at a fast-food place in Delaware. LuEllen said she had to call Duluth, and she used a phone on the wall of the restaurant while I sat in the car and ate a soggy cheeseburger.

"I got the name of a guy in Philadelphia," she said.

"For what?"

"In case you want to buy a gun. No questions."

A few minutes after eight o'clock, going north out of Wilmington, I spotted a chain electronics store in a strip shopping center and pulled in.

"Supplies," I told LuEllen. I ransacked the store's telephone and home-furnishings departments, bought a few general electronics tools, a power drill, drill bits, and a stapler, paid $160, and threw the sack in the backseat of the car.

"Now. Where's this guy with the gun?" I asked.

THE GUY WITH the gun lived in a suburb of Philadelphia, a place with small lawns and aluminum-sided ramblers and a maple tree in the center of each front yard. We found his house after twenty minutes of searching. He met us at the door.

"Mr. Drexel?" asked LuEllen.

"Yes. You must be Miss Carlson?"

"Yes. Weenie called about us. This is a friend."

"Come in," he said. He was a solemn type, tall

and bespectacled, with a ruddy outdoorsman's complexion. He was dressed from the L. L. Bean catalog, with a blue pin-striped oxford cloth shirt and cotton slacks with cargo pockets on the sides. His wife and teenage daughter were watching a movie on television in the living room. The woman said "Hello," but the girl ignored us. We followed Drexel down a short flight of stairs into the basement.

The basement contained a neat, well-equipped woodworking shop and a couple of metal-cutting machines. A full-size unfinished airplane wing hung on one wall.

"Building a plane," Drexel said laconically. "Finish it in a year or so." He led the way to an upright cabinet in one corner.

"Now. What exactly did you have in mind?" he asked.

"I haven't handled a handgun since I was in the Army," I said.

He arched one eyebrow and opened the cabinet. The top was filled with long weapons, M16s and AK47s. The bottom contained drawers filled with shorter arms. He opened a drawer and pulled out two bundles wrapped in oiled paper.

"In that case, and depending on your requirements, I would suggest one of these two weapons," he said. The first looked like it had been made in a high school metal shop, all rough edges and bent, black steel.

"This is a MAC-10. A great favorite with drug smugglers, I understand." He handed it to me. "It's simple to operate, and this model is fully automatic. A submachine gun, if you will." He turned to LuEllen. "You pull the trigger, and a stream of bullets comes out for as long as you hold down the trigger, or until you run out of ammo. I have sixteen- and thirty-shot custom clips for it."

The gun felt big and awkward in my hand. I held it up and sighted down the length of the shop. The front sight wavered in front of me.

"You really wouldn't want to shoot it like that," he said. "Hold it closer to the body, so you can brace your elbow." He showed me.

"What else do you have?"

"Ah. This one. You may be more familiar with it." He unwrapped the second bundle and showed me a .45 Colt, identical to the one I'd qualified with in the Army.

"What do you think?" I asked LuEllen.

She shook her head. "I don't know about guns."

"If I might recommend . . ." Drexel sounded like a wine waiter dealing with a couple of first-time drinkers. "If you need something for immediate self-protection, and don't have time for practice—I got the impression from Mr. Weenie that this was the case—then I'd recommend the MAC-10. Even the rankest amateur can do amazing damage with it, though it is a bit more expensive."

I took it, and he ran me through its operation. He also sold me one thirty- and two sixteen-round clips for the gun, already loaded.

"And for the lady?" he asked.

"Uh, I don't think I want anything," LuEllen said, looking at me anxiously.

"Let me show you this one," he said. He reached back into one of his drawers and pulled out a hand-sized, double-barreled derringer.

"A .32 H&R magnum. Very safe, and very simple to operate. You should use it only in the most extreme circumstances, of course. In this caliber, at five yards, you could actually miss your target. At two yards, or two feet, it's quite effective."

LuEllen looked at the tiny gun for a moment, glanced at me, looked back at Drexel, and nodded. "I'll take it," she said.

"Make sure you pull the trigger with your index finger. It's so small that there's a temptation to use your middle finger and lay your index finger along the barrel. But if your finger overlaps, it's going to catch a lot of muzzle blast. Okay?"

LuEllen nodded uncertainly.

"Just pull the trigger with your trigger finger," he said, smiling.

The two guns cost us twenty-five hundred dollars. We rewrapped them in the oiled paper and went back out to the car, the wife nodding pleasantly as we tramped through the living room again.

"If you need anything else," Drexel said as we got in the car, "don't hesitate to call."

THE NEXT STOP was the airport. I left the car in the long-term parking lot, rented a nondescript Dodge, and transferred the luggage. We were an hour north of Philadelphia before I spotted the right kind of hotel—a long, low, L-shaped place, inexpensive, with two dozen cars distributed up and down its length. I told the desk clerk that my secretary and I wanted adjoining rooms, but without connecting doors.

"I've got divorce proceedings going," I said, trying out a sheepish grin. "I don't want people to think, you know."

He knew, and he wasn't interested.

LuEllen was dazed and heavy-eyed from the stress. "We have to keep going another half hour or so, and then we can get some sleep," I said.

We unloaded the box of electronics supplies in my room. The first item was a compact motion detector—a burglar alarm. I mounted it behind the door, at ankle level. Then I made a few simple changes in the telephone wall outlet. Next, using the power drill I'd bought, I drilled a neat hole through the wall into LuEllen's room, and ran two lines through.

The first line was hooked into the motion detector. If my door opened, the detector would buzz us in LuEllen's room. The second line would allow me to make and take calls in LuEllen's room from my phone. The stapler made the job neat. All the wiring ran under the edge of the carpet, along the baseboards. Even a maid shouldn't notice the changes.

"If it's the CIA or NSA, they could be monitoring everything Anshiser's got. If they trace us, it'll give us a break," I said.

We left the car one space down from LuEllen's room, in front of another room where the lights were on, and carried our suitcases, the portable, and our cash reserve down to LuEllen's.

What?

Can fast check Anshiser house lines for trace?

Yes. 30 minutes.

Need money?

No. Put terminal on receive.

LuEllen had collapsed on the bed and was out, breathing jerkily with an occasional moan, but asleep. I was crumbling when Bobby's call came in, and the terminal automatically answered.

Lines clean.

Thanx.

"Maggie's not back yet, but she's okay. I turned her around at National and talked to her in the air not more than an hour ago. We still don't know what happened," Dillon said. "It's hard to ask the right questions without admitting your guilt."

"What if they don't know what we're talking about?"

"Then we'll have to look into other possibilities. It could be Whitemark, but that doesn't seem likely. Mr. Anshiser was wondering if it might have something to do with the nature of the place you were staying? Some kind of prostitution-related activity, a mistake, just like we thought the first time?"

"That's bullshit," I said. "You don't kill somebody to get the goods on him for a divorce. They knew who we were and they were there to kill us."

"Yes, that's what I think," Dillon said. "Maggie should be back almost anytime. She wants to talk to you. Can you give me a number?"

"Yeah." I gave him the motel's phone number and my own room extension. "Have her call as soon as she gets in."

• • •

LuEllen GROANED AGAIN and said "Dace?" and started to wake up. "Shh," I whispered, "go back to sleep." She frowned and muttered something, but went quiet again. I turned out the light, took off my shoes, and put my head on the pillow, feeling her breathing next to me. That's all I knew until the phone rang.

Chapter 15

THE PHONE SOUNDED like a distant dentist's drill. I'd wrapped it in a heavy synthetic blanket to muffle the ringing, and now I couldn't find it. I twisted off the bed and floundered around for a minute in the darkness and finally stepped on it.

"What?" said LuEllen.

"I got it."

The receiver came free and I said, "Yeah?"

"Kidd? This is Maggie."

"Jesus. You okay?"

"Yes. I just got back. I talked to Dillon and we'll start talking to people in Washington in the morning. But we've got another problem. Something happened to Rudy. He collapsed. He's on his way to the medical center. The ambulance just left."

"A stroke? A heart attack? What?"

"No, no, he started spouting gibberish, babbling. It could be nervous exhaustion, a breakdown, they don't know. I'll let you know when we hear."

"Okay."

"Tell me what happened at the apartment."

I told her in a few words, and she asked if we were sure that Dace was dead.

"If they weren't shooting blanks. Ratface shot him three times from a range of about two feet."

LuEllen grabbed me by the arm; I half turned, and then I heard it: the soft buzz of the alarm. The door in my room had been opened.

"Ah, shit," I said.

"What? What's going on?" Maggie asked.

"Somebody's outside. I gotta call the cops. Talk to you later," I said, and hung up.

LuEllen crawled across to the single window and peeked out through a gap between the heavy fiberglass curtain and the windowsill.

"Don't move the curtain," I said. I fumbled the MAC-10 out of the open suitcase, cocked it, and crawled over beside her.

"There's nobody out there," she said. The alarm continued to burp. "You think . . . wait a minute. Wait a minute."

I looked out over her head. We couldn't see much, but a man in a dark raincoat stepped onto the sidewalk outside my room.

"They're confused," I whispered. "They don't know what to do." The dark shape moved away,

8 8 8 88

and I crawled back to the telephone and dialed 911.

"Is this an emergency?"

"Goddamned right it is. I'm the night clerk at the Knight's Ease Motel and there are two guys with fuckin' machine guns out in the parking lot. Jesus Christ. I gotta go. . . ." And I slammed the phone down.

"Think they'll send somebody?"

"Oh yeah. And if they're good Jersey cops, they'll come in with the sirens screaming. That's in case there really *are* guys with machine guns. It'll give them a chance to get away."

We huddled below the window, listening, the MAC-10 ready. If the hunters were talking to the night clerk, he might tell them about my "secretary." So we waited in the dark until we heard the siren and then risked another look. A few seconds later, two men crossed the parking lot and got into a big red Buick with dark windows.

"That's them," LuEllen breathed. Ratface was wearing a tan gabardine trench coat that looked two sizes too big for him. The other guy was a barrel-chested pug in a cheap double-knit suit. He moved with the easy grace of an aging heavy-weight fighter.

"Yeah." The car pulled away, and we watched it all the way to the freeway entrance. When the phone rang again, LuEllen started across the room. I grabbed her ankle. "Don't," I said. It rang thirty times before it stopped. By then the cops were in the parking lot.

WE LEFT THE hotel twenty minutes later on the heels of the cops, hustling the luggage and the computer into the car. We didn't bother to drop off the keys, but left them with a ten-dollar bill on a bureau. I did clean up the phone and alarm wires, leaving nothing behind but a nearly invisible half-inch hole in the wall.

"We need some sleep before we can think," I said. "We'll head back through Philadelphia and grab a motel somewhere on the other side."

"We're not worried about federal cops anymore?" From the corner of my eye, I could feel her studying my face.

"No."

"You figured it out?" she asked.

"Some of it."

"I'm glad I didn't have to tell you. That was no coincidence, the phone call coming at exactly the same time as those two goons. Maggie fingered us."

"There's more to it than that," I said.

She thought for a minute, then nodded. "That rat-faced guy. He got here in an hour and a half."

"With the car," I said. "The car was the one I saw in Washington. Dillon routed them right along with us. They must have driven up to Philadelphia, then waited for us to call. He told me to call in six hours, which would tell them about how far we'd get."

"But Jesus Christ, Kidd, what are they doing?"

"I don't know."

"Maybe Anshiser cut a deal with the feds."

"I don't think so. The feds wouldn't be interested in knocking off the small guys and letting the big ones go. They'd do it the other way around, if anything. Net the big fish."

"Jesus," she said. "Maggie. Remember her in the Japanese baths, kidding you about burning your balls off? I thought she'd never stop laughing. She was a friend. I thought you two guys were developing into something."

"I thought so too."

"And Dace is dead."

We drove into the Philadelphia airport and retrieved my car. Before we left, I called Bobby from a phone booth, using the portable.

What?

Need everything you can find on Hell-wolf/Whitemark *and* Sunfire/Anshiser. *Crash jobs, full-time. Flat fee $10,000. Need feeds every few hours.*

Leave terminal on answer.

Leaving the airport, we turned back west. The appearance of the two hoods and the inevitable con-

clusion about Maggie kept me awake. I drove all
the way through to Gettysburg, where we
checked into the biggest motel we could find.

I put LuEllen to bed, called Bobby, and took
the first dump of information on Anshiser and
Sunfire. LuEllen slept most of the day, woke up
long enough to eat, and went back down for the
night. I was beat-up but drove into town and
bought another printer so I could dump incoming
files to paper. Late in the day, Bobby was calling
every hour, and the stuff was coming faster and
faster. Most of it was useless: lightweight business-
magazine stuff, public biographies. I'd seen some
of it during the first run-through, before taking
the job.

On the second day, a rainstorm came through
from the west. It killed a spell of late September
heat and replaced it with autumn. The rain left
the park grounds dark and somber. I walked
LuEllen along Cemetery Ridge, pointing out the
path of Pickett's Charge.

"It doesn't look so hard; it's not hardly a hill,"
she said.

"It didn't have to be. The crest was just
high enough to hide the federals and give them
some cover during the preparatory barrage. The
Southerners thought the cannonading had done a
lot more damage than it had. But they came up
the hill into a hornet's nest. The high tide of the
Confederacy. The South was defeated that week.

Lee was turned around here, and out West, Grant was taking Vicksburg. What a time."

We'd gone out to the battlefield during a break in the rain, but now it was sweeping in again, a thin, gray wall coming down from Seminary Ridge, across the peach orchard, obscuring the Roundtops, and up the hill. We turned our backs on it, retreated to the car.

"I was supposed to be in Mexico today," LuEllen said as we went back to the motel. She stared out the window, and tears trickled down her cheeks. I couldn't think of anything to say. We rode back to the beat of the windshield wipers and the sound of wet pavement hissing under the wheels.

Another lengthy file was waiting at the motel. I dumped it to the printer and started working through it. Ten minutes later I found it.

"That's funny." I sat up on the bed.

"What?"

I looked at the source of the article I was reading: one of the popular science magazines.

"I've seen a couple of references to a guidance system called Snagger. For the *Hellwolf*."

"So?"

"So it sounds a hell of a lot like the String system. But I haven't seen anything about String."

WHAT?

*Need word search on all files, references: String
and Snagger.*

It took about six hours to accumulate, but when
we had done it, the facts were clear enough.

"Anshiser never had the String system. Whitemark developed the Snagger. Same thing, essentially. Anshiser didn't have a clue. Then, six
months ago, when preliminary design studies
were due, word got out that Whitemark was onto
something big. Anshiser didn't have anything to
compare with it."

"So Anshiser stole it from Whitemark, not the
other way around?"

"Looks like it. They desperately needed time to
understand Snagger and do a knock-off for their
own plane. That's where we came in. That whole
routine they did in Chicago was an act. Jesus! I
bought the whole thing!"

LuEllen sat hunched on the bed, her hair hanging limp down the sides of her face, her face wrinkled in thought. Eventually she shook her head
and looked up.

"So?"

"So?"

"Yeah. So what?" she said. "So they conned us
into doing a job on Whitemark. What difference
does it make? If they'd told you the truth and offered you two million to take down Whitemark,
you probably would have said 'yes' anyway. They

lied, but that's no reason to start shooting at us. We're no more likely to go to the cops now than if they were telling the truth."

"Maybe not. But it makes what we did a lot more serious, especially for Anshiser. If Whitemark had stolen the String system and Anshiser could prove it, it might have cost Whitemark the contract. Or a lawsuit so big that winning the contract would have been meaningless. But if Anshiser stole Snagger and then wrecked Whitemark to slow them down so they could do a knock-off, and if Whitemark could prove it . . ."

"Then Anshiser is ruined. Absolutely."

"And if Anshiser had hired the job done by a group of outsiders, and one of them was a newspaper guy with a reputation for busting defense industries, and another one was a thief whose name he didn't even know . . ."

"It might make sense to get rid of them permanently," LuEllen concluded.

We both thought about it for a minute.

"Where did they get the gunmen?" she asked.

I shrugged. "Anshiser is a defense industry. They know all kinds of people. They probably found a couple of ex–Special Forces guys looking for a little cash."

"And then you've got a couple of guys who know the story and have killed people because of it," LuEllen objected. "I don't know. It sounds weak."

"They wouldn't have to tell those guys the whole story, just point them at the targets," I said. "I can't think of any other rationale."

THE MOTEL ROOM had two single beds. When we went to sleep that night, LuEllen suddenly said in the dark, "I'd like to come over and sleep with you, but, like, no sex. I just want to sleep with somebody."

"Come on." She snuggled in against me, and we whispered back and forth for a while, and then she drifted away. Her body warmth under the blanket reminded me of Maggie, like a black patch on my mind. I was dozing off when the computer alarm sounded, and I rolled out of bed to look.

Something weird.

What?

Been in newspaper clip files, gone way back. Anshiser old man was in German mob.

What?

Chicago had German mob. Like Mafia. Anshiser father convicted in 1910 extortion, two years in prison, charged 1914 murder and extortion, not guilty. No more charges but mentioned in stories as accountant for German mob. Don't know what that is yet, keep digging?

Look for stuff on Anshiser and associates.

Already got most of it.

Got access to criminal intelligence data banks, FBI?

No. Tried once. Maximum protection.

How about NCIC?

Easy access if got codes. Need codes.

Who got codes?

I find. Call back later. Want mob clips now?

He dumped the clips to the computer. There weren't many of them, but there was enough information to suggest that Anshiser's father was a major crime figure. Exactly what he did was unclear from the clips. I had just finished reading the clips when Bobby called again. He had a name.

When LuEllen woke the next morning, she smiled, a small tentative smile, the first one I'd seen since the shooting.

"I don't know how to break it to you," I said.

"What happened?" she asked, quickly serious.

"We've got to hit another house. We need some more codes." I told her about the background on Anshiser's father. "We need to get into some crime intelligence files. Bobby found a guy for us. He goes into the NCIC—the National Crime Information Center—from his home computer."

"Uh, is this guy . . ."

"Yeah. He's a cop."

Chapter 16

THE COP WAS named Denton. He was the liaison man between the Washington police and the National Crime Information Center, supervising computer-entry work for the city.

"I've never hit a cop before," LuEllen said. She was worried.

"It shouldn't be any worse than the others. Maybe he'll have better locks."

We were leaving Gettysburg. We could see blue sky to the south and west, but the town was still under a dark slab of cloud, and it was raining again. A semitrailer ahead of us on the highway threw up a plume of water and resolutely fought off attempts by the cars behind him to pass. We slowed to fifty, then to forty-five, and settled down for a long trip.

"There might be another problem," LuEllen said. "When Dace and I were going around town, I didn't see many white cops. If he's black and he lives in a black neighborhood, everybody on the block will be looking at us."

"Bobby says he's black, all right, but he and his wife live out in Bethesda," I said. "She's got a heavy job with the Commerce Department, and he's a lieutenant, so they've got a few bucks."

"We need this, right?" asked LuEllen.

"Yeah. We have to know what's going on."

"All right. But if we wind up in deep shit, don't say I didn't warn you."

WHEN WE GOT to Bethesda, the sun was shining and the clouds were blowing out to the northeast. The streets were still damp, with dead oak leaves stuck to them, and everything smelled cool and clean.

The Dentons lived in a low, dark, wood-and-stone house on a lot with tall trees in the back and a narrow, sloping front yard. There were no extra-green tufts of grass. Basement windows were set into the foundation, and the garage was attached to the left side of the house as you approached it. Beside the garage, a tall, gray, board fence separated the Dentons' yard from the one next door.

"Look at that fence. Must not like their black neighbors," I said as we cruised by the first time.

"That's a pool fence," LuEllen said matter-of-factly. "There's a swimming pool back there, in the neighbors' yard. There's a law about putting fences around your pools to keep kids out."

We drove past once more. Everything about the house was neat and in good repair.

"They've got money, all right," I said. "Maybe we ought to check them out for a maid."

"No black cop in the world has a maid, not if he wants to get ahead. Let's find a phone. Let's call them, and if they're working, let's do it. Today. Right now."

"You sure?"

"Goddamned right I'm sure." She sounded fierce, tight, angry. I looked her over and slowed the car.

"If you're doing it because you're scared, or pissed about Dace, that's not good enough. It won't help him if we're busted or shot," I said.

"I'm scared, and I'm pissed about Dace, but I'm not crazy," she said, looking across the seat at me. "The house feels right. There's nobody home. There's hardly anybody on the street. This is the time."

I took a left at the first street and drove to a shopping center. She dipped into her purse for cocaine and took the first hit as we pulled up to a phone.

We got Mrs. Denton's secretary, but Mrs. Denton was in a meeting and couldn't speak to us. We left a message. "Tell her Bob called." We couldn't get the cop on the phone. He was working, a woman said, but he might be out for an early lunch. We called the house. There was no answer. I clipped the phone and LuEllen took a deep breath.

"Let's go," she said.

"You're sure? You're making me nervous." I shoved the phone receiver under the car seat.

"This one feels nervouser. Probably because he's a cop," she said. She had the cellophane wrap of coke in the palm of her hand. "Let's get it the fuck over with. C'mon."

We dropped the car at a park and walked down to the Dentons'. An Oldsmobile passed us as we were approaching the house, and the driver lifted a finger in greeting, as though he recognized us. I nodded and LuEllen lifted a hand. We slowed to let the car get out of sight before we turned into the Dentons' driveway.

A small louvered window, in what was probably the kitchen or bathroom, was cranked open. We could hear the phone ringing as we walked up to the house.

"Hold it a minute," LuEllen said as we walked in front of the garage. There was a row of windows in the garage door, just at shoulder height, and she peered through them.

"All right," she muttered distractedly.

Glancing up and down the street, she took my arm and led me around the side of the house, between the garage and the neighbors' pool fence.

There was a door on the back of the garage, and it hung open. We stepped into the garage.

"Nice and private," LuEllen said. There was a space for two cars side by side. Both spaces were empty. A lawnmower, smelling faintly of gasoline and grass clippings, was pushed against one wall. Several fishing rods hung on one wall, along with a small net. A sack of birdseed and another of fertilizer sat on the floor below the rods. Two bikes hung by their wheels from hooks screwed into the rafters. A pair of green plastic garbage cans stood beside the door into the house.

LuEllen tried the door. It was locked. We were standing on a doormat, and she pushed me away and lifted it. Nothing. Then she scanned the walls, and finally looked up at the overhead tracks for the garage door.

"Can you reach up there?" she asked.

"If I stand on the garbage can." I stood on the can and stretched to the track, slid my fingers along a few inches, and pushed the key off the track into LuEllen's waiting hands.

"Wa-la," she said. "Cops can be as dumb as anyone else." She cracked open the door and used her doggie whistle. Nothing. "Anybody home?" she called. The phone kept ringing. We went inside and she picked it up and dropped it back on the hook.

"We don't have to trash the place. If we can get

the stuff and get out, he'll never know we were here," she said.

The house arrangement was purely functional. A kitchen, dining room, living room, library, two bedrooms, and two bathrooms, along with a miscellany of closets, marched straight down from the garage to the opposite end of the house. The garage door opened into the kitchen, the better to unload groceries. The basement door also opened into the kitchen, directly opposite to the door coming in from the garage. The front door was about halfway down the house.

We checked the top floor, but there was no sign of a computer. We went back to the kitchen and down the stairs. There were four more rooms in the basement. The general utility room had a washer and drier, a furnace and water heater, and a workbench made from an old chest of drawers and covered with a pile of tools. Adjacent to it was a small tiled studio with a floor loom. On the loom was a skillful, half-finished weaving of a vegetable garden. Another weaving hung on the wall. The initials D.D. in one corner indicated that the cop, whose first name was David, was the weaver.

Next was a family room with a television set, a couch, and two comfortable leather chairs. The computer was in a little nook off the family room, along with a two-drawer steel file cabinet, a few computer books, a printer, and a box of disks.

Off the computer nook was the fourth room, a bathroom.

LuEllen was impatient and hurried me along. "Let's go, let's go," she said as I brought the computer up. Denton had one standard communications program, which I copied, but there was no sign of a code list in the program. His file disks all appeared to contain personal budgetary stuff, games, programming languages, and the like. I went through them one by one, the minutes ticking away, the sweat gathering on my forehead.

"Look through the cabinet and around the desk. See if you can find anything that looks like a list or a serial number, maybe," I whispered to LuEllen. "It might be written right on the desk, or on the top of a file . . . anywhere."

"Right," she whispered back. Suddenly we were dealing in whispers.

I unscrewed the plate over the phone line and clipped a bug in place. LuEllen riffled through the files in the cabinet and checked the desk, top and bottom, but found nothing.

"Look under the covers of the books," I said.

She started going through them as I was screwing the strike plate back on the phone outlet. She'd just put the last book on its shelf, and I was dropping the screwdriver into my bag, when the garage door went up.

We froze and looked at each other. There was a

beat of silence, then another beat, and then a car door slammed.

"Shit, he's home," LuEllen hissed, as the garage door came down with a bang. Her face was deathly pale. "And he's a cop. He'll have a gun."

"Did you lock the house door behind you?"

"Of course."

"So now what?"

"Get all the tools. Get everything," she whispered violently. We shoved a couple of extra bugs and the disk copies into the bags.

"In here," she said, pushing me into the bathroom. She stepped back out to the computer area and looked quickly around to make sure we'd left nothing behind. Satisfied, she followed me into the bathroom and eased the door shut.

"Open that window," she whispered urgently.

The bathroom window was one of the slanted type, with the hinges on the bottom. It pulled down forty-five degrees.

"There's no way we can get out of that," I whispered to her. "Maybe he's just here for a minute, we can wait, and he'll leave."

There was a click and a mechanical hum, and LuEllen shook her head. "That was the central air. He's going to be here for a while. And I'll tell you something. He'll find us. He'll be down here in ten minutes."

"How do you know?" Whoever was upstairs

was clumping through the kitchen—heavy foot-steps, a man, and probably a big one.

"Because. Because they always do. It's a rule," LuEllen said. "Something about vibrations. If you hide in somebody's closet, they'll look in the closet. If you hide under the bed, they'll look under the bed. Get that window open."

I pulled it open, and LuEllen said, "Help me." I boosted her up, and she pushed on the screen until it popped outside with a noisy crack.

"Shit," I whispered.

"No sweat, the central air will cover us," LuEllen grunted. "Now push me up as high as you can. Right up against the ceiling." I pushed her higher, and she got her arms out on the grass. Her stom-ach was a solid slab of muscle, and she kept her entire lower body as rigid as a pipe as I fed her over the glass and out onto the lawn.

She was a small woman, and the fit was tight. The chances of my following her were exactly zero.

"Give me my bag," she whispered down to me. I handed it to her, and she pushed the screen back up against the window. "When you hear talking, you go right out through the garage. Out through the garage, around back, and wait behind the fence, you hear? And close this window." I had no idea what she meant. Her oval face looked down at me, and then she was gone. I shut the window and locked it.

One second later, Denton started down the basement stairs. LuEllen was right; he'd find me. I stood back from the bathroom door and set my feet. If I hit him hard, and just right, he'd be down and I'd be out. But if I missed, he almost certainly carried a gun, and he was in his own house. The door to the family room opened and I started shallow breathing.

The doorbell rang. LuEllen. Denton grunted and turned back up the steps. I eased the bathroom door open. From the base of the stairs, I heard him open the front door, and a flustered LuEllen asking about a park, where it was, *tennis, girlfriend apparently gave her wrong directions, decided to walk, smells so good with the rain . . .*

Denton stepped out on the front porch. I crossed the kitchen to the garage door, noticed with unnatural clarity the bologna sandwich on the kitchen table, the three envelopes sitting next to it, the sign on the wall: TRY OUR FAMOUS PEANUT BUTTER & JELLY SANDWICH. It was like a slow-motion pan in a movie. I resisted an impulse to take a bite from the sandwich, silently cracked the door to the garage, closed it slowly behind me, walked around the Ford Taurus now parked in the garage and out the back. In another ten seconds I was beside the house, between the pool fence and the garage. LuEllen was walking down the driveway with her bag, waving and smiling at Denton. I heard the front door close.

"Are you following that lady?"

The voice was only a couple of feet away, and my heart almost stopped. I looked down, toward the fence, and found a pair of small, blue eyes peering between the woven boards. A little girl, not more than four.

"Yeah, we're playing a game," I said.

"What kind of game?"

"Like hide-and-seek," I said. "But it's a secret."

"Are you sure?" she asked suspiciously.

"Of course I'm sure. Haven't you ever seen television?"

I left her with that to chew on, figuring Denton had had more than enough time to get his sandwich and head downstairs again. I walked straight out the driveway, looking neither right nor left, into the street.

LuEllen was fifty yards in front of me. When we were out of sight of the house, I jogged until I caught her.

"Don't talk to me," she said.

"Thanks for pulling me out of there."

"Don't talk to me; I'm too high to talk."

We were back at the car in two more minutes. LuEllen hit the coke as we pulled out from the curb. "Goddamn, that feels good."

"The coke?"

"The whole thing. Going in, getting out. God, I'm so high I could fly."

•   •   •

WE MOVED INTO a downtown Washington hotel with a handy automated switchboard. That night we called into the bug at the Dentons', but nothing went out. I lay on the bed reading an *Artnews* and listening for the tone that signaled a data transmission.

LuEllen was washing her hair. She left the bathroom door open, tossed her clothes on the toilet seat, and went back and forth past the open door, pleasantly pink as always. We slept in the same bed again that night. The next morning we were in spoons, and I woke up with her moving against my stomach. She was still asleep, I thought, until she muttered, "Geez, feels like somebody dropped a pencil in the bed."

"Pencil your ass," I said.

"Oh, God, not that," she said, and rolled away, smiling. The smile slowly faded when she saw my face and she said, "Not yet. It's hard not to tease you, but I'm afraid if we made love, Dace's face would come up. That might ruin it forever. . . ."

WE SPENT THE day around the hotel, in the pool, in a shopping arcade, buying books, and watching movies on television. That night, just after eight o'clock, Denton went into the NCIC. We watched the entry transaction come up on our screen, and I was flabbergasted. There were virtually no screening protections at all. He signed on

with his own name, a backup code—"weaver"—
and an account number. Then he was in.

What?

Got NCIC entry codes. Would prefer you do
search, all known execs Anshiser and associated
companies.

Send codes.

We slept in the same bed again that night, and
it was easier, but shorter. The computer started
beeping for attention shortly after seven in the
morning. Bobby said there would be multiple
dumps. I plugged in the printer and routed the incoming data to paper as it arrived.

It was all there, in the NCIC files, if you knew
where to look. Anshiser was involved with the
mob all the way back to his teenage years. His father had been an accountant—a banker and
money-mover for half of the organized crime syn-
dicates in the country. He was trusted, with im-
peccable books.

Anshiser took his father's methods a step further. He laundered the mob's dirty cash with a variety of money-making and money-losing ventures:
vending machine companies; trash-hauling con-
cerns; hotel casinos in Atlantic City, Reno, Las
Vegas, and the Caribbean; hotels in Chicago, Los
Angeles, San Diego, Dallas, Miami, Philadelphia,

Freeport, and a half dozen other tourist destinations. Federal cops suspected him of recirculating big-time drug money through his casinos. The process was simple enough. A drug dealer has, say, a suitcase full of ten-dollar bills—an awkward way to carry your money. Take it to Anshiser, pump it through the company, and out comes a handy pocket-size packet of thousands, ready for a trip to the third world. Less, of course, a ten percent handling fee.

More sophisticated opportunities were available for investors in the trash-hauling firms. One deal had Anshiser executives locating a failing trash-hauling company with old, screwed-up equipment but reasonably good potential. An unnamed dealer supposedly had two million in cash that he wanted to use in the U.S. but couldn't explain to the Internal Revenue Service. He gave the two million to Anshiser and got back in return fifty thousand dollars in stock in the failing trash hauler. Anshiser sent one of his hard-nosed executives in to run the company. New equipment from other Anshiser trash haulers was transferred in, at no charge to the new company. In a very short time, the dealer had stock worth a million and a half, and Anshiser bought him out. The dealer paid his taxes and, instead of two million in impossible-to-explain cash, had a perfectly legitimate, IRS-sanctioned, million-dollar bankroll. Anshiser's people took out a half million and owned a thriving garbage hauler.

We read through all the printouts before ten o'clock, then went down to the shopping arcade for croissants and coffee. I sat in the booth and found it hard to think.

"I really got took," I said finally. LuEllen was watching me across the table. "There was so much money, I didn't want anything to be wrong. We should have gotten out after we bumped into Ratface the first time. That was never right, we knew it wasn't right. And I had Bobby on the other end of the line, and I didn't use him. I should have given him an open account to keep running stuff on Anshiser and everybody else involved. If we'd known about Whitemark's Snagger program, we would have known something was wrong. If we'd known Anshiser's old man was in the mob, we would've been warned."

"Pigs and wings," LuEllen said. She was looking at the light fixtures.

"Thanks. I needed that."

"Stop whining, for Christ's sake," LuEllen snarled. "Tell me why they sent Ratface the first time. I still don't understand that. They had Maggie right there watching us."

"They were paranoid," I said. "Remember how she'd call Chicago to tell them what we were doing? Talking to computer people? When I laid out the attack for them, and they began to see what could be done, in detail, they really started to get worried. I think they wanted a better line on us. Maggie told them what she could, but she's not a computer tech. If they'd gotten a bug on our line, they could've looked at the attack programs in detail. And that's why it was such an old-fashioned bug—we were dealing with the mob, not the NSA or the CIA or the FBI or any other fuckin' alphabet."

"The fuckin' mob," LuEllen said. She thought it was funny.

"It doesn't seem to be a mob. It seems to be a whole bunch of people who float around in rackets."

"What do you think a mob is? Italians in zoot suits with violin cases under their arms?"

"I don't know. This doesn't seem so organized. It seems like they just . . . know each other."

"That's what a mob is. People who know each other. Our mob got started because you knew me and Dace," she said.

"We're not exactly a mob," I said dryly.

"Oh yeah? Then what are we?"

I thought about it for a minute. "A gang," I said firmly. "We're a gang."

"Okay, so we're a gang," she said. "What I don't understand is why Anshiser does all this stuff. He's already got more money than God."

I shrugged. "Maybe he likes it. Maybe they don't give him a choice. And it must be profitable.

They've probably got a hundred of these scams going all the time," I said. "Who knows how much they take down? Thirty or forty or fifty million a year, all of it hidden? I bet there aren't five people in Anshiser's company who know all of it. Anshiser, Dillon, Maggie, maybe a couple more in that working group at his house."

"So. What do you think, Kidd?" she asked. "Is this better or worse than dealing with the feds?"

"Better. Much better," I said. "The problem with the federal people is that once a decision is made, it becomes part of the bureaucracy. Nobody beats a bureaucracy. If they seriously want to get you, they'll do it. If it was the feds, our best bet would be to run. Brazil, or someplace like that. But if we're dealing with a company, especially a one-man gang like Anshiser's, we might be able to develop some leverage."

She considered it for a moment, and nodded.

"Something else," she said, her face cold and intense. "When I thought it was federal people, I couldn't figure out what to do about Dace. I mean, federal people are like cops. But these guys are just hoods.

"We can get back at them for Dace," she said. She reached out and gripped my wrist so hard that the nails bit through my skin. "I want them dead. Like Dace."

Chapter 17

DREXEL THE GUN salesman wasn't surprised to see us back. He seemed pleased.

"Trading up? Or adding to?" he asked as he opened the door.

"Adding to," I said. "I need an M16."

"What range will you be shooting at?" We followed him through the living room and down the basement stairs. There was no sign of his wife or daughter.

"I don't know. It could be fairly long."

"Ah, you are in luck," he said happily. He opened the gun cabinet. "I've just been out to our farm. I happen to have on hand a scope-sighted weapon. An M16/A2, to be precise. I sighted it only three days ago. The mount is quite sturdy."

He stroked the weapon a few times, gazing at it fondly as if it were a female friend, and handed it to me. It was dead black, and long, and cold, and heavy. "Much like the one you probably used in the service," he said.

"Yeah." I looked through the scope at a dart board at the end of the basement. I could see the dart holes.

"There are some differences," he said, "though you don't need to worry about them. The main thing is that you'll be shooting a heavier slug, the sixty-eight-grain Hornady hollow-point. They'll give you excellent accuracy. It's dead-on at a hundred and fifty yards. The weapon does have a tendency to ride up on full auto. If you're shooting that way, at a significantly closer range, you could drop down to a pelvic hold and allow it to ride up. That should cover all the bases."

Or all the people I intended to kill.

I bought three banana clips and four cartons of shells. He threw in a long cardboard box that said "curtain rods" on the side.

"Minimal camouflage, should you be stopped for something," he said, sliding the weapon into the box. "Be careful not to jar that scope. It would be best to brace the box in the trunk so it won't rattle around. If you have a little leisure time before you deploy, you might find a quiet place and check it. Just in case."

"Better safe than sorry," said LuEllen.

"A stitch in time saves nine," Drexel shot back.

I gave him another twenty-five hundred for everything. As we were going out the door he asked if we'd had a chance to shoot the other weapons.

"No, we haven't," LuEllen said.

"I'd like to hear how they perform, if you have a chance," he said pleasantly. "I do have a fifty-percent buy-back policy for all weapons in new or near-new condition, after you are finished with them. Lesser amounts if there is damage."

"Thanks. We'll keep it in mind," I said.

"That guy is a lizard," LuEllen said as we drove away. "He's like a cross between Beaver Cleaver's dad and Alfred Krupp."

I nearly drove the car over a curb.

"Alfred Krupp?"

"I read books," she said defensively. "You act like I'm a fuckin' dummy."

DACE HAD TAKEN LuEllen to his cabin in West Virginia only once, and it was before Maggie showed up. LuEllen didn't remember mentioning it to her.

The cabin, LuEllen said, sat over a pool on a small stream that allegedly harbored a trout or two, though Dace admitted he'd never seen one. The nearest cabin was half a mile downstream. There was nothing at all above him.

"He liked it because it was remote," LuEllen said. "The land is no good for farming, the timber is all bad second growth. The only thing up there are a few cabins along the stream. Dace said you can't even get in or out if it snows. He came up here once in the winter and almost froze his ass off before he could get out."

The road, she said, wasn't on any map. I wasn't so sure. We stopped at the county courthouse and bought a large-scale county map.

"You were right," said LuEllen, after we unrolled it on the hood of the car. "This is it." She traced a narrow track along Greyling Creek. It ran through the lower reaches of the mountains between two all-weather gravel roads.

"It's a good thing to know. Dillon will find this thing. If I give Maggie directions, the shooters will come in the other way. Count on it."

The road to Dace's cabin ran parallel to the creek, which lay off to the right. To the left was a partly wooded ridge that rose two hundred feet to the ridgeline. We followed a single strand of overhead electric wire along the road, past a half dozen cabins and two broken-down barns. The wire ended at Dace's place. The cabin was high on the bank, thirty feet above the stream.

Like the other cabins along the creek, Dace's was small and primitive, built from four-by-four timber and rough siding. The roof was covered with green tar shingles. A one-holer outhouse sat on the upstream side of the cabin, surrounded by a screen of pines, with a new moon cut in the door. Nearby, a strand of plastic-covered rope, tied between two trees, served as a clothesline.

"Dace said they get terrific floods through here every few years," LuEllen said, as we pulled onto the dirt patch that served as a parking place. "They cut down most of the trees upstream, and there's nothing to soak up the water."

I got out and looked around. The weather had broken, and though it was cool now, the day was a pretty one. Dace had thinned the trees between the house and the creek, and there was a pleasant view down to the water. In Minnesota and Wisconsin, the fishing would be prime, the muskies carrying late-season weight. I needed some time on the water.

As I walked around the yard, LuEllen tramped through the falling leaves to an herb garden beside the porch. She turned over a rock, took a bottle out of the ground, unscrewed the cap, and dumped a key out.

"His emergency key," she said.

The cabin was as simple inside as it was out. There was a two-burner electric range, a wood stove for heat, a table, a few chairs, a couch, a stack of old magazines, and two beds and a bureau behind a partition. I unloaded the luggage and we got comfortable.

We spent that day and the next walking the neighborhood. On the hill above the road, there were large areas of grassy hillside that at one time might have been pasturage. There were no animals to be seen. The grass was broken by patches of wild raspberries and clumps of ragged, second-growth timber. The strip below the road, along the creek, was heavily wooded.

We found an acceptable ambush site two hundred yards downstream from the cabin and an excellent one seventy yards above it. The site above the cabin was better. And that's where I expected to see them.

"I WANT TO talk to Maggie."

There was a long pause. "She's here," Dillon said. "It'll be a minute." He put me on hold. A long minute later, Maggie came on.

"Why did you do it?" I asked. My voice grated out, angry and cold. I wasn't pretending.

"I didn't," she said urgently. "I knew you'd think so. But it was Rudy. He was so frightened of what we did to Whitemark and what could be done to us, that he panicked. He's sick. He's in the hospital, and he may not get back out. They're not sure, but they think now it's a brain tumor. But believe me, I had nothing to do with it. Dillon didn't either."

"Huh." LuEllen, standing with her ear close to mine, turned her head and mouthed "Dace."

"What happened to Dace?"

"He was killed," Maggie said simply. Her voice sounded low and hurt. "These assholes shot him and killed him. They would have killed you, too, and LuEllen. When you called Dillon, Dillon confronted Rudy. The argument brought on the breakdown, or whatever it is. As soon as we figured out how to do it, we called these men off. They're already out of the country."

I let the silence build until she said, "Hello?"

"What happened to Dace's body? Is it still in the apartment?"

"No. I was told they . . . disposed of it. I really don't know the details." LuEllen squeezed my arm and closed her eyes. Tears started around the lashes.

"Explain how they knew where we were," I said, pressing. "How they got up past Philadelphia, if they weren't tipped off by Dillon."

She had the answer. "They put some kind of radio signal device on your car," she said. "They couldn't follow you exactly, but they knew when they were close. They tracked you up north, and then, they said, you picked a motel out in the middle of nowhere. They followed the signal right in. They took the beeper off the car when they got there, so if they . . . found you . . . the police wouldn't find it on your car."

"Jesus Christ."

"Do you believe me?"

I let the silence hang for a moment, then said, "I don't know. It sounds okay. But I don't know."

"Where are you?"

"I don't want to tell you that. Not yet. I've got to talk to LuEllen. I'll call you back."

"When?" she asked.

"Half an hour."

"I'll wait," she said. "I'm terribly sorry about Dace. It's awful. But I had nothing to do with it. Goddamn it, Kidd, you've got to believe me." Her voice cracked. I could see her standing over the desk, one hand on it for support, her head bowed, talking into the phone, pleading.

"I'll get back," I said, and hung up.

"WHY NOT TELL her now?" LuEllen asked.

"So she'll think we're talking about it. She's going to be suspicious anyway. If we hold out for a while, she may be less suspicious."

"She was awful good," LuEllen said after a while. "Would you have believed her? If we hadn't left your car at the airport?"

"I don't know," I said. "Maybe. I'd kind of believe her. But I'd still be careful."

DURING MOST OF the attack on Whitemark, I'd gone to bed late at night, after three o'clock. One night Maggie woke up and rolled onto her back as I sat on the edge of the bed, pulling off my socks.

"You wouldn't ever hurt me, would you?" she asked.

The question was a stopper. I turned and looked toward her in the dark. "Hurt you? You mean beat you up?"

"No, you dope. I mean dump me for a sixteen-year-old with up-pointy tits."

"Your tits are up-pointy."

"You know what I mean."

"We're not going to come to that," I said. "I do what I do, and you do what you do. They don't mix. Neither one of us will change. We're too old. Too committed. When you get back to Chicago, I'll come and see you. You'll come to St. Paul a time or two. Then it'll start to take up too much time, there'll be other people, and eventually we'll fizzle away."

"You're really the great romantic, aren't you?"

"I'm trying not to bullshit you," I said. "You're not stupid. You know all this. But I wouldn't be surprised if you came through St. Paul every once in a while and got laid. In between the other-people relationships, I mean. We could be friends for a long time."

She might have agreed, or she might have demurred, or might have said something about the abstract nature of the analysis. She might have laughed. She didn't. What she said was, "You'd never beat me up, would you?"

WE GAVE IT a half hour, sitting in a greasy spoon in a nondescript West Virginia hill town, idling over coffee and cheeseburgers. It was the afternoon coffee hour, and the local merchants drifted in, said hello to each other, casually looked us over and drank coffee and ate lemon meringue pie. The pie was listed on the menu as the *pie du jour*. The joke was, the city folks would wonder whether it was a joke. . . .

"I WANT TO talk," I told Maggie. "LuEllen doesn't but she'll go along. She's afraid of you and the Anshiser people. And we have a gun. We bought a gun. We're at Dace's cabin in West Virginia, and there's only one way in, and we'll be watching it. You fly into Washington, rent a car, and come up alone."

"You don't believe me," she said.

"We kind of believe you. We're not sure about Dillon," I said. "We're not going to take any chances, after what happened to Dace. We want to talk. Bring the money."

I told her how to get to the cabin. "When you turn off that road, follow the electric wire. There's only one, and it ends at Dace's place."

"I'll see you tomorrow afternoon," she said. "I'll bring the money. You've got to believe me."

Chapter 18

BEFORE WE LEFT town we bought a seventy-dollar boom box from an appliance dealer. Crossing the street to a hardware store, we picked up two light timers, the kind used in greenhouses, and two hand-held CB radios. As we were checking out, I went back and got a shovel. At a discount chain store we bought insulated coveralls in a camouflage pattern, daypacks, cheap rectangular sleeping bags, plastic air mattresses, and two pairs of binoculars. At a convenience store we bought bread, lunch meat, mustard, cupcakes and cookies, and a twelve-pack of Coke.

"Even if the shooters were in Washington, they couldn't get here before dark," I told LuEllen on the way back. "And I don't think they'll come in the dark, in unfamiliar territory. Dillon will research it for them, find a map, and see that the road goes through. The shooters will probably come in one car, from the top end of the road. Maggie will come up the way I told her, from the bottom. If she comes at all."

"You think she might not?"

"If they see this purely as a clean-up, she might not risk it. But I think she will. They'll want to talk, to find out if we've tried to protect ourselves—you know, letters to the FBI, that kind of thing. I don't think she's scared of me. She might be scared of you."

"She should be," LuEllen said, with a dangerous rime of bitterness in her voice.

"She'll probably have a radio in the car. When she sees us, she'll signal that we're in sight. Then they'll come in. She'll try to get us down in the vicinity of the cabin. They'll hit us there. Talk first and then shoot. Or just shoot."

"What do we do?"

"The first thing we do is cool off." I looked over at her. Her mouth was tight and her chin was up, ready for the fight. "If you go after her too soon, we both might wind up dead."

"I'm cool," she said. I looked at her and she gazed back unflinchingly.

"All right. You'll be up on the hill, above the bottom of the road, covering Maggie. It's possible that Dillon won't find the map, and the shooters will trail her in. You see her coming, you call me on the radio. We'll work out some codes. If she's alone, I want her to see you. Just a glimpse, and it has to be convincing. Run across an open space, down toward the cabin; let your upper body show. Wear that light-blue shirt of yours. After you've given her a couple of chances to see you, sneak back up the hill and get back in the camouflage."

"What if there's somebody with her?"

"Lie low and call."

"Where will you be?"

"I'll be on the top end of the road. I think that's where the shooters will come in."

The shooters, I thought, would show up a few minutes before Maggie, moving into position around the cabin. They would leave their car a mile or so out and walk in, following the creek. They would stay off the high ground because it was too open. The woods along the creek would give them good cover.

Some seventy yards out a rough, steep-walled gully, too small to show on even the largest-scale topo maps, carried a feeder creek down the ridge. The shooters could jump down the ten-foot walls, wade the stream, and climb the rocks on the other side. Or they could slip back up the road where the gully was crossed by a low-railed wooden bridge. The bridge was only twenty-five feet long, and it was well out of sight of the cabin. I thought they would take the chance.

If they crossed the bridge they were dead men.

I'd be in the brush on the hillside, twenty-five yards away, with the M16.

"What about Maggie?"

"I don't know," I said. "She's not a pro, so she'll probably make a run for it. You can try to hold her, but we can't worry about her until the shooters are down."

"You mean *dead*."

"Yeah."

"What if the guys who show up are completely different people? What if they aren't the people who shot Dace?"

"I don't know. What do you think?"

"They'd be killers. They'd be there to kill us." She was troubled.

"Yeah."

We turned off the blacktop highway onto a gravel side road, and she watched the landscape rolling by, the tan fall grasses in the roadside ditches, the fat milkweed pods, the wild marijuana.

"I'd let them go," she said finally.

I nodded. "That would be best. We lie in the briar patch like Brer Rabbit, and we never come out."

At the cabin we ate and made sandwiches for the next morning.

"We stay on the hillside tonight, just in case," I said. "We'll put the lights and the boom box on the timer. If they come in early, they'll see the lights changing around and hear the boom box go off and on. Not too loud."

Half an hour before dark I took the M16 and a sheet of paper outside, pinned the paper to a tree, and fired four shots at it from twenty-five yards. I'd have to hold it just a bit low. I fired a few more shots at a hundred yards and at 150, and found that the rifle was, as advertised, dead-on at 150.

When I finished, I reloaded the clip, and we walked up the hill and found a comfortable nest in the deep grass. We were eighty yards from the cabin and a hundred feet above it. In the dying light and cool still evening air, the sound from the radio drifted up the hill. We'd chosen a rock classics station. Most of the music was distinctly non-classic and in some cases barely rock, but there were interludes of Pink Floyd and the Doors and REM.

"You remember way back, when Ratface first showed up, and I did that tarot spread, the magic spread, for you and Dace?" I asked.

"Yeah."

"The cards that came up were the Emperor and the Seven of Swords. I just figured it out."

"What's that?"

"The Emperor is Anshiser. The Seven of Swords is a betrayal card. I didn't even think about it at the time."

"Too late now."

• • •

WE TALKED ABOUT the next day, setting up radio voice codes and practicing them. At 11:15, a timer turned off the light. A few minutes later, the other one shut down the radio.

"What's the worst thing that could happen tomorrow?" LuEllen said in the sudden silence.

I thought about it for a minute. "If they are deeper into killing than I think, it's just barely possible that they'll come over the hill with a helicopter and a half dozen guys in camies and flak jackets and automatic weapons with the experience to use them. They'll take both the hillside and the woods and sweep us right out in front of them."

"What do we do?"

"Run, if we can. Fight if we can't."

"What's the best thing that can happen?"

"Jesus, LuEllen. The best thing that can happen tomorrow is that we kill some people."

We sat in silence until LuEllen stood up and shivered and said, "I'm cold." We pulled on the coveralls and lay back on the sleeping bags and looked up at the stars. We were far out in the countryside, away from the lights, and the Milky Way looked like a huge illuminated milk-bowl.

"You know any of them? The stars?"

"Some. Everybody who goes outdoors knows a few. The North Star, Polaris." I pointed it out. "And there's Cassiopeia, the W. And that's Orion.

The three bright stars are Orion's belt. You know the good thing about them?"

"What?"

"The belt's very close to the celestial equator. When the middle star hits the horizon, either coming up or down, it'll be almost due east of west. Within a degree or two."

"Did you learn this stuff when you were a teenage nerd?"

"Right," I laughed. "That's when I learned it."

We were quiet again for a while, and finally she said in a small voice, "Where'd you put the shovel?"

"Beside the outhouse," I said.

We slept off and on until daylight. My watch alarm beeped, and I woke to find LuEllen watching me. She had circles beneath her eyes but she said she was okay. We ate from the cooler and drank Cokes, and we packed Cokes into our daypacks with the extra ammo. The radio handsets had pagers so we could beep each other.

"I thought of something during the night," I said. "There's a good chance they'll come in early, earlier than we should expect. Like in the next hour. Trying to catch us off-balance. But there's also the possibility that they'll come later than we expect, like two o'clock in the afternoon. Hoping that we'll break cover to talk it over, or to eat, or get a drink, or pee, or whatever. When you get up there, stay put. I'll call if we should move. Victory goes to the iron butt."

She waved and went off to her hiding place.

MY AMBUSH SITE was a shallow depression on the edge of the ravine, behind a clump of brush and dried-out weeds. I retrieved a three-foot chunk of rotted log from the ravine and placed it on the edge of my hole, so I could brace the M16 on top of it. I settled in, using the sleeping bag as a cushion, and got comfortable. The camouflage coveralls were warm, and I was tired. I drank a Coke for the caffeine, and then another. A fat black-and-yellow bumblebee floated around me for a few seconds, and I started to worry that I might be on his nest. He left, and I settled back again, more awake now.

They came neither early nor late. It was eighteen minutes after noon when I saw the motion in the trees below. It was hard to follow, and at first I was uncertain whether it was really there. Then I saw it again, and then another movement, again slow, but farther up the hill and closer to me. Two of them, at least. In camouflage. I let out the breath I was holding.

Moving like molasses, I eased the binoculars up to my eyes and found them. They were walking unaccountably slowly, until I realized they were trying to pick their way silently through the fallen leaves. Given the choice between the woods and the open hillside, they chose the cover, but the leaves underfoot were giving them fits.

I beeped LuEllen and said, "Two. Two." She returned with, "Two." A few minutes later she beeped back and said, "Blonde." I returned the call. The Blonde code meant Maggie was on the way in, alone, as far as LuEllen could tell. I looked at my watch. Two minutes since I spotted the first movement. I began scanning the woods behind the two men I had already spotted, looking for a backup. LuEllen should be running down the hill. . . .

The shooters were only sporadically visible as they moved closer, about fifteen feet apart. Then one of them lifted a handset from his belt and listened. I clicked around the channels on my CB, but there was nothing. Their sets were more sophisticated than ours and probably used dedicated channels.

Their conversation went on through several exchanges. It meant, I hoped, that Maggie had seen LuEllen running across the hill and believed we were at the bottom of the road. The man with the handset hung it back on his belt, said a few words to the other, and they moved up, a little quicker now. They were only fifty yards away, coming up to the ravine. They stopped on the lip, looked down at the creek, talked for a moment, then turned uphill.

As they got closer, I eased the M16 into position over a low tangle of vines and brought it to bear on the bridge. My heart was thumping wildly, and it was suddenly hard to breathe.

The first one stopped below the bridge, where I could see only his head, and waited for the second one to come up. When he arrived, they talked for a second, and I was afraid they would decide to cross the bridge one at a time, providing cover for each other. Then they both scrambled up on the road, crouching, their heads turned down toward the cabin. The big guy dangled an Uzi from his right hand. Ratface was two steps behind him, carrying a police shotgun with a pistol grip below the stock. With my cover, the Uzi was more dangerous, so I decided to take the big guy first. Once on the road, they moved fast. Staying low, they scuttled onto the bridge, using the low railing as concealment from the cabin.

I let the big one get two-thirds of the way across the bridge, held the M16 at waist height, and when he was about to intersect the sight, I pulled the trigger. An M16 doesn't roar so much as clatter; it clattered in my face, and the first squirt pitched the big guy over. I tracked back to where Ratface had frozen for a split second, and I was almost there when he simply leaped off the bridge, head first.

The move was so startling that I half stood and instinctively dumped the rest of the clip under the bridge, punched out the used clip, and fed in a new one. There was no thrashing around in the brush below the bridge, and I said, "Shit," and started sliding to my right toward the road.

The beeper on my radio went off. I said, "What?" and she said, "Maggie's out of the car and heard the shots. She's just standing there."

"Well, we got problems," I said. "It's the right guys, but one of them jumped off the bridge and he's on the loose. He may be hurt. It was a hell of a fall, and I sprayed the place down."

"I'm coming down," she said.

"You keep an eye on Maggie," I said.

"Fuck that."

I tossed the radio on top of the backpack and crawled along the upper edge of the road until I was thirty yards from the ravine and around a shallow curve. There was no sign of Ratface. If he was uninjured and sat tight, he would be almost impossible to get at. On the other hand, he might be unconscious under the bridge, helpless from the fall. Either way, he might not expect me to be on his side of the road. I moved up the road, ran across, then dropped flat on a game trail. Nothing. Moving slowly, slowly, I turned back toward the ravine. Still nothing. I stopped, waited, moved up, stopped.

I was fifteen yards from the bridge when Maggie gave him away. They had radios, handsets, and his had been clipped to his belt. She beeped him. I heard the beep, high and electronic, as distinct in the woods as a raven call would be in a computer lab. It came from the near bank of the ravine, over the lip. Was he still with the radio, or had he dumped it? There was no second beep, and I crouched, watching, ears straining.

LuEllen broke the impasse when she came down the hill over my old position. She touched a tree, or stepped on some brush, and Ratface heard it and moved. He was hurt, all right. His face was covered with blood, one leg was apparently twisted at the knee, but he still had the gun. He dragged himself up beside the roadbed opposite my ambush site. I waited until he was fully in the open and brought the M16 down on him. At the last second he apparently sensed me behind him, because he twisted and threw out a hand and, like Dace, said, "Wait." I unloaded the M16 into his side and back. He was dead before the bullets stopped shuddering through him.

"LuEllen!" I shouted across the road. "Two down."

"Are there more?"

"I don't think so. I didn't see a backup."

"Maggie."

LuEllen started running along the hill parallel to the road, an awkward galumphing in the camouflage suit. I followed on my side. We came through the bend and saw Maggie running back toward her car.

"Shoot her," LuEllen screamed.

I dropped to one knee and put the scope on her back. She ran so well. I watched as she took five steps, ten, long, lithe strides like a college runner. . . .

"Shoot," LuEllen screamed again.

"Ah, shit," I said, and took the gun down.

LuEllen looked at me, looked at Maggie, close to her car now, put up her MAC-10, and sprayed out the whole clip. A MAC-10's effective range must be about thirty yards; she was shooting at more than two hundred. I saw one slug hit the dirt road perhaps fifty yards behind Maggie. The rest must have gone into the woods or the hillside. Maggie got back to the car, climbed in, and cranked it around in a circle. She stopped abruptly, a bag flew out of the window, and she was gone.

GRAVEDIGGING IS BRUTAL work.

With Maggie gone, I ran back to the bridge, dragged both bodies into the brush above the ravine, and scuffed dirt over the bloodstains, while LuEllen picked up the brass from the M16. If a car came down the road—an unlikely occurrence—nothing would be visible. That done, LuEllen and I climbed the hillside together, all the way to the top, toward the lower end of the road. Once over the ridgeline, we doubled back toward the top end. We found a good clump of trees above the road and crawled into it and lay there for three hours, and never a thing moved. Later on, we walked back down the road and looked at the bundle Maggie had thrown out of the window. It was the rest of the money.

"Maybe she wanted to deal," LuEllen said doubtfully.

"If she had to. If we'd come up with something she couldn't fight," I said.

"We did, I guess," said LuEllen. We looked at the money for a while, glumly shuffled through it, and carried it back to the cabin.

"Let's get the shovel," I said finally.

We buried Ratface and his large friend a hundred feet up the hill, in a small natural hollow where I could work out of sight. LuEllen sat on the hill above me with the MAC-10. I first cut out the clumps of sod and put them to one side and then threw the dirt on a tarp. I dug for two hours in the yellow, sandy soil before I was both satisfied and too tired to dig anymore.

Getting bodies up the hill was as bad as the digging. I checked their pockets, found car keys and wallets, kept the keys but left the wallets with the bodies. I dragged Ratface up the hill by his coat, but the big man was too heavy, so I tied three loops of rope around his waist to use as a handle. Their heads and hands rolled loosely and their skin was as white as candle wax. When I dropped them in the grave, they made an untidy and unholy pile. I tossed the M16 and both of their guns in on top of them.

It took another half hour to get the dirt in, and the sod tramped into place.

"Should we say a prayer?" LuEllen asked as I fitted the last of the sod back in place.

I said nothing and finally she said, "Ah, fuck it."

There was some extra dirt left on the tarp, and I dragged it down to the ravine and dumped it in the creek. LuEllen loaded the car and shut down the cabin. I found her wiping the table, the stove, and the woodwork.

"I hope it doesn't come to that," I said.

"Remember what Maggie said? Why take a chance?"

We left the cabin, going out the back way, at seven o'clock. The red Buick was parked near the intersection of the all-weather road. I checked the front seat and trunk as LuEllen waited, and found a box with fourteen thousand dollars in it. I took the money and drove the car out to the main highway, with LuEllen following. We eventually left it at a turnoff by a historical marker, fifteen miles from the cabin. I wiped it down before we left it.

"Now what?" LuEllen asked.

"We got their shooters. They might have more, but they'll be cautious. And now Maggie knows that we know, so there'll be no more bullshit."

"Is that good?"

"Maybe. I've got a couple of ideas. I've got to get on the terminal and talk to Bobby. You ought to get out of here. Back to Duluth. It'll all be computer stuff from here on. If we travel together, we'd just be easier to spot."

"You think they could spot us? They're not the cops, they're just a bunch of hoods."

"Yeah. But like Maggie said, why take a chance?"

"You're right," she said after a while. "But I'm not going back to Duluth."

"Where?"

"Mexico. Right where we were going. I'm all packed." And she started to cry.

WE DROVE NORTH through Cumberland across into Pennsylvania and arrived outside of Pittsburgh in the early morning hours, running, in the end, on pure adrenaline. We slept late, and in the evening I put her on a plane to San Diego.

"Take care of yourself, Kidd." LuEllen kissed me on the cheek and went through the gate. Unlike Maggie, she never looked back.

What?

Need long talk.

Call 3 A.M.

Chapter 19

E ARLY THE NEXT morning I laid out a program for Bobby.

Big bux.

Yes.

Need 2 more hacks.

OK.

10K each for hacks.

OK.

25K for me. Cash. Pay when we win.

I pay out front. If we lose, I might not be able to pay. Give PO Box.

Leave terminal on answer.

I woke at midmorning to the terminal alarm and a squirt of data—a post office box in Memphis where I could send the money and registered mail, and also the names of the other two hacks. They were both from California. Bobby called them Cal Tech and Stanford. I couldn't remember either one, but Bobby said that Stanford met me on a Vegas gaming board a few years before. Bobby said he would begin checking Anshiser phone lines for incoming data.

Anshiser company/house show no incoming data lines. Must have private exchanges. Major pain.

Yes.

Most computers are hooked into the local telephone exchange. In simpler days, the data-line numbers were often variants of the telephone number of the company that owned the computers. If the company's number was 555-1115, the computer number might be 555-1116.

Hackers got onto that right away. Whole nights were spent exploring the guts of various expensive on-line computers. A generation of computer fanatics learned their jobs by doing it. The first illegal entry I made, way back in the early seventies, was to a call-in board that regulated the heating, cooling, water, and other systems of one of the biggest office buildings in Minneapolis. I could have turned off the building's heat in the middle of a January night, but I didn't. I left a note for the operator, though, and the next time I called, entry was more difficult.

A little later, computer security got tight enough that data-line numbers were moved well away from the company's regular phone—but still in the same exchange. Hackers fought back by producing autodial programs that would dial all of the ten thousand numbers in a given exchange. Whenever the modem got a carrier tone, the computer would note it. If there was no answer or a voice answer, the computer would hang up and move on. A computer could call a thousand numbers overnight, and it was a sad night that didn't produce a dozen new computer lines.

Eventually, security-phone companies began creating their own exchanges. The secret exchanges were not listed in the phone book. Only a few numbers out of the ten thousand possible for that special exchange would be used as data lines. That meant that even if hackers knew that Company X was running an open computer on a hidden exchange, they would first have to find the exchange. If they tried to do it randomly, they would have ten thousand calls for each exchange tested. Most of the time it wasn't worth the effort.

THERE WAS A way to break the hidden exchanges. Bobby was deep into the phone system.

If he monitored a number of Anshiser businesses, and one called into a hidden exchange, we would have it. I worked through our Anshiser research again, and isolated five hotels most likely to use regular phone lines to transmit reports. Bobby would watch them for a few days, and if nothing happened, we'd look at different ones.

While Bobby was working, I took off again, heading south through Kentucky and Tennessee, dipping into Alabama and Mississippi. I spent a day at Vicksburg, down on the river, painting, then turned south and into Louisiana. The idea of New Orleans was tempting, but I was known there. I turned back north through Arkansas and into Missouri.

Each night I'd do between a dozen and a hundred tarot spreads, figuring the possibilities. The Fool was back, and that was okay. After the tarot, I'd call Bobby for progress. There was none until the fifth night, when I put into a tidy little Ma-and-Pa motel on the edge of the Ozarks.

Got exchange.

Great.

Not great. Dipped in. Have very heavy security. No on-line help. Get zero. Think one-time codes. Think probes spotted.

Traced?

No. But guard up now.

One-time codes are essentially unbreakable. There is no pattern, and they are used only once. Sometimes the operators on opposite ends of a phone link literally have identical pads of words: one is used, then that piece of paper is ripped off and thrown away, and the next one is used. The words may be of any length, pulled at random from a dictionary. Or they may be lists of numbers produced by a random-number generator.

Our problems were compounded by what Bobby thought was individual call monitoring: when we tried to get in, it set off an alarm. They knew somebody was knocking on the door, and without the correct codes. They would be watching for us.

THE NEXT NIGHT we went back into the exchange, intending to proceed most delicately. It was empty. They had changed it again.

Unless we get codes we locked out. Watched Anshiser/Vegas Hotel data line, there was call-in call-back, enough data that may be two-way one-time codes, maybe simultaneous voice monitoring and clearance.

Okay. Hold probes. Need time to think.

Call when need us.

Sometimes, in high-security environments, a clerk from a remote computer, like that of Anshiser/Vegas, would be brought into the home computer installation. He would go to a company-sponsored lunch and dinner with the home computer operators, often with a shrink or "enabler" present. The shrink would keep the conversation going, both in person and over internal telephones.

When the clerk returned to his remote site, he would call one of his new friends at the home base before each computer entry. They would chat until his identity was confirmed. Some companies even used voice-print analyzers as a backup. Only when the identity was confirmed would they begin the sign-on procedure. Since the procedure was a two-way affair, with conversation and code going both ways, it was essentially unbeatable. While there might be ways to read the transmissions, there was no electronic way to get inside and work with the computer itself. We would need a different route.

How good is access to credit computers?

Read-only or read-write?

Read-only.

Good access.

Need complete run on all Anshiser lower-level execs with likely computer access. Find worst credit, forward names.

OK. Tomorrow.

While Bobby was running the credit reports, I went back into the NCIC computers using the codes we'd stolen from Denton, the Washington cop. This time I wasn't looking for anything deep, just the standard rap sheets. And I wasn't looking for felonies, I was looking for sleaze. I came up with a half dozen possibilities. When Bobby sent his list of bad credit reports the next day, we had one match.

I dumped the car in St. Louis and flew to Miami the next afternoon. Our man, Phil Denzer, was in the book. There was no answer at his apartment up to eleven o'clock that night. I found his apartment on the map, in a complex in North Dade County, and the next morning drove up to talk to him.

Denzer lived in a run-down complex of town houses surrounded by several acres of hot asphalt. The parking lot featured redneck specials, Firebirds and Camaros and five-liter Mustangs, most of them several years old, along with broken-down Dodge Swingers with rusted-out taillights. Sickly, yellow-leafed palm trees lined the lots. The town houses were arranged in a donut shape around two swimming pools. It was a hot and cloudless day, and a few women in bikinis, and one guy wearing shorts, a gold chain, and loafers, were arrayed on lounge chairs around the pools. Nobody was actually swimming.

I got Denzer's apartment number from the manager. The jalousie windows on the door were cranked open, and disco music poured out through the glass slats. I peered in and could see a guy in a white T-shirt and black slacks dancing to the music, by himself. Practicing moves. I knocked, and Denzer came to the door.

"You a Witness?"

"Do I look like a Witness?"

He thought about it and eventually shook his head. "No. They dress neater. What'd ya want?" He talked past a cigarette and, on his way to the door, had picked up a plastic plate with a half-eaten slice of cherry pie on it, which he was now holding.

"I've got a proposition for you."

"Oh yeah? You gonna make me rich?"

"There might be a few bucks in it."

"Tell me in ten words. I gotta get to work."

"That's what I'm interested in. Your work. You work on a computer, right?"

His mouth actually dropped open.

"Hey. I bet you're one of the guys trying to break into our system, right?" He pointed a fork at my chest and I looked for a place to run. "Well, shit, come on in," he said, holding the door open. He was delighted. "I hoped you'd call me, but I didn't really think you would."

I stepped inside. It was cool and damp and smelled like beer.

"I'm just having a beer and piece of pie before I take off for work. You want a beer?"

"Sure."

He got one from the refrigerator, popped the top, and handed me the can. "Sit down, sit down," he said. "How much can you pay me?"

I sat on a rickety armchair that might have been stolen from a budget motel. "Depends on what you've got."

"I want some money up front. They told us you were well-heeled. 'A well-heeled operation,' is what they said."

"How about five hundred?"

"Fuck, how about five grand?"

"We're not that well-heeled. I'll give you a grand now, and if it's worth more, I'll give you another."

He scratched his head. He had long black hair, combed straight back. He must have held it down with grease or wax, because you could see tooth marks from his comb.

"All right." I had three thousand in my pocket; I took it out and started counting. He looked at it greedily. I stopped counting for a second.

"Look, Phil, I know all about your money

problems. But don't think about taking this away from me, okay? I'd just beat the shit out of you."

"Hey, man . . ."

I handed him a thousand and he counted it, folded it, and put it in his front pants pocket and sat back.

"Okay. So here's what I know. And this was why I was so happy to hear from you. 'Cause all I can tell you is that you can't get in. Even if you put a gun to my head, and marched me in there, and made me sign on, and we got in, it wouldn't do you any good. Things are so tight that almost nothing moves anymore. It's all voice-backup and it's all one-way. We dump it into a computer on the other end that's physically separated from the main data banks. Then they've got operators to put all of the data up on the screen from the dump bank, and they scan it for code. Only when they're sure it's clean, they call up the main bank on their own internal line and dump it. There's no way in from the outside."

"What if you need to go interactive with something in the main banks?"

"Well, they're trying not to let that happen. If it's really serious, then they'll download the interactive program to the remote computer; you'll interact there. They sterilize the input before they ship it back to the main banks. I mean, there's one way to break it: you have to get to the systems programmers. And that won't happen. I'll tell you, man, this is a pretty good company, but they've got some rough customers roaming around. You know what I mean?"

"Yeah. I think so."

"Just in case you don't, let me lay it out in a couple of sentences. Their top systems programmers are taking home maybe a hundred grand a year, plus options and benefits and bonuses. That's good money. That's the golden goose. If they get greedy and go for some small change from you, they'd be fired and blackballed and maybe, you know, hurt. The chances of those guys taking your money are slim and fat, and slim is out of town." He took a gulp of Bud.

"So why are you talking to me?" I asked.

"Because you gave me a grand. And because about two seconds after you leave here, I'm going to call them up on the phone and tell them you came to see me. I won't mention the grand, though. I'll tell them I told you to take a hike."

I stood up to leave. "You ought to think about that for a while, Phil. Like you said, there are some hard guys with Anshiser. They might not believe you, and you'll wind up in an oil barrel on the bottom of Biscayne Bay. Because if you call them, and they come after me before I can get out of Miami International, I'll tell them you got ten grand and suggested a couple ways I might get in. And they just won't want to take the chance with you, will they?" I slapped him lightly on the cheek. "Thanks for the information. It was worth a grand."

I LEFT HIM standing there with an empty beer can and two bites of pie. He scared me, though, and an hour later I took the first plane to any-where out of Fort Lauderdale. As it happened, it was going to Tampa. From there I flew to Atlanta and then back to St. Louis.

What?

Talked to Anshiser guy about system, it's no go for now, may have to find different route.

Let us know.

I spent three days at Lake of the Ozarks, fishing out of a rented boat, letting the problem cook. In the evenings, I'd sit on the porch of my rented cabin, look out at the lake, and drink beer. If I didn't find anything, it wouldn't be the end of the world. I could go underground for a while, call Emily, arrange for her to take care of the cat, pay the bills. In a couple of years, three or four years, I might even be able to go back.

But it was a sour solution and sent me to bed half drunk. I couldn't sleep on it, but lay awake twisting the sheets around my legs, flopping around on the bed like a beached carp.

On the third night, I got out the cards, and instead of game-playing the problem, I laid out a magic spread, the Celtic Cross. I did it three times, and three times the Tower of Destruction came up in association with the Magician. The Magician I'd always related to computer freaks—the power of thought in all its forms, including mechanical. The Tower of Destruction is usually interpreted as meaning disaster or crisis, although it can mean a sudden awakening or awareness.

It was all hopeless bullshit. I dropped the cards on the table and went for another beer, walked back, and looked down at them. The Tower showed a medieval stone tower shattered by a bolt of lightning, with two men falling from the top. The woman who taught me to read the cards warned me not always to depend on book interpretations, or even on her interpretations.

"Sometimes," she said, "you just have to look at the cards."

I looked at the cards . . . the magician, the tower, the bolt of lightning . . .

"Sonofabitch," I said.

What?

I got it.

You got it?

The answer was typically tarot: outside what I'd considered the parameters of the problem, elegant, and slightly twisted. It took two days to confirm that it would work. It took three weeks—all four of us working twelve to fourteen hours a night—to get the code written, tested, and shipped out.

For the first two weeks I wandered aimlessly up and down the Mississippi River valley, sleeping late, painting in the afternoons, writing code at night. Twice I sent tubes of paintings to Emily in St. Paul to hold for me. I always mailed them from places I was leaving. In the third week, I turned west, across Arkansas, Oklahoma, a piece of Texas, New Mexico, and Arizona, heading for Las Vegas.

My rational tarot was talking, now that the possibilities were finite, and I spent a lot of time thinking about the cards. The time wasn't too bad, except for the loneliness. I was fond of my life in St. Paul, the apartment, my friends, even the cat. I wanted to get back.

We close now.

You debug last batch?

Stanford doing that. He close.

We should run command tests.

Yes. Start tonight.

We ran the tests. There were a few final bugs to hunt down, and then the attack programs worked fine. I was in Phoenix, in a nondescript motel off Interstate 10. It was hot, and the air conditioner smelled like somebody had dropped an aging cheeseburger on the compressor unit. I sat in my underwear and sweated and ran the tarot.

If you run the cards long enough, everything comes up; it's all meaningless. But it seemed that I saw a lot of the battle cards, the Five of Wands, the Seven of Wands, the Seven of Swords. None showed defeat, but none projected a clear victory, either. I finally turned the deck around and tried to run a spread from Maggie's point of view. That's not supposed to work. I came up with an Eight of Swords as the outcome, a woman blindfolded with her arms bound, surrounded by swords stuck point-down in the earth. That was good enough, and I quit.

The next day was a Wednesday, the last in October. It would be getting cold up north, but if I could back off the Anshiser crowd, I might be able to get my boat over to Vilas County, Wisconsin, for the November muskie rush. It's not that there's a rush of muskies; there's a rush of muskie fishermen, crowding in before ice-up. I decided to call Maggie the next day.

Chapter 20

Y EARS BEFORE, WHEN I first started doing
   unconventional computer work, I had taken
the trouble to construct an alternate identity. It
wasn't particularly hard: a phony birth certificate
acquired in Chicago, along with the Social
Security number of a dead teenager who would
never use it, got me a passport in the name of
Harry Olson, of Eau Claire. A few customs
stamps and stapled-in visas gave the passport a
wearied look. Presented at a Wisconsin driver's
examination office, the passport and Social
Security number were good for a driver's license.
The license and Social Security number produced
a bank account. The bank didn't ask too many
questions, since the documents were accompanied
by a fat cashier's check.

That summer I rented a place on Grindstone
Lake, near Hayward, in the name of Harry Olson.
I spent the summer writing code, painting, hunt-
ing muskie, and collecting my mail, which in-

cluded credit cards from Visa, Amoco and Exxon, and the local library.

When I left Hayward, I changed the address for the credit cards to a post office in Hudson, Wisconsin, just across the St. Croix River from St. Paul. I carefully used the credit cards and promptly paid the bills. I renewed the driver's license and over the years collected a variety of other forms of ID in Harry Olson's name.

Harry Olson checked into the Anshiser/Vegas at three o'clock in the afternoon. The desk clerk ran the Visa through the credit-checking machine, smiled, and handed me a room key.

"Let the bellman know if you need anything. The movies are turned on for your room. The key to the refreshments cabinet is on the credenza," he said. The bellman had a number of suggestions for the evening, including a private party with a couple of showgirls. I declined, but gave him ten dollars.

"LET ME SPEAK to Maggie."

"Kidd?"

"Yeah. I want to talk to Maggie."

"Just a minute." Dillon sounded stressed, but controlled. I had been out of sight for a month, though they suspected I'd tested their computer security. If Denzer told them about my visit to Miami, they would have that. Nothing else.

"Kidd." It was a statement, not a question.

"Yeah. How are you?"

She ignored the question. "What do you want?"

"Peace and quiet."

"That's going to be hard, now."

"Yeah, I know. I thought we should talk. Face-to-face."

"Where are you?"

"Flagstaff. I'll be in Vegas tomorrow. I'll meet you at the Anshiser/Vegas."

"What time?"

"In the afternoon, about three-thirty or four o'clock. I'll call your room."

THAT EVENING, I dropped seven hundred dollars at the blackjack tables.

Blackjack can be beaten. There are several methods of shifting the odds in your favor by keeping track of certain cards as they're dealt. You make your biggest bets when the deck is most in your favor; the rest of the time, you tread water. Casinos don't like card-counters.

With that in mind, a mathematician friend at the University of Chicago once spent some time refining a common card-counting routine. In essence, he built in a randomizing factor that disguised the bet-building. In my case, the disguise more than worked: I lost my shirt.

In the process of losing it, I thoroughly confused the dealer. She spotted me for a card-counter, I think, but I was leaking money at a ferocious rate. When I finally walked away, her eyes followed me all the way across the casino floor, as though she expected me to come back, pull out a surprise bet, and recoup all the losses. No such luck.

High-tech computer-assisted programs sometimes get out in the real world and get their ass kicked. Something to lie in bed and think about, as we made the torpedo run on Anshiser.

THE CASINO WAS a bad idea. I'd picked one a few blocks from the Anshiser, just in case somebody was looking for my face. But on the way back, I almost bumped into Maggie.

She went through the lobby with a thin, dark-complected man in an expensive banker's pinstripe. His nose had been broken a long time ago, well before he acquired his current sheen, but he did not look at all like Mary's Little Lamb.

I was standing in the hotel gift shop, looking at magazines, and caught a flash of her in a mirrored pillar. I turned away and gave them time to get through. I bought a few magazines while I waited, plus two paperbacks. This time, I would stay in the room.

What?

Everything set?

> Set and checked. Hacks on line. We'll trip you off exactly at 4. Then we'll have a cascade on the other plants.

Timing would be delicate. I debated calling her as early as 3:30, but we wouldn't have that much to say to each other. On the other hand, she might have people scattered around the hotel. She'd want them together before she came into the room. So when to call? I rehearsed the probable moves and finally decided there would be at least ten minutes to talk. And I should be able to stretch it out, if need be.

I would call at 3:40. At three o'clock, time started to slow down. I risked a trip to the Coke machine down the hall, got three, drank two, and looked at the clock. 3:15. I did a few desultory tarot spreads: not enough time now for the tarot to help. I watched television, paced. 3:30. More pacing. A pit stop in the bathroom, dumping the processed Coke. Last-minute thoughts. At 3:39 I dialed the operator and got her room number. She picked up the phone on the first ring.

"This is Kidd."

"Yes. I'm here."

"I'm in Room 2406. It's almost right straight below you. I'll wait five minutes, then I'm gone. And Maggie—you may be tempted to send in some shooters to take care of the problem. That

would be a major mistake. You would remember
it for the rest of your life as the mistake that ruined you. I don't have a gun, I just want to talk.
Okay?"

"I'll be down."

I did have a gun, the MAC-10. I glued a fat
strip of Velcro to the grip and stuck it on the side
of the easy chair where I planned to sit. It was out
of sight, in an unexpected place, all cocked and
ready. It was too big and would be an awkward
draw, but if they came in shooting, I would make
it more than a simple execution. That was the
idea, anyway.

After Maggie hung up, I unlocked the door,
pulled the drapes, turned on the TV set and ad-
justed the sound until it was barely audible, got
the last Coke, and sat in the chair. At 3:44, there
was a knock at the door.

"Come in."

A short, tough-looking blond with a brush
haircut pushed the door open with his finger
while he stayed in the hall. He looked at me, nodded, took a slow step inside, glanced into the
bathroom. The dark man with the broken nose
was behind him, dressed in a different, but
equally conservative, pinstriped suit. He waited in
my line of sight, watching me, while the blond
went into the bathroom and pulled back the
shower curtain. The blond came back out, opened
the coat closet near the door, looked in, then

came into the room. The beds were on pedestals, but he looked between them and behind the one next to the wall. Finally he turned to the dark man.

"It's okay," he said. The dark man stayed where he was, and the blond went back to the hallway and came in with a briefcase. He opened it and took out a debugging loop and started working his way around the room.

"Look, it'll take an hour to find a bug if I put one in. . . ."

"We don't think you did. Nothing heavy, anyway. We're just making a quick sweep. We'd be embarrassed if you had something as crummy as a cheap tape recorder."

"I don't."

He smiled and followed the loop around the room. When he was satisfied, he folded it and shoved it back in the briefcase.

"I think it's clean," he said.

The dark man stepped into the room. "Mr. Olson," he said, nodding at me. Maggie was a step behind him.

"Kidd," she said. Her face was taut. Not frozen, but ready, like an athlete on the starting blocks.

"How's Anshiser?" I asked. The blond shut the door without locking it, and the dark man sat on a corner of the bed, looking at me. Maggie perched on the other chair.

"He's out of it," she said. "They're off the tumor theory. They think now it may have been a series of ministrokes over a period of time, killing his brain in such tiny increments it was impossible to find. They're still not sure. One of the doctors said the only way they'll ever be sure is with an autopsy. He's now in what they call a vegetative state."

"Tough. It's a bad way to go." I nodded at the dark man. "Is this the new boss?"

The dark man smiled, his even teeth glittering against his olive skin. With the broken nose and the good teeth, he would be devastating with women.

"I'm afraid you've got that backward, Mr. Kidd," he said mildly. "The board has chosen Ms. Kahn to run Anshiser. She's asked me to work as her executive assistant. Essentially, I have her old job."

"What about Dillon?"

Maggie shrugged. "Dillon is Dillon. He does the same thing. That's all he wants to do." When she first came in the room, her face was deathly pale. Now the color was coming back and the tension was seeping out. The situation was under control. The red numerals of the digital clock on the bedside table said 3:52.

"How's LuEllen?" Maggie asked.

"She's fine. She went back home."

"Was she the one who shot at me, back at the cabin?"

"Yeah. She was pissed about Dace."

"I thought it was she. I knew you were in the Army, and when I heard that machine gun going, and I didn't hear Frank's shotgun, I had an idea what happened. When I saw you coming around the corner with LuEllen and those guns, in those camouflage suits, I thought, Dear God, he's going to shoot me in the back."

"I thought about it," I said. "I had the scope right on your shoulder blades."

She shuddered.

"What happened to Frank and Leonard?" asked the dark man.

"I'm afraid they're, uh . . ."

Maggie glanced at the dark man and then looked back to me.

"Most of the people involved in the decision to shoot Dace now agree it was a mistake. But it's a mistake that will be hard to walk away from. You and LuEllen could cause us an infinite amount of damage with a letter or a phone call, and you may have reason to do it. To get back for Dace," she said. She was using her business voice. The small talk was over.

I shook my head at her. "We won't do it. We want to cut a deal. You don't mess with us, ever, and we'll never mess with you. We've got our money and it's all over."

She glanced at the dark man again, and he said, "Ms. Kahn has suggested that you were too smart to expose yourself this way unless you had done something that would give you protection. Would you like to tell us what it is? A letter with a lawyer or something? A letter in a safety-deposit box?"

"Ah, no." I glanced at the clock. 3:56. "That, I'm afraid, could be managed. People could be bought, the charges denied, especially if LuEllen and I weren't around to back them up. Somebody might say the whole thing was a fantasy . . . and even the people who would believe it wouldn't have any way to prove it for sure. Besides, the instigator of the whole thing is a vegetable. You can't put a vegetable on trial."

"So what did you do?" Maggie asked.

I shrugged. "Same old shit you saw in the Washington apartment. A computer blitz. The fact is, if you mess with me or LuEllen, our friends on the computer net will take Anshiser right down the toilet. Right down."

Maggie glanced at the dark man again. He frowned and tipped his head back and stared at me, figuring, and finally said to Maggie, "I don't know."

She thought she did, though. She had decided it was a game, and looked at me with what may have been genuine regret.

"I'm disappointed, Kidd. We thought you'd be

better than this. Let me tell you what we've done. We have the best people—the very best, better than you—watching every move that's made on those computers. It has been a major inconvenience, and it cost us a lot of money, but we'll get it back with the *Sunfire* contract. In any event, we know you're not in there. Just in case, we have backups of all our software, and all the daily work. We can shut down and sterilize our system in half an hour, and be back up with completely clean software. Everybody who does anything on the system is logged in and out, and the input is studied by the security crew. There isn't any way you can reach us. You just don't have the leverage for a deal." She shook her head and stood up. "I think it's time to leave," she said to the dark man.

The clock said 3:59.

"By the way, don't try to use your telephone. It won't work," she said, showing a few teeth. "I couldn't figure why you stayed in an Anshiser Hotel. You must know we could control the place."

"Don't go," I said. "We have more things to talk about."

"I don't think so," she said. A note of triumph had crept into her voice. The clock ticked over to four, and she started toward the door, the dark man standing to follow. The blond opened the door, and she walked away, giving it a little extra effort as she walked. At the door she paused, and seemed about to say something.

Then the lights went out.

Everything else went with them—the clock, the TV, the air conditioning. There was a stuttering, and emergency lights came on in the hallway. Somewhere, a smoke detector screeched, and doors started popping open down the hallway.

I had pulled the blackout drapes over the windows to intensify the effect. I waited for a few seconds, and reached back and pulled the drawstring. Daylight flooded the room, and the blond was standing just inside the door, pointing a small-caliber automatic pistol at my chest. A long, fat silencer was attached to the snout.

"Why don't you come back in and sit down?" I suggested.

Maggie looked shocked, but came back in. "What have you done?"

"I've shut down Anshiser," I said. "Or at least, my friends have."

"What are you talking about, we have the best security, there was no way . . ."

"It's awful good," I agreed. "Too good to penetrate in the time that we had. So we had to do something different."

"What did you do, Kidd?"

"We went into the power company computers. We couldn't get every little dinky Anshiser operation, but we got all the good ones. All the hotels, all the factories, your headquarters back in Chicago. Not a single one of the big operations has power. If you call up your airframe fabrication plant you'll find they don't have a computer problem, they've got a problem with everything. They can't run a fuckin' power drill."

The Tower of Destruction. The lightning bolt. Power plants, of course. And it had been shown in conjunction with the Magician, the computer-freak card. It was all coincidence, but a timely one—I really don't believe in that magic shit.

"This can't last. . . ." Maggie blurted.

"Yes, it can. Believe me: Anshiser is shut down. Unless I tell my people to bring you back up, you'll be down for three or four days before the electric people find the fault. And then the next bomb goes off. If you're really efficient, you might get fifteen or twenty days of work out of your companies in the next year."

She sank down in the chair opposite me, and the dark man said, "Sonofabitch." He looked at the blond and said, "Put it away." People were shuffling through the hall in the dim light, moving toward the stairwell. The smoke alarm, apparently triggered by the power shutdown, was still screeching into the gloom. The blond stepped inside and shut the door.

"How long will it take to get us back up?" Maggie asked.

"Probably two or three hours. We have a lot of

them to deal with," I said. "But we don't want to bring them back up too soon. We want to give you a chance to call around. Find out how bad things can get. See if you can fix it yourself."

Maggie looked at the dark man. "What do you think?"

He shook his head. "What I thought in the first place. We cut the deal and walk away. And keep his phone number in case we need his help sometime."

"No chance," I said.

"Don't shut any doors," he said. It didn't sound like a threat. It sounded like advice.

Maggie was still looking for a way out. "We could go after your computer friends."

"No. The National Security Agency has gone looking for Bobby, and came up empty. A bunch of hoods aren't going to find him. And if you come after me or LuEllen, if there's even a hint of it, Bobby'll take Anshiser apart."

"What happens if you're hit by a car?" the dark man asked.

"You better pray I'm not, because you'll be out of luck," I said. He nodded. That was the kind of deal he understood. One that had no options.

"Look," I said to Maggie, "in a couple of years, anything I say about this whole Whitemark deal, or about Dace, will be ancient history. Nobody will pay any attention. It'll be like if you called up the FBI and said you knew who killed

Judge Crater. Nobody would give a shit. So if we can make it through a couple of years together, you'll be safe. And there'll be no percentage at all in coming after us. You'll have that whole big company to work with."

"He's right," said the dark man.

"Okay," said Maggie, deciding. She stood up again. "It's a deal. Turn the power on."

Chapter 21

I WAS WORKING on the sandbar below St. Paul. I'd dragged the anchor halfway up the bar and buried it, and the boat swung placidly on its line as the towboats streamed by. It was hot, the first real heat of the coming summer. She crossed the levee, pushed through the willows, and walked out on the bar. She was wearing gym shoes, jeans, and a peek-a-boo blouse. She had a nice tan.

"Neat picture," she said when she came up. She said "pitcher."

"Thanks. How was Mexico?"

"All right. A lot of foreigners." She laughed and I smiled and she said, "Old joke."

"No kidding." I laid in a long vermilion horizon.

LuEllen did a critical pout, cocked her head, and nodded. "Not bad," she said.

"Thanks."

"Seen Maggie lately?"

"Not since I called you—not since Vegas. There's a mutual lack of interest."

"Still think we're safe?"

"I think so. We put ourselves outside the percentages. Have you been back to Duluth?"

"Snuck in and out a week after you called. Moved some money around, and went back." She wandered around, looked in the boat. "I saw that old man Anshiser croaked."

"Yeah. Maggie's running the place. A new guy took her job, Dillon's still number three." I dropped in some very liquid ultramarine and feathered it into the vermilion.

"I could never do that," she said. "Paint, I mean. Like you put in that hill, with purple. Who would think that a hill with green trees is purple? But it kind of is, isn't it?" She looked across the river at the hill.

"Yeah, it is."

"Have you thought about Dace at all?"

"You mean, do I feel guilty?"

"Yeah."

I stopped painting and looked at her. "Yes. I do. I thought I knew what we were getting into, and I didn't. And Dace paid. But there's nothing I can do about it. I could go after Maggie, I suppose. But I can't do that, either. And I like it here. I don't want to spend the rest of my life running from somebody, the cops, or the mob, or whoever."

She nodded. "That's where I got to, sitting on the beach. I kept thinking, Dace would want us to do this, or Dace would want us to do that. Then one day I figured, Dace doesn't want us to do anything. He's dead. It's like they turned out a TV. It's like thinking a TV show wants you to do something, after you've turned it off."

I went back to painting and she watched for another minute or two, then ran off down the sandbar, stopping to look at the flotsam. She was back in five minutes with a wasp-waisted seven-ounce Coke bottle.

"Must be twenty years old," she said.

"I don't want to break your heart, but you can still buy them like that."

"Oh yeah?" She looked at me suspiciously, but when I nodded, heaved it into the river. She had a good arm. The bottle hit and bobbed up, its neck sticking out of the water.

"Been stealing anything?" I asked.

"Nope. I'm too rich," she said. "But I'm thinking about it anyway."

"Playing the ponies?"

"A little."

"How about the nose candy?"

"Yeah, a little."

"Were you faithful to me down in Mexico?"

She snorted and threw a driftwood stick after the Coke bottle and watched them both float away. A tow jockey ran his harbor boat by, heading toward the coal dump downriver.

"Are you, you know, involved with anybody?" she asked.

"Nah."

"What are my chances of getting laid?"

"Pretty good, if you play your cards right," I said.

"Okay," she said. "All right."

She looked happy. She found a flat rock and tried to skip it side-armed out in the river. It skipped once and crashed.

The river itself was dark and black and snaky, the currents and crosscurrents bucking up along the bar. We spent most of the afternoon there, painting and talking and watching the clouds roll in, up from the south, over the Mississippi.